"Literature, the most seductive, the most deceiving, the most dangerous of professions."

John Morley, 1st Viscount of Blackburn,
in his book on Edmund Burke (1867).

For

My daughter Maria

My granddaughters Leisel and Dawn

&

My seven great-grandchildren

ACKNOWLEDGEMENTS

Some of the work in this collection has appeared
in the following publications:
Beatlick News; Bloody Quill; C.P.R.;
Kneeling in the Silver Light; Medusa; Of/With;
Poetry Cornwall; Poetry for Pleasure; Quarry;
Terror Tales of Wales; The Horror Zine;
The Renegades of Prose; The Song Is…; Tigershark;
Worlds of the Unknown; Voices from a Coma;
and various titles from the Atlantean, Malfunction,
Rainfall and Tickety Boo presses.

"Ain't That The Truth"; "El Homestead Notorious";
"Locust Day"; "Oh Babylon"; "Singing Sad Songs";
"Space Jocks: Yes! No! Yes!"; "The Place of Small
Misdemeanors"; "The Road To Salamis"
and "Trumpet Involuntary"
all appear here for the first time.

CONTENTS

The Poems

THE HOUSE THAT TIME FORGOT

When I was young I yearned for my own
     Lady of Shalott
A lady fair
A love so rare
When I was young I'd hurry past the house
     that time forgot
I kept away
No place to stay
As time went by I learned to lose the purity of youth
Love turned to lust
An end to trust
As time went by I learned how to compromise the truth
What's wrong is right
What's black is white

The house that time forgot is a place where
     time stands still
A house that's never learned that time will one day kill
Somewhere the house is standing, a place
     where I could stay
If I can only find it, before time has its way

The house that time forgot

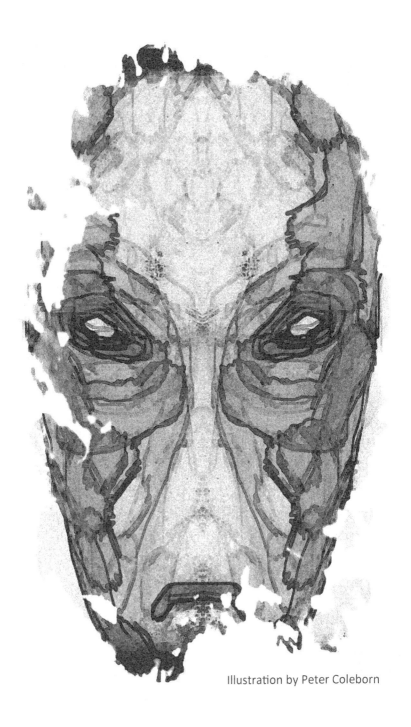

Illustration by Peter Coleborn

BRYN FORTEY:
THE OLD MAGIC NEVER DIES

FUNNY HOW CERTAIN things keep recurring throughout an individual's life: people, places, literary works, a certain song or musical piece. I've lost track of the number of times *Macbeth* has cropped up in mine. Or "Lucy in the Sky with Diamonds". Or Newport, Wales.

Yes, you heard me, Newport, Wales.

A modest city, not far along the southern Welsh coast from Cardiff, its more illustrious big brother (though you do not say that in Newport). Once it was home to some of the biggest docks in the world, a thriving centre of trade. I know this because my great, great (great?) grandfather, a native of north Devon, and a stone mason by trade, worked on those huge docks.

My own first visit to Newport was in September 2017, on the occasion of the eightieth birthday of Bryn Fortey, whose second collection of stories you are about to read – certainly you should be. Bryn is a native of Newport, a true Silurian Celt, and has lived there all his life. Me, I'm a Celt too, though my genes are a little more confused, being Dumnonian and Hibernian, with more than a dash of Silurian to boot. Whatever – Bryn's ancestors and mine very likely spent time swapping punches with the Roman invaders.

Bryn and I have more than just our Celtic heritage in common. We write, of course, and we love our football. Our champions are not the mighty multi-national powers of the Premiership. No. We favour the sleeping, one might say comatose, giants. Bryn, naturally, supports his home town Newport County, while my own colours are pinned to the mast of Plymouth Argyle. In recent times these two clubs have had occasion to slog it out with each other more than once, and these tumultuous tussles have spiced up our correspondence accordingly.

There was the FA Cup tie, a soulless 0–0 stalemate at Plymouth, and a televised replay on the notorious sand pit at Newport's Rodney Parade. The prize for the winner would be a money-spinning tie at Liverpool, something to play for given the financial plight of both teams. I watched the game on television, imagining Bryn seated beside me. The form book favoured Plymouth – we were strongly placed for promotion, while Newport was bottom of our league and seemingly doomed to relegation and non-league football.

The pitch, however, was a great leveller, a soggy, sandy bog that made slick passing and skill difficult. Even so, I expressed my confidence that Plymouth would triumph to the imagined figure beside me. Naturally it poured scorn on my suggestion. Plymouth added to my concern by fluffing a number of good chances to score. They went one better – or worse – and missed a penalty. It had been a dreary, cold night and now a bank of thick mist threatened to roll in and completely muddle affairs. I could sense my invisible companion's spirits lifting, potentially tasting the outrage of a Plymouth defeat. But a rush of blood in the Newport defence gave Plymouth another penalty and this time it was duly despatched, and soon after the match was over.

That had been in December 2016. By April, the

fortunes of both teams had remained positive for Plymouth and gloomy for Newport. Bryn's team were still bottom, with a handful of games left to save themselves. They went on a remarkable run of winning 1-0 a few times, lifting themselves! Four games from the end, Newport came to Plymouth. Argyle needed a draw to be promoted. Newport still had work to do to survive. Bryn and I remained polite. I sat in the grandstand at Home Park, again imagining Bryn beside me. My joy at the result, a thumping 6-1 victory for my team, was tempered by my genuine sympathy for Bryn's.

Well, this isn't an arena of death threats and hurled obscenities. No. We rise above that. In the end, we are brothers in arms. It's life and its vicissitudes we really have to contend with. And Bryn's life has been blighted with personal tragedy, more so than most of us. The fortunes of Newport County, and indeed, of Plymouth Argyle, pale into insignificance beside Bryn's crippling experiences.

He has already expressed himself, vividly, in his earlier Alchemy Press collection *Merry-Go-Round*, particularly in his beautiful, moving poems, and I'm delighted to say he's included fresh poetry in this volume. His stories here reflect a clear understanding of the human condition and he imbues his characters with knowing insights. The tales vary from stark, unnerving urban horror, to blackly humorous, almost preposterous fantasy, although even these hugely entertaining yarns are seated in reality. Bryn knows his terrain, of course, both the external cityscape and the fractured, bruised inner landscape of the human condition. And it's typical of his modesty that his writing is often understated, making it all the more poignant.

As for Newport County football club: well, they did survive that battle against expulsion from the Football League – in a fairy tale ending to the season, winning their last crucial match with a late, late goal. There seemed to me to be a sense of justice about their triumph. And as I write this, half way through another campaign, they are pushing hard for promotion. In a typical quirk of circumstance, the side they are most likely to replace in the higher division is … yes, yes, okay, dammit, Plymouth Argyle.

At 80, Bryn probably doesn't think of himself as a phoenix, but in these latest tales, we see the man writing at the top of his form, deserving of a move into a higher league. Unlike our football counterparts, though, I very much doubt his work will be allowed to slip back into lower league obscurity. At that eightieth birthday I mentioned, he asserted his determination to hold an equally celebratory ninetieth birthday. Ten years on … wow, what new gems will he produce for us in that time?

Adrian Cole
Devon, December 2018

AIN'T THAT THE TRUTH

ALASTAIR DRAKE WAS one of the go-to guys when it came to the blues. After first being turned on to the music by a chance hearing of Frankie Laine's version of *West End Blues* he'd spent his teenage years scouring second-hand record shops for rare American imports, then later becoming a regular at both the London Blues and Barrelhouse Club and the Ealing Club. Hearing visiting Americans such as Muddy Waters and Memphis Slim live confirmed his love for the genre.

As the Sixties moved on he'd played a small part in organizing some of the Folk Blues Festivals, featuring artists such as Sonny Boy Williamson, wrote articles for the music press, and worked with various record companies. Most of the performers, those who had stayed faithful to their roots and not been tempted into more commercial avenues, had been largely forgotten in their native America. Their careers were being kick-started as part of the UK blues boom, which gained them reawakened recognition in their homeland.

This sudden resurgence of interest was an unexpected career boost for people such as Lightnin' Hopkins, a master of post-war down-home blues, whose former popularity had been in serious decline for the previous ten or more years. Bukka White was another successful rediscovery, and the small body of recorded work by the late – and generally ignored – Robert Johnson elevated him to superstar status.

Howlin' Wolf and John Lee Hooker both had crossover pop chart hits without having to dilute their music, and respectable sales were achieved in general across the blues spectrum, and the record companies took note.

The search was on to find more forgotten titans of the genre. Men to be rediscovered, recorded, and sent to tour Europe before being reintroduced to a newly interested American audience.

THOUGH HIS PARENTS thought he had wasted a good university education, doing what he did they had to admit he was happy enough. His work was his hobby and it enabled him to travel the world, though his mother wished that he would settle down and start providing her with grandchildren.

Dreadnought Records, Alastair's employer at the time, wanted a blues veteran of their own. "Someone straight from the plantation," said the order from high. "Signed, sealed, and in the studio." Most of those with remembered reputations had already been brought back but if anyone could unearth a lost gem, then Alastair Drake was the man to do it, and he already had someone in mind.

The man-mountain piano virtuoso Roosevelt Sykes had been the first to mention the name in Alastair's hearing, during a general discussion about Delta guitarists. All of the usual names had been talked about before Roosevelt suggested: "Then there was Jackson 'Truth' Monroe, who was never remembered enough to be forgotten, but he ranked with the best."

Nobody else gave the man a mention and the discussion itself was soon over and done with, people moving on, and other conversations starting. The next day, with the blues package moving on to the next town, Alastair asked the piano-man about the guitarist he'd named. "Don't pay no mind to him, Al," said Sykes, "just me shouting my mouth off." Then he'd changed the subject completely but Alastair Drake was intrigued by the prospect of a Delta bluesman he was not aware of, filing the name away for possible future investigation; and maybe now was the time.

PROBABLY BECAUSE HIS love for the blues was so genuine, he got on fine with most of the musicians he came into contact with and many were happy to respond when he wrote or phoned seeking information or help.

Mississippi Fred McDowell had a vague recollection of having heard the name but was certain he had never met the man nor heard him play. Sleepy John Estes didn't think he ever left the Delta and never recorded: "No way, never did." The guy seemed a shadowy figure, more heard of than met, which made him more intriguing than ever to someone like Drake.

Was he still in the Delta or a long-time gone north?

He had never recorded for a major label, that had been easy to establish, but there were so many tiny independents he could have cut a few sides for.

Was he even still alive?

Roosevelt Sykes, the only person to have commented on the man's actual guitar work, now claimed Drake had got it wrong. "I must have been talking 'bout someone else, Al. You just misheard, that's all." But Drake knew that no way would he have just dragged the name out of thin air. This Monroe person was real enough but for some reason nobody wanted to talk about him. His breakthrough finally came in the shape of Gypsy Sam Arnold, a disciple of the Muddy Waters urban blues style and one of the few white men to be acknowledged within the idiom.

"Jackson 'Truth' Monroe?" cackled Gypsy Sam in his tobacco-stained voice. The veteran bluesman smiled knowingly. "I bet you've got a sack full of questions, but an empty bag of answers."

"Just about," agreed Drake.

"It's Hoodoo Voodoo, man. His daddy was a Houngan and his mammy a Witch Queen, and the Delta is like a separate nation within the United States. Throw in a helping of secrecy, a dollop of criminality, and as many names as he cared to use. He wasn't born Jackson Monroe and the 'Truth' nickname only applied to his music. For the rest he was a psychopathic ju-ju man who was feared and hated in equal portions.

"His guitar playing and vocal abilities were such that if he had concentrated on a musical career he might well have gone far. I'm pretty sure he did cut some tracks for back-room labels that were gone almost as soon as they appeared. If you could find them now, Al, I am sure they would create a stir, but you will get no help."

Drake didn't understand. "There have been other unsavoury characters who nevertheless enjoyed reasonable careers," he said. "Surely this guy can't be that much worse. It's as if he's been written out of history."

"You'd better believe it, Al. People went missing, but although bodies were rarely found it was known where to point the finger; not that anyone did, of course. That would have seen your name added to the list."

"So where do I start, Sam? I don't even know if he's alive or dead!"

"Last I heard, some years back now, he was doing time. Try checking the Delta prison system. It was almost guaranteed he would end up a Big House inmate."

ALASTAIR ENJOYED THAT side of things, digging into dusty old files, and in this instance it paid off. In spite of Gypsy Sam's assertion that Jackson Monroe was behind a number of killings, it was only when he handed out a bad beating to the son of a prominent Riverton businessman that the law came calling. What would probably have only been a short sentence escalated when he then put two deputies into hospital. A twenty-year stretch in America's largest maximum-security prison, the Louisiana State Penitentiary, was handed down. It was a place that broke many of its inmates, but Monroe seemed to have survived since he was released after serving twelve years, and then he just seemed to vanish.

So okay, Alastair could find no further trace of the man in the Delta, but maybe it was at this point, if at all, that he took the time-honoured route to the north, which in so many cases had meant Chicago; and again he struck lucky with prison records. Monroe might have been better served using one of his other aliases, or even his real name, which would have made tracking him more difficult. Having been found guilty after a gang-related killing spree, Jackson Monroe was at the Stateville Correctional Centre at Crest Hill, near Chicago, serving a life sentence without any possibility of parole.

GYPSY SAM ARNOLD slammed the phone down and reached for his whisky bottle. "Fuck it!" he said aloud, to himself since he was alone. "Damn and fuck it!" He hadn't been drunk when Limey Al Drake had asked him about 'Truth' Monroe, but he had supped enough to loosen his tongue. It would have been better if he'd acted dumb like others had.

Jackson Monroe was bad news, big time. Always had been.

Curly Calhoun had gotten quite angry when Sam told him about it, and that wasn't like his old sideman at all. Curly had been a mouth harp player of some repute in the old days, but that had been before losing all his teeth. He had still been able to play but the sharp control he was known for was lost. They had been friends and drinking buddies for many years, and Gypsy would always call to see him when he visited the Delta.

"You shouldn't have told that Englishman nothin', Sam. Of all people, not you!" Curly had told him, and he'd been right.

Gypsy stared hard at the telephone, as if blaming it for whatever words tumbled down the wire. So Limey Al had traced Monroe to the Big House in Crest Hill, and was going to visit him there. Jackson Monroe was a sleeping dog best not woken. Voodoo stuff was less controlling now than it had been, even in the Delta, and Gypsy had never been a believer in the supernatural aspects of it all, but some things were hard to explain. If only the man's violent nature could have been curbed there was no telling where the blues might have taken him.

Oh that voice!

That bottleneck guitar!

A sinner for sure, but what music he'd played. No wonder they had called him 'Truth'.

Gypsy Sam lifted the whisky bottle to his thin bloodless lips and drank deeply, trying not to think about Louella.

THERE WAS, ALASTAIR Drake knew, a tradition of bluesmen doing time and getting out. Leadbelly's singing was said to have been instrumental in gaining his release on two separate occasions. Both Son House and Bukka White were reprieved, at different times, from jail terms at the notorious Parchman State Farm. He could not help but wonder whether he might be able to engineer something similar for this Jackson "Truth" Monroe, if he did indeed turn out to be good enough to warrant it. Probably not, things being different now, though you could never underestimate the pressure highly skilled record company lawyers could bring to bear.

The hints were that Monroe might have been talented, but that music was just a hobby, a passing fancy to be indulged in between his more serious ju-ju and criminal personas. Well, whatever, he would be meeting him soon. Future consequences, if any, would become clearer after that.

He had received a strange and rather garbled phone call from Gypsy Sam Arnold though, asking him not to carry out the prison visit. "Don't do it, Al," he had demanded. "Let the bastard rot!"

Drake initially thought the man was drunk, a not unusual state for Gypsy, but his voice wasn't slurred. As diplomatically as he could, he pointed out that his time in America was limited so he had to get done what he could before work constraints sent him flying back across the Atlantic. "Well at least wait till I get there," insisted the other. "I've got a gig arranged and I'll be in Chicago next week."

What the heck was that all about? Drake had not

promised to wait, and not said he wouldn't, leaving himself freedom of choice either way. Not that he was really considering even a postponement. He had an appointment to see an Assistant Governor, and then he would meet the man himself.

"I DON'T MAKE a habit of talking to visitors, Mr Drake," the Assistant Governor told him, "but you are the first to want to see Monroe in years, certainly going back to before I started work here, and there are certain peculiarities relating to his incarceration that I think you should be made aware of." And by the time the man finished, Alastair knew there would be no early release for this inmate.

Early in his sentence he had only barely been stopped from killing fellow prisoners, leaving four in need of hospitalisation. He picked fights for fun, needing no provocation, and was willing to take on guards as well as other prisoners. It finally reached a situation where he was spending more time in solitary than out of it. Fellow inmates wanted nothing to do with him and there were even a couple of guards who threatened to quit rather than work anywhere near to where he was.

The final solution was an isolation cell, a cage-like construction with bars from ceiling to floor. It wasn't solitary confinement since anyone could speak to him, and he could see them, though he himself did not encourage it. Anybody with reason to go into this area was warned not to stand close enough for him to reach between the bars and grab them. In spite of passing years he was still a man of great strength, ferocious temper, and was not to be trusted.

With a final warning ringing in his ears, Drake was

taken in and directed to a chair a good few feet away from the cage. The man on the other side of the bars was a bit shy of Willie Dixon's six foot-five and 250 pounds, but not by much, and whereas the Chess Records stalwart was big and genial, this man was big and threatening; maybe even more than that.

"So you're my visitor. Not had many of those and don't want them. You hear me, Limey Al?"

Drake tried to suppress a shudder, feeling the hairs on the back of his neck stand up. "My name is Alastair Drake and I work for Dreadnought Records," he said, trying to sound business-like. "There is a good deal of interest in veteran blues performers, which is why I have come here to meet you."

"Well you've wasted your time then, haven't you! Huh?"

"That would depend on whether you're as good as I've been told. If you are, and if you were interested, I could try to arrange for you to record your music here at Stateville. Right here in this room if need be."

Monroe's laughter was not a pleasant sound. "Someone told you I was good. Now who might that be?"

"Well, Gypsy Sam Arnold for one."

"Gypsy Sam!" roared the man, his dark face twisting with anger as he grabbed the bars that held him captive. "Just a no-talent white-assed rattlesnake! You tell him from me that Louella cursed him before her end."

"Mr Monroe..." Drake started to say.

"Time for you to go, Limey Al," interrupted the man in the cage. "Come back after you have spoken with Arnold and tell me what the skunk had to say." And with that he turned to face away while his visitor left.

That was the first time ever, thought Drake as he

journeyed back to Chicago, that he had been in the presence of someone who came across as truly evil. He felt unclean for having been in the same room, breathing the same air. It was only later he remembered that Monroe had twice called him Limey Al, the nickname a lot of Americans used behind his back. How could he have known it? Drake himself had definitely not told him.

And who was Louella?

GYPSY SAM, STILL performing after all these years, was regarded by many as a living legend, someone who had actually played with all those dead giants from the past. It was never expected that he should be at the top of his game every time he strapped on his guitar and stepped up to a mic. People made allowances.

The Chicago gig however, even after taking everything into consideration, was something of a disaster. Gypsy showed only disinterest and had merely gone through the motions. Even the grizzled humour he normally spiced his act with was missing.

Was he drunk? No, he did seem sober. Yet Alastair could remember occasions when, barely able to stand, bottle in hand, he had staggered onto the stage and been absolutely terrific. But not tonight.

"You went to see him then." It was a statement more than a question.

At least Gypsy had not gone straight into his usual after-the-gig drinking. Not yet anyway. "I had to, Sam, after all the effort I put into finding him," said Drake.

"What did you think?"

"He makes Sonny Liston seem like little Lord Fauntleroy."

"Don't he just!"

Both men were silent for a moment, then: "He became angry when I mentioned your name," said Drake.

"I should have told you not to do that."

"You two have personal history?"

"Sort of."

Alastair had thought himself in two minds about passing on Monroe's words, being unsure about the gruesome undertones they contained, but he didn't hesitate now the time had come. "He sent you a message, Sam."

"And that would be?"

"He said to tell you that Louella cursed you before her end."

Gypsy, white-faced and drained of colour, made a couple of harsh throaty sounds. Drake, for a moment, wondered if his friend was having a heart attack, but he recovered sufficiently to speak. "The bastard..." he said weakly.

"You want to explain any of this? Or if it's none of my business, just say so."

"It goes back to when Jackson Monroe was bossing the Delta with a sense of entitlement, due to his Voodoo connections and physical power. He had 'wives' all over, though not one ever saw a wedding certificate, but he had home comforts in every part of the area."

"And this Louella was one of them?" suggested Drake, and Gypsy nodded his agreement.

"What a beauty she was, Al. An ebony goddess, and I was smitten the first time I set eyes on her, and she felt the same about me. He was always moving, up to his skulduggery, so all his 'wives' had time free of him, and we thought we were so clever and careful. I was planning on moving her up north, away from the Delta, just as soon as my next European tour was out of the way.

"It was while I flitted from Berlin to Paris to London, that all hell broke loose back there. We had been fools to think we could keep our love hidden. Someone had told Monroe about us. Louella disappeared, I later learned, and was never seen again. People who knew her in the Delta suspected she was dead. Nobody crossed Jackson Monroe and got away with it, but without a body nobody could or would say anything. I guess I only survived by being out of the country, and by the time I did venture down there to try and find her he was doing his first stretch in the State Pen, and the Delta was free of him. There have been other villains since, of course, but none as bad as him."

"And yet, you told me, his music was good..."

Sam Arnold's face twisted into a painful grimace, making him look more ancient than ever. "More than good, Al. People don't talk about him because of the person he was, and no-one hated him more than me, but the blues that poured from him could spear your heart. His life was full of lies, corrupt and obscene, but his music was great. It was his blues that were called 'Truth'. The rest of him was 'Trash'." Enough was enough, and some memories were more painful than others. Gypsy finally reached for his after-the-gig bottle.

ALASTAIR DRAKE, THE English record company man, knew that he was playing a cat-and-mouse game with Jackson Monroe. He had asked for permission to bring in a guitar and was still waiting for the Assistant Governor's decision. Monroe, for his part, blew hot and cold on the possibility of recording but kept asking Drake to bring in Gypsy Sam Arnold for a visit, claiming he wanted to put things right between them. Not that Drake believed him for one instant; nor did Gypsy, who totally refused to consider a visit under any circumstances.

Drake knew that Monroe was toying with him, showing just enough interest in his plans to keep him hooked. The Englishman, for his part, was beginning to doubt that any recording would ever take place, but nevertheless felt a need to hear the man's music, even if without any commercial end product. He wanted to find out for himself whether the implied contradiction between the pure nastiness of the hulking figure he saw, and the claimed beauty of his blues, was as extreme as Gypsy Sam said.

"Bring Sam in to see me. Give me the chance to put things right," asked Monroe, with underlying threats and violence inhabiting even the calmest of words.

"Drop it, Al, I beg you," pleaded Gypsy. "Go back to the UK and forget you ever heard of Jackson Monroe."

"Having given the matter full consideration," decided the Assistant Governor, "I will allow the prisoner to have a guitar in his cell."

Alastair Drake did wonder if he was already in too deep but knew he couldn't stop when some sort of end was coming into sight, and he already had an album title in mind: *Ain't That the Truth*, even though it might never be used.

JACKSON MONROE SAT, a brooding and immobile figure, looking like something carved out of granite, and then painted black. The faceless dumb-ass authorities, who thought they ruled every facet of his existence, had intended this cell to be a place of punishment. The fools! Here, with no outside distractions to interfere, he led a mind-based existence: reliving the past and sharpening his skills.

There were many interpretations of voodoo culture and beliefs. From its West African beginnings, where it was an officially recognised religion in Benin, slavery had carried it to the Americas. As well as the better-known Haitian and Louisiana versions, there were Brazilian, Cuban, Dominican and Caribbean varieties. Each had differences peculiar to themselves, and hidden beneath what was allowable for public perception there were secret and darker elements where magic and control were not mere entertainments but very real.

The self is in the structure, he had read, and it was. The ego, the id: all was fluid. Contained, but not lacking the power of control and movement. For years he had taken the basic building blocks given him by long-time dead Delta magic men and shaped and moulded, layer upon layer. Reading book after book, which they let him have to keep him quiet, so that he could add other persuasions into the mix. Techniques by such as the Yamanara Clan, refined and adapted to suit his purpose, and improved beyond all recognition.

Time was a-coming.

He hummed a short blues motif, quiet enough so no-one passing near might hear.

Oh yes, Jackson Monroe's time, and that was the truth.

ALASTAIR DRAKE SAT rooted to his chair. Not even the keen sense of anticipation that led to this moment had prepared him for what he had just heard. Jackson 'Truth' Monroe had played what he claimed to be an original song called "Delta Darling Died in Shame", which Drake recognised as being based on Robert Johnson's "If I Had Possession Over Judgement Day", which was itself in debt to Hambone Willie Newbern's "Rollin' And Tumblin'". All part of a blues tradition of reworking older songs for newer days, and it had been all that he had hoped for.

Not having the usual metal or glass tube to slide up and down the strings to obtain the deep vibrato bottleneck effect, Monroe made do with a plastic beaker, and he made it work. His voice leant towards the Howlin' Wolf style of highly masculine vocalising, and the whole performance was as emotionally charged as the blues were meant to be.

The song itself was obviously based upon Louella, and Drake was mentally shredded to hear him sing about a girl he might well have murdered. Thank goodness Gypsy Sam had stuck to his refusal to visit. It might have finished him off completely. But in spite of the subject matter, no wonder the man's music had been labelled as 'Truth'. Drake knew, even before the song had ended, that although this man might well be Satan himself, he had to get him recorded.

"You want to cut a deal then, Limey Al?" boomed Monroe. "You've talked me into it, got me playing again. Now I want to do it."

Was it going to be this easy? "I'll get Dreadnaught to draw up the contract and we'll start putting pressure on the prison to allow recording here."

"No, Mister Executive, take off your record company hat. I don't like words on paper, but I know that you are a man I can trust." Monroe held out his right hand, between the bars of his cell. "Shake on it, Al," he said, "and that will be as binding as any contract."

Drake didn't really want to have physical contact

with the man, and all the warnings he'd been given rang through his head, but he did so want to get his music recorded. *Ain't That the Truth.* He could see the CD in the shops already.

Crossing to the cell Drake took hold of Monroe's offered hand and accepted the shake.

"Got you," murmured the big man under his breath.

ALASTAIR DRAKE HAD been momentarily disorientated but shook his head as the dizziness passed. He felt big, lumpy, and somehow he seemed to be on the wrong side of the metal bars.

Looking up, he saw *himself* leaving!

Looking down, he saw that he had big *black* hands!

He fainted then.

Jackson Monroe, meanwhile, was on his way to Chicago and trying to get used to the skinny white body he now inhabited. The switch had been much smoother than he could have wished for. It was all very well accumulating knowledge and devising theories, but you couldn't be certain until you'd actually done it.

And he had!

And it worked.

He was now Alastair Drake, in appearance at least. And free.

Women, liquor, further mastery of the black arts. It all spread before him, and each would have their turn, but there was one thing above all else that had to be dealt with first. He had to find Gypsy Sam Arnold and kill him – slowly, painfully, bit at a time. He had to pay for trying to take Louella away.

Nobody could be allowed to better Jackson Monroe, and that was the truth.

THE KING IS DEAD

I SUPPOSE THE person we can blame most for it all is Thomas Thorne Baker, an electrical researcher who in 1907 had been hired by the *London Mirror* to develop a way of sending photographs over telephone lines. He came up with a primitive version of a fax machine, which he called an electrolytic telectograph. It did indeed produce recognisable though grainy images, but was considered too costly for further development. Baker, though, remained convinced that within what we now look back as being a "Golden Age of Electrification" he could find both fame and fortune.

An electric lock which was opened by the playing of specific musical notes failed to catch on, but never mind, he had bigger fish to fry. Well maybe not actually fish. Baker switched to a study of electromagnetic fields, theorizing that they could be just as beneficial as the sun's rays. Maybe they could even stimulate growth.

Since he could see potential custom from within the food industry, Baker's first subjects were peaches and Camembert cheese, exposing both to fields of electromagnetic energy. Both, so it seemed, ripened more quickly. Encouraged, he moved on to chickens. Soon twelve birds perched on insulated wires that were charged with five thousand volts for one hour each day, and the results were promising. The testcase chickens reportedly weighed thirteen percent more than those in a non-electrified coop.

Mr Randolph Meech, a chicken farmer from Poole, was sufficiently impressed to allow Baker to carry out trials on a building which housed around three thousand birds. He wrapped the entire construction in insulating wire and was soon announcing that the chickens so treated grew fifty percent larger in half the time.

Despite such grand claims, the relatively conservative chicken farmers of Great Britain did not queue up to switch to his electrically treated methods. Baker's only other convert was over in America where a Brooklyn dentist named Doctor Rudolph C Linnau stopped pulling teeth and electrified chickens instead. Baker himself moved on to larger subjects, thinking he might find a cure for shortness in humans. He even used his five-year old daughter Yvonne in some of his experiments, as reported in the *London Mirror*.

But Baker's moment in the public eye was fading, being overtaken by bigger and grander studies. Svante Arrhenius, who had won the 1903 Nobel Prize for Chemistry, electrified a whole classroom of children in a Swedish school. A five-year old daughter in a cage could not compete with that.

Baker's most successful accomplishment, however, gained him no credit whatsoever. Indeed, he himself had no knowledge of it at all. Within the confines of the test building on Randolph Meech's chicken farm, Stag Beetle larvae were feeding on rotting wood. Just why Stag Beetles responded so well to the theory of electrically enhanced growth was never investigated since it remained unknown. Mr Meech himself did spot a twelve-inch specimen at a later date but he merely said "Ugh!" and stamped on it. An act of violence not lost upon the growing insects.

IF GOD HAD not meant Stag Beetles to be judged by the power and dexterity of their antler-like jaws, then why had they been given such mighty appendages?

All hail the Mighty God Elvis, King of Rock & Roll.

Lucky Lucanus had crushed all opponents to win the leadership of his particular burrow, which didn't make him the smartest insect there but did mean that nobody wanted to take him on in a fight. Stag Beetle Superior had come a long way since the original larvae group had been the accidental beneficiaries of Thomas Thorne Baker's chicken experiments. Each succeeding generation had become that bit bigger until now, over a hundred years later, when the growth rate of Stag Beetle Erectus had tapered off at an average four foot.

As their size increased, so had their intelligence; not sufficient to have produced a Stag Beetle Einstein yet but they were way beyond the unaffected insects. With wings now redundant and lifespan much increased they lived in underground colonies and kept away from humans. The horrific story of the murderous Randolph Meech was an ever-present syllabus highlight in all larvae schools. Though raiding groups would make carefully controlled trips to the surface in search of bounty, human contact was to be avoided. On the thankfully rare occasions when they had been seen, the human was killed and the corpse disposed of.

Our thanks, God Elvis, for the gift of mighty jaws.

The only semi-contact allowed was via the radio, which the Stag Beetles had developed just as soon as their technology had allowed. That way they kept up to date with surface news and listened with keen enjoyment to any music being broadcast; which was how Elvis Presley, the King, became their God. They could relate to how he had grown increasingly larger before ascending to Rock & Roll Heaven.

The Stags didn't always exercise full and proper understanding of the surface world.

"General Franco Sinatra did things *his way* during the Spanish-Mafia wars," said Lucky, pausing long enough for his underlings to show support for his statement.

"He sure did."

"Right on!"

"True enough, boss."

"And I'm going to do things *my way* now," he finished.

That usually meant doing extensive damage to someone with his all-conquering antlers, so his subordinates were relieved that on this occasion personal violence was being sidestepped. "I want two patrols out tonight, looking especially for discarded newspapers. There might be mention of starting dates, that sort of thing."

"The radio only said they were proposals, boss. Nothing definite yet," said one who was a little braver than his fellows.

The Leader's handsome reddish-brown body glowed with irritation while his black wing cases glistened. "We can never trust the humans," he rasped angrily.

IAN BARTON HAD dreamt of a show-biz career for as long as he could remember. From amateur talent shows and local bands to a singer/songwriter solo act; though he did prefer to forget his time with Cardiff punk group Gobby Arseholes. Those safety pins really had hurt. None of it had ever amounted to more than a bit of local notoriety and he had rarely gigged outside his South Wales stamping ground. Not until the day someone suggested his voice to be well suited to Elvis Presley material.

Impersonators, most people called them, but Ian was more ambitious: he was an Elvis Presley Tribute Artist. He had read *Just Pretending* by Kurt Burrows, cover to cover, taking all his tips on board and practising hard with the five karaoke backing tracks provided with the book.

He was good, everyone said so, but that alone was not enough in such a highly competitive and crowded show-biz sub-genre. Early Elvis, GI Elvis, Las Vegas Elvis, Black Elvis, Asian Elvis, Gay Elvis, and so on. There was already a Welsh Elvis, much to his initial annoyance, but Ian had soon zoomed in on a gimmick he was fast making his own. Ian Barton was Dead Elvis, stepping from an onstage coffin in full Las Vegas regalia and returning to it at the end of his act, and his reputation was growing with gigs all around the UK. One day he would make it to America where hundreds of Elvis acts congregated at conventions and in competition.

He could see the headline now: DEAD ELVIS WOWS AMERICA!

Where was he playing next week? Ah yes, Salisbury. Wiltshire might not have the same ring to it as Texas or Montana, but every gig was another brick in the career Ian was building for himself.

GREAT THOUGHT HAD gone into choosing the sites for their underground habitations. After some narrow squeaks had unfortunately resulted in human fatalities, it had been decided to burrow deep beneath surface structures that mankind appeared to cherish, so would be unlikely to dig there themselves.

There were a number of these subterranean townships hidden across the UK, and the one Lucky Lucanus was in charge of was directly below Stonehenge. Though why a pile of old stones, however large, was so important, he did not understand. It wasn't as if God Elvis had ever appeared there.

"Humans think it's a *good luck charm*," was one theory.

"Just as long as they leave us alone, *way down* here," said one of his henchmen.

"*I just can't help believing* we are missing something by only ever seeing it in the dark."

"*Well, I don't care if the sun don't shine*. It's just a building site. It's no *promised land*."

"*A Little Less Conversation*," decided Lucky.

God Elvis: The Lyrics was required reading and no self-respecting Stag was without a copy, but not even the much-loved rhymes of "Rock a Hula Baby" could help in this current situation. Mixed in with various human transport proposals was a suggestion that a duel-carriageway tunnel be dug beneath Stonehenge; something about ending A303 bottlenecks and doing away with long traffic queues. Not that the reasons mattered, human behaviour being way beyond beetle understanding; God Elvis apart – and look what they'd done to him! – he had been too forgiving when allowing lesser beings into the Million Dollar Quartet; even letting in the great betrayer Judas Lee Lewis. No wonder they called him The Killer! But God Elvis had put the frailties of chart success behind him and had entered the Land of Grace.

Lucky Lucanus lowered his head and rattled his mighty jaws. Human intrusion had grown over the years but up until now beetle technology had kept them safe, successfully blocking and diverting sonar probes and the like. But a tunnel was something else!

WHEN THE SURFACE parties returned from their foraging duties that night they brought with them a few discarded newspapers as ordered, and much consternation and twitching of feelers resulted. There were no mentions of the proposed tunnelling to be found, but one small item tucked away in an entertainment section provoked challenges not experienced in generations.

A small headline read: DEAD ELVIS TO APPEAR IN SALISBURY.

The Stags were split between those expecting a Second Coming and others who thought the whole thing a blasphemy. Never had beetle opinions been so divided. Males clacked their antlers with threatening intensity, arguing finer points of faith, while the females hid in nurseries and kitchens. Stag society was strictly antler orientated. Those with, the males, ruled. Those without, the females, did as they were told. It was a system that worked and was accepted. Killer jaws guaranteed compliance.

In the end, Lucky Lucanus called a Big Hall meeting that only males were allowed to attend. It was too big a topic to let go without an official line being decided upon.

"God Elvis is delivering a Big Comeback Special again," insisted some. "He will stop the tunnelling."

"He died only to be reborn as the King of Rock & Roll Heaven," countered others. "He cannot become a Dead Elvis a second time."

"Maybe we've got *suspicious minds*," decided Lucky after the arguments had raged to and fro for some time, "but I tend to agree with the sceptics, and the only way to find out for sure is to see for ourselves."

THE STAG TACTICS of secrecy and isolationism had undoubtedly been the best way to ensure survival during their original transformation and development. But they were beyond the stage now where human contact might result in extermination and specimen jars; at least so reasoned Lucky Lucanus. Might was right in his book, and the occasional confrontation had shown that men were no match for the beetles' superior jaw power. Maybe this Dead Elvis thing was a sign that they should return to the surface and stomp on whoever got in their way.

"Why should we live *in the ghetto* of this underground existence," he declared, convincing himself that action would be the best policy. "No good *crying in the chapel*. It's time to hitch a ride on the *mystery train* and *return*, not *to sender*, but to the surface."

IAN HAD DRUNK his usual honey-laced linctus to sooth his vocal cords, and a can of Special Brew to calm his nerves. Feeling edgy before a performance was good. It showed he wasn't taking anything for granted. "Thank-you-very-much," he muttered, copying the way Elvis ran the words together, and nodding to himself. He was sounding more like him all the time.

This venue at – where was it? Salisbury? – yes, Salisbury, boasted a proper stage and curtains. Not all places he played could say the same but the Dead Elvis routine could cope with any situation. His coffin, in an upright position so he could open the hinged lid and step out, was hidden behind his own electrically controlled framed curtains. Once in his wooden box he would hear the announcer introduce him and know that the stage curtains were parting to reveal his own personal smaller curtains. These would then open at the press of a button and Ian would sing "Love Me Tender" from inside the coffin, before stepping out to continue his act.

Everything was going to plan, except for the audience being the noisiest he could ever remember. It had started all of a sudden while he was being introduced. Shouting, yelling, what sounded like booze-fuelled shenanigans. This was something he did not need, a drunken audience.

Opening the coffin lid, he stepped out, breaking into another ballad, "Are You Lonesome Tonight". He would normally up the tempo with a couple of fast rockers next, but not this time. Ian did not even finish his second song. He hadn't drawn a large audience. Indeed, he doubted that even the real Elvis would have achieved a full house here, but the hullabaloo he'd been hearing was because everyone in the place were fighting. People were struggling, grappling, winning, losing, even dying! They were being killed by *giant insects!*

Though Ian had stopped singing he had not turned off his backing track and it seemed rather suitable that "Paralysed" was playing, because that is what he was. He just stood there, open-mouthed and motionless, unable to believe his own eyes. *Giant insects* with *big horns* were taking his audience apart.

"*It's now or never,*" Lucky had told his troops before leading them into battle. A couple of lines of "Love Me Tender" from behind a curtain had been sufficient. This was a charlatan, a copy, not the real God Elvis returned from Rock & Roll Heaven. This was a crude blasphemy!

Ian Barton stared with uncomprehending eyes as the creature clambered onto the stage and came towards him. "This is *too much,*" he gasped weakly, feeling unable to move even an inch. No more booze, he promised himself, no more funny fags, pills, or needles. Just let me wake up!

Lucky Lucanus clicked and clacked his fearsome jaws in eager anticipation. This False Elvis had to die. "I know who you are," he shouted. "You're the *Devil in disguise!*"

"*Don't be cruel,*" begged Ian unbelievingly, then the thing was upon him.

SO ENDED THE first skirmish of what would soon become an all-out war as the two species battled for supremacy over the British Isles. A vicious war it was too, but the story of that is best left for another day.

SPACE JOCKS: YES! NO! YES!

THE AREA 51 conspiracy theories grew and multiplied until they reached cottage industry proportions; the stronger the official denials the more widespread the general belief. Did a flying saucer crash on Earth in 1947? Did the occupants later die? Was an alien autopsy carried out? What, if anything, could the boffins learn from a study of off-world technology? Were decades spent in back-engineering an alien device?

Then, many years later, came the sudden appearance of a near-Earth wormhole, soon called the Hawking Singularity. Official reports claimed the two events were far apart and unconnected but non-stop speculation linked them in a variety of far-flung scenarios.

Sometime later Government sources started to drip-feed odd snippets of information relating back to 1947 and Area 51. If these sudden admissions were intended to satisfy and calm a worldwide population that was already starting to question the ruling elite, then they failed. The general opinion was that America would only admit that some earlier conspiracy theories had been correct if, by doing so, they covered up something even bigger and scarier. Something like a reinterpreted alien device having been responsible for the sudden appearance of the wormhole. If the Hawking Singularity worked, then visitors from other worlds were not only possible but likely. Humanity was going to have to accept that mankind was not alone in the universe, and that was panicky.

This could all be totally true or a bag full of fictional make-believe, or even a bit of both. Take from it what you will, if anything, but if you do then please don't complain. This is no money back offer. There were no Space Jock Heroes, or if there were then their names were different and the mission they undertook was something else entirely. Maybe wormholes should be confined to the pages of science fiction. How many spacecraft have you seen in the sky today: that many, that few; ten, one, none? The Space Jocks were the cream, just out of training and raring to go. If there were such things as wormholes, then they would have been the lads to explore them.

JOEL ABERCROMBIE WAS chosen to be the first to enter the Hawking Singularity. The one-man module was fitted with every recording device known. "Just a daytrip," the experts told him. "In and out, job done." The various *...ologists* might air their opinions, but nobody really knew what the inside of a wormhole would be like. Some thought that unmanned drones should be used first, but the public wanted heroes and the Space Jocks, so named by the popular media outlets, fitted the bill.

Abercrombie's H-S1 module was piggy-backed to as near to the singularity entrance as the carrier rocket could take it. "Have the coffee boiling," he said in a live statement being broadcast around the globe. "Same time tomorrow: two sugars, no cream." The module lifted free, approached the wormhole, and entered.

Neither Joel Abercrombie nor the H-S1 module were ever seen or heard from again. Not a single message.

Not a peep.

The second member of the Golden Generation of fearless space explorers to volunteer was Bruce M'Banga. He could have been challenging for one, or all, of the Heavyweight Belts if that had been where his ambitions lay. Big-chested and powerful; well suited to sucking in deep breaths of air in less than ideal conditions, the stars had always beckoned him. If brute strength was needed to conquer the wormhole, he had enough and plenty to spare.

"Maybe we were too ambitious," worried the experts. "Start recording before you actually enter the hole … and keep up a non-stop conversation. One hour in and then back: let's get the entrance sorted first."

Bruce spent his last free hours in the gym, toning up his already fantastic physique. His whole philosophy insisted that a fully functioning intellect needed to be housed in as perfect a body as possible. The next morning, obeying instructions to the letter, his H-S2 module flew into the wormhole, and as he crossed the threshold and disappeared from view all recording and transmissions from his craft ceased. As had been the case with Joel Abercrombie, Bruce M'Banga vanished completely.

Does it seem believable? Or just a little unlikely? The Hawking Singularity, named after a noted physicist from the past, seemed better suited to a space opera trilogy rather than scientific journals. America, as the leader in what was ostensibly a worldwide endeavour, huffed and puffed and tried to present these disasters in an optimistic light. America did not take failure easily. Europe, and particularly Britain, were more forgiving. They had a history of glorifying gallant losers. Russia was worried that the missions might have been totally successful but that America was keeping all the information to itself.

There were also some disaster-hit parts of the world that really did not give a damn. They were too busy just trying to survive. The most unbelievable thing of all though was when a third person put his hand up to enter the wormhole.

Pete Mandel felt his group were duty bound to follow one another, each in his turn, into the wormhole, and he would be next. There was widespread belief that Abercrombie and M'Banga had perished but it was not an opinion that Mandel subscribed to. Those brave Space Jocks were missing, presumed dead by many, but you couldn't have a funeral without a body. It could be that they were merely lost, totally so it would seem, but if that were the case then finding them was a possibility, however tiny. He would go in, aiming to fulfil all mission requirements but also to find out what had happened to his fellow astronauts.

"Straight in and out," they told him. "No recording, no audio; just fly in, turn, and fly out. Future exploration can start to map the thing, if we can only master the art of wormhole survival."

Pete Mandel kissed the badge and saluted the flag. Once in he would be his own man and he would look for signs of his lost brothers, whatever the controllers thought. His H-S3 module would go wherever it needed to and if he suffered the same fate as Joel and Bruce, whatever that might be, then he hoped and trusted that further attempts would follow in his footsteps.

Three was more than enough. As with the two before him, Mandel was lost the moment he entered the wormhole. There would be no more attempts and the depleted group of Space Jocks would be split up and transferred to more ordinary and mundane space and aviation programmes. As far as Earth was concerned, the Hawking Singularity was off limits. And so it remained for ten years, until the first alien vessel emerged coming the other way. Day trippers, in a way, looking for a new planet to experience, and Earth fitted the bill.

THERE WERE, IT transpired, specific rules to using a wormhole. You didn't just blunder in, gung ho, as those brave but foolhardy Space Jocks had done; but Earth had not known better back then. Soon two-way traffic was achieved, with sufficient visitors coming in to require a permanent Alien Registration Centre to deal with the influx. Mostly they were tourists or traders, but there were occasionally some with hidden agendas and they had to be weeded out and sent back to wherever they came from.

All went smoothly for five hundred years. Interspecies trade agreements were hammered out and signed while galactic tourism grew and flourished. Mankind was doing okay, thank you, and memories of those three lost Space Jock Heroes faded. Ask a man-in-the-boulevard who Abercrombie, M'Banga and Mandel had been and he might well guess them to be the Manchester United midfield the last time they had won a trophy; such was the lack of concern for both old space failures and minority interest sports. That last bit is probably fair comment, even if the rest of it is debatable. There was one stir of the pot missing though: a sci-fi blockbuster needed interplanetary conflict.

THE TROLLICKS CAME pouring out from the Hawking

Singularity with all weapons blazing. They were warriors, pure and simple, with no interest in anything but expanding their empire. Most species wilted under their non-stop aggression and quickly tried to get the best surrender terms available, but when they attacked Earth the Trollicks finally found themselves up against beings as bloody-minded and determined as they were. After every defeat, and there were a few, mankind merely retreated, regrouped, and set up new defence lines. They simply would not give in.

After more than a year the conflict drifted into a stalemate, neither side able to achieve any sort of real supremacy. This wasn't the way Trollick commanders were used to conducting their expansionist policies and they began to doubt the wisdom of continuing.

There were no talks between the two sides, and no official halt to hostilities. The Trollick forces merely withdrew, entered the Hawking Singularity, and were gone. Areas of the planet were devastated but the aggressor had given up. The message was blunt: Don't mess with Man.

A number of things followed. A lot of resources were poured into healing the extensive battle damage and making the planet whole again. Politically speaking, the old open borders policy regarding alien visitors had to be scrapped. If Earth had been able to close the wormhole they might well have done so, but since they couldn't then at least it had to be kept under strict control. To that end, a fully armed squadron of sentinel-class battle cruisers were permanently posted at the wormhole. Any vessels arriving were escorted to the newly rebuilt, and much less friendly, Alien Registration Centre. Not many were granted access to Earth, and those that weren't were promptly sent on their way. And the years passed.

To sit was pain. To stand was pain. Both were concepts that maybe meant something once but did no longer. With flesh into metal and metal into flesh, positional changes were impossible anyway. He was flesh, blood, metal, all hurting in a hundred different ways. He knew pain at every conceivable level. With eyes that ached, and sometimes blurred, he kept up a constant surveillance of the needles and dials on the panel before him and responded to what he saw. He was a merger of two opposites. A blueprint conceived in the Halls of Beelzebub. He had been different once: a person, named, but that had been then. Now he was both man and machine. Now he flew the black wastelands between the stars. Now he was pain personified. Reduced, at best, to a dull ache, or raging to excruciating levels. So much a part of what he was, he feared he would not survive without it.

What threatened his sanity even more than the pain was an itch on the end of his nose that he needed to scratch but couldn't, not with hands welded into the vehicular control system. Sometimes he wished they had let him die, stranded in non-space where no stars twinkled and no planets spun their time honoured orbits. If fate had ordained that he should be rescued it was a cruel twist that it should be by a Dordorationist.

The Dordoration research vessel had been taking non-space readings when they happened upon him; barely alive, hallucinating, as near to death as is possible without tipping past the point of no return. Being skin and bone, with only limited flesh, which could have been natural but wasn't, a severe lack of nourishment was obvious. The Dordorat belief system was based on scientific knowledge and achievement, with life being relatively unimportant. Their first reaction was to leave this old and battered vehicle alone. The being it contained would soon be dead. It was not their concern.

So it would have been, had the Research Commander not had a brainwave. His number three male offspring had volunteered his main parent to provide a classroom challenge, and this could be it. The being, brought back from the brink of death, would never know that he had merely been a college project for fourth year students. They had rebuilt both man and vehicle, merging them into a single entity. It was both a scientific and an engineering success, but with little or no thought given to the trauma of living tissue so totally manipulated. And when they had finished, and before he awoke, they shot him back into space. The entity had no memory of ever having been on the planet Dordorat.

BECAUSE EARTH'S STRICT controls were rigorously enforced, aliens knew better than to merely visit on a whim. Only those with legitimate reasons made it to the planet, and they were usually pre-planned well in advance.

Captain Starling, the officer-in-charge of the Hawking on-duty task-force, was suitably surprised when his surveillance officer informed him that an unknown craft was travelling through the wormhole and was estimated to exit in exactly one hour. At his command, the six strong unit adopted a standard hold-and-contain formation.

"Whoever it is, hold them at the entrance," ordered the Alien Registration Centre. "We will decide on a course of action once we know who it is, and what they are after. Keep this channel open and tell us every last little thing."

Captain Starling clicked his heels and saluted at the screen. It would have to be when he was on duty. Captain Nightingale, his opposite number, would be happily snoring alongside his current partner of choice; while he, Starling, faced goodness knew what; but he was a conscientious spaceman and would act accordingly.

"Here it comes!"

The six cruisers blasted "HALT AND AWAIT INSTRUCT-IONS" at the emerging craft, in all the languages at their disposal. It was only a small vessel that came into sight and did indeed stop as ordered. Old too, if the pitted surface was anything to go by: modern craft were no longer affected by space dust.

"Can you read the insignia?" asked the Captain of Cruiser Four. "H something, but it's faint."

"H-S3!" exclaimed Starling, but that couldn't be right … could it?

Only people looking to qualify for a career in Space remembered anything about the three lost wormhole pioneers. It was part of their syllabus, and H-S3 was the module of Pete Mandel, the third and last of the brave but thoughtless Space Jocks.

"Blanket all communication," ordered a bigwig at Alien Registration Centre, "and bring it in."

PIERRE JACKDAW WAS the top Regenerative Surgeon on the planet, Walter Buzzard the number one Engineer, and Yusef Finch the most acclaimed Psychiatrist, but not one of them had ever seen anything like the man/machine they had been called in to examine. Pete Mandel was unique on Earth. No one there had seen his like before.

He had survived for all these years on a single meal, and that in itself was mind-blowing. That one meal had gone through his digestive system with the waste products being removed by tubes and taken to a mini-recycling plant, where it was transformed into a nutrient-rich mulch which was reintroduced into his body via more tubes; the process being repeated at regular intervals for what appeared to be the rest of time.

Are you getting this? Any of it? The best brains on Earth were flummoxed but maybe common sense will grab more than high-falutin theorists. The experts did their best though. There was no way they could separate flesh and metal but they did make the union less stressful, and therefore less painful, and for that the man/machine was grateful. Also, Doctor Finch did break down some memory barriers and promoted a certain degree of self-awareness. Some things were hard to assimilate though.

"So how long was I wandering space?" he asked.

He was probably going to find out one day, so maybe it was best to be truthful. "From the time you entered the Hawking Singularity until the moment you emerged from it, ten thousand years had passed."

Pete Mandel never really accepted that. They told him about the war with the Trollicks, and all the other amazing things that had happened during his absence, but he never could get his head around it being ten thousand years, and who could blame him. If I'd been him I wouldn't have believed it either. If I were you, I'd have my doubts.

Finally the experts declared themselves finished, and that was when Earth's problems really began. What could they possibly do with him? He was unique and a machine, but his human half made it impossible for him to be a museum exhibit. A one-man module might be small in comparison with other spacecraft but was way too bulky for run-of-the-mill accommodation. Space was always at a premium, even with the current multi-storied Earths-within-Earths system; but Pete Mandel was a Space Jock Hero and a living legend. It was suggested that he be granted a portion of land and on it they would build an all-purpose hanger, sufficient for the comfort of both man and machine. But they need not have worried. Pete Mandel had his own ideas and settling back into Earth society was not one of them.

HE HAD SURVIVED, somehow, for ten thousand years, so they told him. But what about the two who had gone before him? What about Joel Abercrombie and Bruce M'Banga? As the second had followed the first, so he had followed them both; and then Earth had cut them off, had forgotten about the three of them. Pete Mandel had expected, should he too be lost, that a fourth Space Jock would make the attempt; then a fifth, a sixth, and so on. But it would appear that Joel, Bruce and he were not merely expendable but left to rot, dead or not. Pete wasn't sure he wanted to settle back into a world that treated its Heroes so coldly.

He had entered the Hawking Singularity, that endless tunnel with a thousand exits, and lived to tell the tale. Changed, admittedly, but still alive. Somewhere, lost within the multitude of possibilities that existed within a wormhole universe, his buddies might also be experiencing some form of life. They might be dead, and he accepted that, but there was only one way to find out, if at all.

Pete Mandel was determined to spend the rest of

eternity, if need be, searching for Joel Abercrombie and Bruce M'Banga. Or at least finding out what had happened to them. Whatever he had now become, maybe first of a new breed of man/machine, he was content within himself. Earth had updated him with their wormhole knowledge. He was much better prepared this time.

PETE MANDEL: SPACE Jock Hero, man/machine, a strange interlocking of flesh and metal, said his goodbyes to Earth for a second time. With a feeling of relief, he aimed his module/body at the wormhole entrance. H-S3 entered the Hawking Singularity for the second time and set out on another amazing journey.

CHARLEY PATTON
FATHER OF THE DELTA BLUES

Small man – Charley
Ever picking fights he could not win

Small man – Charley
Part European
Part African
Part Native American
A Puerto Rican-looking man
Said Howlin' Wolf

Small man – Charley
But the Patton pattern
Saw his Delta style
Extended all the way
To Chicago and beyond
Making stars of many who followed

Physically small – Charley
But a big man nevertheless

THE DEATH OF
BLIND LEMON JEFFERSON

*Blind Lemon Jefferson had a heart attack in the back seat of
his snowed-in car during a Chicago blizzard in the winter of
1929. Deserted by his panic stricken employee, he froze to
death.*

He was a street-singing Daddy
A superstar
Sing *Jack O' Diamonds* Lemon
Sing *Black Snake Moan*
Records gave him money
And a big flash car
Sing *Crawlin' Baby* Lemon
Sing *Matchbox Blues*
He was a sharp-dressed guy
With a chauffeur man
Sing *Broke and Hungry* Lemon
Sing *Bad Luck Blues*
Because when bad luck
Did come calling
That chauffeur man just ran

ELLAS McDANIEL

Ellas McDaniel would have laughed
At being lumped with
The Jazz & Blues Giants
He thought himself a rock 'n' roller
An entertainer
The man who invented rap
And the psychedelic guitar
The baddest cat alive
Rock 'n' roll – certainly
R&B – yes
But rooted in the blues
(And where would jazz be without them)
With a nod to the field hollers
That preceded it all
Ellas McDaniel: the boy violinist
Who tuned a guitar like a fiddle
And grew up to be Bo Diddley

MIGHTY WOLF

This is where the soul of a man never dies
                              Sam Phillips (Sun Records)

Chester Burnett was a farmer
Bone stupid
Said some
With an ingrained suspicion
A man who knew how to bear a grudge

Big Foot Chester
Became Howlin' Wolf
Still difficult
Brooding
Not an easy man
But sounding like no one before or since

The blues would never be the same

THE ROAD TO SALAMIS

AM I BEEF? Of course I am. These muscles don't come natural, or cheap. Then there's my super-sensitive hearing and sharper-than-sharp eyesight, all topped up with a pounds-per-square-inch power-ratio that can see me punch through a brick wall. You want to try me, bro?

There are bigger and bulkier to be hired within the security sector, of course. It's like an addiction with some, piling muscle upon muscle in a never-ending search for the ultimate in size and strength, looking more grotesquely alien than human, in the end. Big and strong they might be, but lumbering with it, sacrificing speed. I like to think I judged it right and knew when to stop.

Beef for hire – anything that comes under the security umbrella: from bodyguard duties to roughing someone up. Some guys double as hit-men but not me. I've had to see off a couple in self-defence, or protecting a client, but contract killing would not rest easy on my shoulders. Guess I'm just a big softy really. Not academically gifted but with an innate intelligence that sees me get by, or so I like to think. Marty is a streetwise kid. That's me, by the way, Marty Butterfield, and I had an appointment to see Arman Kazemi, sometimes referred to as the Sultan, though I had heard it was not a nickname he liked.

He wasn't one of those celebrity criminals who

everybody had heard of but law enforcement could never pin down. Mr Kazemi was more of a shadowy figure, maybe the money man who bankrolled whatever appeared lucrative enough to be of interest. Or so the rumour mill suggested, and I try to keep up to date with both players and the games they play. I was sure he had muscle aplenty near at hand; people like him always had permanent security, so why had he set up a meeting with me? There was only one way to find out.

Drugs, people trafficking, illegal armaments: those were whispered to be areas of special interest, but the metallic plaque merely stated GULF ARTIFACTS (Imports & Exports). The office suite was situated in a genteel area, all shiny and expensive looking, as was the receptionist, boasting a classy chassis and a voice that purred. "Ah … Mr Butterfield. Mr Kazemi is expecting you." When she stood I saw long shapely legs that pointed to heaven but I suspected that if climbed they would only lead to plastic.

Arman Kazemi was not totally unknown to me, though we had never actually spoken before. I had seen him at functions when in the employ of a fellow attendee. While he fixed me with his unreadable eagle-like eyes I took in his large hooked nose and thin-lipped mouth. It was the face of someone who always got his own way.

"I wish to employ you," he told me. It wasn't a request. "Bodyguard duties at a scientific research facility with accommodation provided. A minimum of three months at double your standard contract rates."

I liked the double-pay bit but the rest needed to have meat put on the bone. "Why me?" I asked for openers. "I'm sure you already have plenty of security, so why bring in an outsider?"

Kazemi cocked a thumb in the direction of the seven-foot tree-trunk impersonator who stood guard by the door, beefed-up Beef to the ninth degree. "Ray is very good at his job," he explained. "He does what he's told, to the letter, without question, but the gears slow down under any requirement for independent thought. Very good for day-by-day routine but for this particular job I want someone who can think for themselves; you have been recommended as being able to do so, Mr Butterfield. There will be a couple of my regulars on site but you will be in charge of them.

"If all goes well, and there is nothing to suggest it shouldn't, your presence being purely a precautionary measure, a generous bonus will be added to your account. I have stipulated three months but a certain amount of flexibility might be required."

A generous bonus on top of double rates! I offered up a silent thank you to whoever had recommended me for this particular gig. It sounded more attractive every time the man opposite opened his cruel mouth. "Who is it I'll be babysitting?" I asked, seeking a little more clarity.

"A group of three," replied Kazemi, "Professor Andris Irbe and two assistants. Does his name mean anything to you?"

"I'm afraid not."

"I didn't think it would. He is a noted physicist, lauded within his field, but hardly a public figure."

"You said it was a scientific research establishment," I said, thinking a show of interest might be appropriate. "What is this Professor's speciality?"

"All in good time, Mr Butterfield. I'm sure it will become clear once you are integrated within the facility but until then all you need to know is that it's an area of great concern to me personally. It is a private endeavour, funded by me and for me, with no involvement from any other source whatsoever."

"When do you want me to start?" I asked. "I have a few loose ends that need to be tidied up."

"Of course! Will two days be sufficient for you? A vehicle will pick you up at 9:00 a.m. on Thursday morning. Welcome aboard, Mr Butterfield."

He didn't offer a handshake and his whole bearing suggested it unlikely we would ever share anything approaching a buddy moment. "Thank you, Mr Kazemi," I muttered, and Big Ray opened the door for me to leave.

I KNEW WHICH type of bar Dipper Campbell was likely to be in at that time of day and scored a home run with my first port of call. Even at this relatively early hour Le Hostelry stank of cheap wine, low-grade hash and stagnant piss. He would move on to better class places as the day progressed.

"Arman Kazemi's credit rating is beyond the ability of credit agencies to put a figure on. Even his legitimate business makes a good annual profit and what goes in and out of the back door would cover many a third world country's national debt. Tread very carefully in your dealings with this man, Marty."

I shrugged dismissively. "Tell me something I don't know, Dipper."

"There's been a suggestion that he's been releasing assets for a private enterprise, which might be this research facility, whatever it is. In many ways he is a very shadowy figure, but there are times he leaves no shadow at all. I'm not being much help to you, Marty, but if I had any hard facts to pass on then he would not be the man that he is, and he would probably be sending a super-Beef or two to stomp all over me."

I knew he was right. Dipper would help if he could. Maybe it was time to switch from Kazemi to the Professor. "What about this Andris Irbe guy?" I asked.

"His great-grandparents were part of the mass migration from what was once Latvia," said Dipper. "He was fully respected in his field until recently. His last paper on curved space-time apparently rehashed the old and discredited Tippett-Tsang theories, and was not well received, making him something of a laughing stock in certain quarters.

"Not long after that he resigned his position at the University of New Delhi and has not been heard of since."

"That could be when Kazemi scouted him for this hush-hush research thing," I suggested.

"Looks that way," Dipper agreed. "Watch yourself, my friend," he continued. "This is a bit outside your comfort zone and the Iranian is not a man to be trifled with."

OUTSIDE MY COMFORT zone? Well fuck you, Dipper mate! Playing nursemaid to three scientific boffins in a locked-in environment would be child's play compared to some of the jobs I'd had in the past. Bringing me in was just Mr Kazemi being ultra-cautious, according to Edward, the GULF ARTIFACTS employee who arrived in the chauffeur-driven limo at nine on the Thursday morning and accompanied me on the ride. The dark-tinted windows made it difficult to see just where we were going, apart from the realisation that we eventually left the urban sprawl, and Edward wasn't any help. He did talk about our eventual destination though, comprising laboratories, workshops and living quarters. The Professor's two assistants were Clifton McClennan and Chantal Pelletier. The two permanent security men were Lenny and Sam. They all knew about me.

Edward's own opinion was that I was a safeguard against possible industrial espionage. He didn't know what was going on at the facility and didn't want to, but if Mr Kazemi thought it worthwhile then others would too, and they might try to steal the information. It was an explanation that had already crossed my mind, so one up to my travelling companion.

The tightly packed group of buildings were surrounded by protective fencing that would fry to a cinder anyone stupid enough to try and climb. The single-entry point was being operated by either Lenny or Sam, who opened up to let us in.

"Come on," said Edward. "I'll introduce you to everyone before I leave."

I followed him into the nearest building.

By the second day I had organised Lenny and Sam into regular patrols of the buildings, in and out, and apart from undertaking an occasional shift myself had very little with which to occupy myself.

"What is it you're doing here, Prof?"

I was even willing to listen to a bit of scientific babble.

"You have not been told, Mr Butterfield?"

"No, Mr Kazemi thought it best if I established myself here first … and call me Marty. I don't go much on titles except those that have been earned – like yours, Professor."

He was a thickset florid sort of fellow with a mop of iron-grey hair. "How shall I word it without you thinking us crazy?" he said. "We have been, uh, investigating the possibilities of time travel."

"Time travel?" I exclaimed, echoing his last two words but turning them into a question.

"Do you wish to return to your room now to have a good laugh at the mad scientist? Or are you willing to listen to what I have to say?"

Well I could always laugh later and I had nothing better to do just then.

BENJAMIN K TIPPETT and David Tsang had created a mathematical formula that used Einstein's General Relativity Theory to prove that time travel was possible, the Professor told me. Its acceptance was not helped by them calling it a Traversable Acausal Retrograde Domain in Space-time, thus TARDIS – the name of a time-travelling machine in a popular visual entertainment of the day. They were unable to move from theoretical to practical because what they were suggesting needed to be constructed from what they termed Exotic Matter, which had not yet been discovered.

That sounded like a convenient get-out clause to me, and probably to most of Tippett and Tsang's contemporaries. Their theory had lain dormant for years, ignored and unremembered, until Andris Irbe, tucked away in the University of New Delhi, dusted it down and took an interest, that seemed to me to have grown into an obsession.

Most of the technical data he threw at me, curves and bends in space-time and squares within bubbles that flew backwards or forwards as required, went floating way over my head, but the Prof didn't seem bothered by that. I think he found it a relief to expound his mad theoretical cleverness to a non-judgemental audience like me. The condemnation and attacks he had received when publishing his findings had obviously left their mark. Only one man, and a non-scientist at that, had taken him seriously, Arman Kazemi, and seriously enough to fund Irbe's continued research.

"All he wants in return," said the Prof, obviously in total awe of the man, "is for me to aim our trial run at a spot in history of his choosing."

There had to be more to it than that, I thought, but kept to myself. Kazemi was no philanthropist. There had to be an eventual profit margin to cover such an immense outlay, but as long as I received my double-time credit plus fat bonus, then the rest of this nonsense could go whistle.

Boy, would I have a tale to tell Dipper Campbell when all this was over!

"But if Tippett and Tsang couldn't try out their theories, how does Professor Irbe plan to overcome the same obstacles?" I asked.

"By being cleverer," replied Clifton McClennan. "Yes, he has added refinements to their original calculations, but their main failing was to need material that had not yet been invented."

"Exotic Matter," I suggested, pleased to have remembered as much as I had from the Professor's rambling.

"Exactly," agreed McClennan, "but Irbe has gone that one step further, inventing it, and we have produced sufficient to build the machine."

"He has actually invented Exotic Matter?"

McClennan chose his words carefully. "Well he has invented something," he said, "and with it we have constructed what he claims will be a working method of time travel, but we won't know if it is indeed Exotic Matter until we try it out."

Even though he was one of Irbe's assistants, I had the feeling he was something of a sceptic. "You've got doubts though, haven't you?"

"Nothing is proven until tested." He shrugged and shook his head a little. "It's been interesting work and I wouldn't have missed it but, deep down, I don't really believe that time travel is possible under any circumstances. I just don't think the Universe would allow it."

Chantal Pelletier, the other assistant, was more tight-lipped. Her loyalty to the Professor and his work did not allow for any arguments against either. "The man is a genius," she insisted. "Even if our first attempt should fail his work will continue and will eventually bear fruit."

"But what about the time-travel paradox?" I asked. "Going back and killing your own father. If you're never born how could you go back so you would be born."

It was nonsense, all of it. All I'd want would be to go back to this morning with a list of this afternoon's winners in my pocket.

"Things are only impossible until they've been done," decided Miss Pelletier, a pleasantly attractive woman, even though she didn't make the best of herself. She didn't seem that friendly with her fellow assistant, which surprised me. Given the circumstances I thought they might have been bonking buddies by now.

"We will soon find out," she added, "Just as soon as the Professor and Mr Kazemi sort out the details of our first attempt."

THE PROFESSOR WAS angry, red-faced angry. He kept in regular communication with the man paying the bills but this last time had been more than him just giving a progress update, and the physicist had not liked the way the conversation had gone, and he'd gathered us all together for the news.

"Mr Kazemi will be joining us tomorrow and will be staying for the duration of our first use of the Tippett/Tsang/Irbe Time Machine. I would have preferred some short-hop test-runs before attempting something major but, uh, under the terms of his funding Mr Kazemi owns this facility and his word is, uh, law!"

"Don't keep us in suspense, Professor," interrupted McClennan. "Where and when are we aiming for?"

"Wherever or whenever," added an excited Chantal, "you will still be mankind's first ever time traveller."

"If only, my dear, if only…"

"Don't tell me Kazemi wants that honour for himself!" exclaimed McClennan.

"Not quite, Clifton. He has nominated one of his employees, a Raymond Fuller." Irbe was having trouble maintaining a calm exterior. He must have been chewed-up inside. "And we will be sending him back to 480 BC, to witness the naval battle between the Greeks and Persians at Salamis. Again, Mr Kazemi's, uh, choice."

"And this Mr Fuller," asked McClennan, "I take it he's a scientist? What is his area?"

The Prof just shrugged, silently, so I stepped in. "He's a Beef," I told them, "just part of the Security

Team."

Big Ray, beefed-up to not far short of exploding point: mankind's first time traveller! It was getting odder and odder. What strange game was Arman Kazemi playing?

IF NOTHING ELSE, it got us looking up Salamis. I for one had never heard of it before. Greece: yes of course, often in the news, making the sort of threats and demands that bankrupt countries could never back up. Persia was an old-time name, which made me think of Ali Baba, Aladdin and magic carpets, but maybe I was getting my Arab nations mixed up.

"Salamis was the turning point in the decade-long Persian War, giving the Greek city-states belief that they could win," offered Clifton McClennan, obviously gearing himself up in full lecture mode.

"But what has that got to do with Kazemi?" I asked, butting in.

"Well Iran used to be called Persia," said Chantal.

"And Kazemi is Iranian," I added, completing her train of thought.

"Quite!" she agreed.

So there was a vague connection but not enough to throw a punch at. Why was Salamis so important to Arman Kazemi?

XERXES, THE GREAT King, intent upon both avenging his father's defeat at Marathon and stubbing out the potentially damaging threat posed by the Hellenic experiments with radical democracy, entered northern Greece with the biggest force Europe would see until WW2's D Day invasion by the allies in 1944. Initially they swept all before them, small Greek city-states having to choose between destruction or surrender.

I've got to admit, it was exciting stuff. Some I got from Clifton, some from Chantal, and some I even looked up for myself.

The Greek cities, bickering among themselves and unable to agree a common strategy, stood on the brink of total defeat. Previous attempts to stem the tide had failed leaving Salamis as their last chance to stop the Persian onslaught.

"Cometh the hour, cometh the man; in this case the Athenian Statesman/Admiral Themistocles," lectured Clifton McClennan. "His plan was to pit his much smaller fleet against the numerically superior Persians in the narrow straits between the island of Salamis and the Greek mainland, where the lack of space would nullify many of their advantages, and his sturdier ships could ram their flimsier opponents."

"In spite of having twice as many vessels," butted in Chantal, "the Persian Admirals were outthought and their fleet was outfought. Within a few days of the loss Xerxes took an infantry guard of 60,000 men and returned to Persia."

The end was predictable, as I found from my own research. The remaining Persian land force, demoralised by the defeat, now lacking the support of a victorious fleet and the leadership of their king, was defeated at Plataca.

The war had been the last chance for the East to check Greek culture in its infancy, and the outcome was that the democratic principles that would eventually emerge as Western Civilisation were allowed to flourish and grow.

"All very interesting," I agreed, "but what has it got to do with Arman Kazemi?"

Neither of the assistants knew or would hazard a guess, and the Professor didn't take part in our brainstorming sessions. The next day the moneyman himself would be joining us but would be unlikely to satisfy anyone's curiosity on the matter.

"HOW HAVE THINGS been down here, Butterfield?" he asked, having summoned me for a face-to-face.

"Fine, Mr Kazemi," I replied, "everything smooth and easy."

"No attempted infiltration?"

"No."

"Or signs of unwarranted observation?"

"No."

"Good!" He paused for a moment before continuing. "Things have not been so straight forward back in the city."

"Oh?" was the safest comment I could come up with.

"An Info Hack, or Data Salesman as I believe they like to call themselves, suddenly started to take too much of an interest in my affairs."

"Might have been just a random sweep," I suggested, hoping it hadn't been Dipper. "It probably had nothing to do with what's going on here."

"Only fools take chances," said Kazemi. "The threat, real or imaginary, has been removed, permanently. A man named Dennis Campbell."

Dipper!

Dead!

On the orders of the man who sat only a few paces from where I stood. Dipper had been the closest thing I'd had to a friend in the last year or two, but dead was dead and nothing I could do now would make any difference to that. "Stupid guy," I remarked with what I hoped would pass as a disinterested shrug. Sorry Dipper, but you're dead and I am still alive and I want to keep it that way. "How does Ray feel about being the first ever time traveller?" I asked, thinking a change of topic might pay dividends.

"He does whatever I tell him to do, no questions asked. A perfect employee in many ways, and the role of messenger is well within his capabilities."

"Messenger?"

Kazemi smiled knowingly. "I'd hardly be sending Ray back to engage in philosophical discussions, would I?"

I would love to have planted my fist in the middle of his smirking face but I did nothing.

"Be extra vigilant over the next few days just in case the Info Hack was already acting on behalf of a client."

"Of course, Mr Kazemi," I said.

Yes sir, no sir, three bags full sir. Whatever your plans I hope they get fucked! But I stood straight and tried to make sure that my feelings didn't show on my face.

I COULDN'T GET Ray's own thoughts on what he would soon be attempting because he was being tutored by Irbe in a crash course on all things relating to the Time Machine, but I did manage a late evening chat with Clifton McClennan.

"What's going on? What are the plans? Come on, Clifton, spill it!"

"480 BC is the definite year, aiming for the end of August, some weeks before the big sea battle. Fuller will wear period clothes, already made to measure before they left the city, so he should be able to blend in. All he'll take with him will be a leather pouch containing documents, but don't ask me what they are about because Kazemi's not saying, and I don't think Fuller knows."

Documents! Clifton was as frustrated as me.

"Artificially introduced mastery of both the Greek and Persian languages of the day will enable him to converse with whoever he might meet," continued McClennan.

"That will wear off though, won't it?" I asked.

"Not for six months."

"You're talking as if it was all going to happen," I suggested. "I thought you didn't believe time travel was possible!"

"I don't! Not really! But I can't help being carried along by the enormity of the moment; and the total conviction of others can be quite contagious."

"I hope it goes wrong," I said, thinking of Dipper. "Kazemi needs to experience failure."

"IT WORKED! YES, yes, yes! Or at least it appeared to. Everything happened just as the Professor had predicted."

Chantal Pelletier was beside herself with excitement.

"Tell me!" I begged, security personnel having been barred from being present.

"The man, Fuller, entered the box and operated the controls in sync with the Professor on the outside. The bubble, made of Exotic Matter, started to revolve, slowly at first. Left-right, up-down, past-future, would all have been merging within the spinning boundaries at this point. Communication with the inside of the square would no longer be possible."

"Yes?" I prompted. "What happened next?"

"The spinning got faster and faster, until it was

nothing but a blur of bright light and colours. The box could no longer be seen properly."

"If it was going that fast surely it would have injured or even killed anyone inside."

"It's hard to explain to a layman, Marty, but to the occupant it would not appear that the box was moving at all. He will know nothing until reaching the pre-set date, at which time the bubble will stop spinning and go into a temporary collapse, and the square's entrance will automatically open."

"But how can you tell here at our end?"

"We saw the spinning stop, and everything was gone. No bubble! No box! No Mr Fuller! All gone! Back to 480 BC. We did it. We must have!"

And she threw her arms around my neck, kissing me with a passion that surprised me. Never one to miss an opportunity, I kissed her back.

LENNY, SAM AND me had our regular surveillance duties to carry out. Well the other two did and I tried to make myself appear busy in front of the boss man. The others though were very much on edge, waiting for proof of success, or otherwise. Kazemi, for instance, was in constant communication with the city, barking questions and instructions at whoever he was con-tacting.

"But what sort of proof are you all expecting?" I asked him, taking a chance on whether or not he would welcome a show of interest from me.

"Between you and me, I don't give a damn about Irbe's scientific mumbo-jumbo. I sent Ray back to carry out a specific task. If he succeeded then repercussions should have echoed down the ages, bringing changes that will show in our present-day world."

"And those changes have not yet shown?"

"No!" He pierced me with his cold eyes. "Keep our conversations private, Marty. Irbe and his team have their own areas of concern, and I have mine. I prefer it kept that way."

With the rift between him and Irbe growing maybe he saw me as a safe pair of ears he could talk to. "Whatever you say, Mr Kazemi," I said, dutifully.

Later I discussed it with Chantal. In bed, since I was willing to approach what was going on from whatever angles I could fashion. "His side lost at Salamis," she said, lying alongside me. "I think he might have hoped to influence the outcome of the naval battle."

"Whatever it was, Ray seems to have failed." I reached out for her. "The changes Kazemi was hoping for haven't materialised."

"Changes!" exclaimed Chantal, pushing my hands away. "Don't you realise, if the Persians had won at Salamis they would then have conquered all of Greece. The whole of history would have been changed and the world today would be a completely different place. Many of us, maybe you and I, would never have existed. If I am right then the changes Kazemi is looking for are not small or insignificant. He is looking to impose a New World Order, and has been willing to risk his own existence, and ours, to achieve it."

I lay in a nice warm bed, a hot body alongside mine, but an icy chill coursed through my veins. It was more madness, it had to be, please, but Chantal thought it all possible

EDGY DAYS STRETCHED into nervous weeks, and still nothing was heard from, or about, Ray Fuller. September came and went back in 480 BC. The sea battle was over, whether he had delivered the documents or not.

"Operate the damned thing!" I heard Kazemi shout.

"It would be best done by your man at his end," countered the Professor.

"Best, worst, whatever … I know you can do it. McClennan has kept me informed."

"Clifton, have you been playing the Judas role?"

"Mr Kazemi's money has made all this possible," responded McClennan angrily. "He deserved to know everything."

"For a price, I am sure."

"Enough!" thundered Kazemi. "If you won't do it then McClennan can take your place at the controls."

At this point I felt that voices had been raised sufficiently to justify action on my part, so I opened the door. "Ah, Butterfield," said Kazemi as I entered, "you might be needed to remove the Professor."

"Whatever you are being asked to do, Prof, why not just do it," I suggested. "You wouldn't want to miss out on any part, would you?"

"You are right, Marty." He turned back to glare at the moneyman. "It is against my better judgement but, uh, if anyone is to operate the machine it should be me."

"I don't care who, just get that box back here into our time," said Kazemi. "We have to know what Ray saw, and exactly what happened."

Professor Irbe positioned himself at the controls, pressing buttons, flicking switches, studying information that appeared on screens. "We shouldn't be, uh, forcing it like this," he muttered, more to himself than anyone. "It should be in tandem with the person riding the timelines." But the flashing lights and colours returned as the spinning bubble reasserted itself. Round and round it flew at speeds that could only be imagined, before suddenly slowing to a halt.

The bubble collapsed, as it was supposed to, but the box remained, and a door swung open. Being the nearest, Chantal stepped forward, looked inside, screamed – then fell to the floor in a faint.

The rest of us rushed over, stepping across where she lay, more keen to see what was inside the box. Looking after Chantal could wait until after that.

"My God!" exclaimed McClennan, turning away to vomit over his own shoes.

Neither Kazemi nor Irbe said a word but I noticed that both their shoulders slumped.

"Is he there?" I shouted, squeezing between the two older men to look inside.

Ray was there alright, but obviously dead. His body had been quartered, butchered into four fairly equal pieces. The leather pouch and contents had been destroyed as well, littering the blood-stained floor of the box.

"Shit!" muttered Kazemi, breaking the silence.

Shit indeed, I thought. This wasn't the way his projects were supposed to end.

LENNY AND SAM were given the task of cleaning the box and disposing of the body bits. There being no bar on site, which was a real shame because I could have done with a shot myself, I made Chantal a coffee and patted the back of her hand.

"Stop fussing," she told me. "It was a shock, but I'm over it now."

"I can understand that sometimes killing is necessary," I said, "but did they have to cut him up like that?"

"Disembowelment and other forms of mutilation were common at the time. When Pythias the Lydian asked for his son to be excused military service, Xerxes response was to have the young man cut in half – and marched his soldiers between the two pieces."

"So McClennan was feeding Kazemi all the little titbits the Professor kept from him," I said, changing the subject. I'm not the squeamish sort, but I don't see why even death can't be straightforward and business-like.

"Clifton was good at his job, but there was always something about him I could not take to."

"There's no accounting for likes and dislikes."

Chantal did smile a little at that. "You mean like us?" she asked. "Not a promising pairing, a Scientific Research Assistant and a Beef, but it seems to be working."

"It is for me," I said, and surprisingly enough I meant it.

MY ENHANCED HEARING meant that there wasn't much I was not able to listen in on, so was well aware that the relationship between Kazemi and the Professor remained icy. Irbe either did not know just how dangerous the Iranian could be, or he simply didn't care.

"No, no, no!" he shouted when told to prepare for a second return to 480 BC. "The Tippett/Tsang/Irbe Time Machine was intended as an observational tool, a method of learning from the past, of correcting misconceptions, and preparing for the future. It was not meant as a vehicle for private vendettas by people like you!"

"Without me you'd still be giving lectures in New

Delhi," shouted back Kazemi. "Your machine is mine, bought and paid for, and only you and the girl are not on my immediate payroll. You will follow my instructions or be removed, and I don't care which one you choose. With either you or McClennan at the controls I will get my way."

Ray's death had not put him off and Kazemi was determined to try again.

"I made a mistake," he admitted to me later, "in thinking it would be a straightforward messenger job. Whatever complications Ray faced, he was no longer able to cope."

"What was in the pouch?" I asked, feeling more confident in my dealings with him.

"The Greek navy battle plans and suggestions as to how to overcome them. If Xerxes and his Admirals could have seen them the Persians would have won."

"And that would have resulted in what?" I wanted to hear it from his own mouth.

"Greece would have been swallowed up," said Kazemi. "All of Europe and beyond would have eventually become part of a mighty Persian Empire, ruling much of the world. There would have been no need for the 1979 revolution which led to the monarchy being abolished. To this day a Shah would still sit on the Sun Throne in the Mirror Hall of Golestan Palace in the royal complex at Tehran."

"But maybe you and I would not have been born in your new world." I pointed out. "Maybe our particular lifelines would never have existed."

"A small price to pay."

"And who do you intend sending back this time, Lenny or Sam?"

"No, I've learnt my lesson," said Kazimi. "This time I

will go myself!"

Professor Irbe, standing alongside the controls, made one final plea. "I beg you to reconsider. Abandon your mad plan and let science dictate the machine's use."

But there was no stopping Kazemi now. McClennan had seen to the language implants and new copies of the naval battle plan had been prepared. He wasn't properly dressed for the period but if anyone could see it through and get it done, it was him.

"Fuck science!" he declared. "This is for the glory of Persia. To right a wrong that denied my nation its true place in the world."

He looked at each of us in turn. "Just in case I am not successful in returning, the accounts of those due payment have been fully credited, and generously so." Well, that was one of my concerns settled.

"You're mad!" said the Professor, his voice shaking. "You have made me mad too. I, Andris Irbe, the man who took the Tippett/Tsang theory and turned it into reality, claim the right to destroy what I created." He lifted a hammer while speaking, with the obvious intention of smashing the controls.

"Stop him!" screamed Kazemi, and both Lenny and Sam drew weapons and fired.

"Someone help me, please," called Chantal as she rushed to the Professor's aid, but the two security men were not going to miss from such a short range and Irbe was dead before he hit the floor. I let her check, to see for herself, then drew her into my arms while Lenny and Sam moved the body away from the controls.

"Take over, McClennan," ordered Kazemi and Clifton, pale-faced and shaken, moved unsteadily to do as he'd been told. If all went to plan he would arrive a week before Big Ray's appearance in 480 BC, and if successful might even be able to prevent his death. A super-Beef at his side might be a good move, but trying to work out all the possibilities sent my mind in a spin.

"Let's do it!" said the Iranian, and he entered the box.

This time I saw it for myself: the reformed bubble starting to spin, the colours and lights flying faster and faster as the box – the square within the bubble – blurred until it could no longer be seen. Then, with a suddenness that startled me, it was over, gone, and Arman Kazemi was all those years in the past.

"HOLD ME TIGHT, Marty," she said, burying her face into my shoulder, sobbing quietly. "It is such a waste."

"I know," I said quietly. Chantal was thinking of the Professor of course, and I agreed with her, but I was also thinking about Dipper Campbell. The whole thing was such a mess.

"If he succeeds, and if we are not a part of the new world, how will it happen?" I asked.

She couldn't know of course, could only guess, but I felt a need to fill spaces with words. "It won't be like dying," she replied. "No pain and no awareness. We will just never have existed."

It was a concept I had trouble getting my head around. Was Salamis that important?

"Make love to me, Marty," she asked, holding me tight. "If Kazemi does succeed and I am surplus to requirements I want to flick out of existence with my last heart beat matching the exquisite joy of your steady thrust.

So we lay together, Chantal and I. Yes, it was fucking, but love too, as we waited to find out if the world still had a place for us … or not.

THE PLACE OF SMALL MISDEMEANOURS

Biff Brescia: We, well, Izzy Abelman and I, long ago decided that this place must probably be a hotel; a large one mind, the size of a small planet, with guests coming and going at a fair old rate of knots. Izzy and I, however, seem to be permanent fixtures, not having moved on from the day we arrived. Some only stay a day or two, and we don't even learn their names, while others hang around for up to a month or so, or sometimes even longer.

Izzy Abelman: Calling this place a hotel adds an element of reality to our rather insubstantial existence. We even go so far as to refer to our level as the Fourth Floor, though we might just as easily call it the four-hundredth. Same with people passing through; have I seen a dozen, a score, or is it thousands?

Marcus Flaccus, a top bestiarius during his time in Rome, was an interesting guy. Biff, especially, because of his boxing background, was always keen to hear the way animals were trained for performing in the arena. I preferred the tale of a wealthy Roman noblewoman who paid vast sums of money to be serviced by his specially trained jackass. From an initial worry that the lady might be putting herself at risk, Marcus eventually became more concerned for the welfare of his valuable animal. We were both quite sorry when the time came for him to move on.

Though nothing has ever been made official, it does seem that our particular landing is for low-level misdemeanours, maybe waiting for a final judgement. It could be that Biff and I were at some stage partially forgiven and sentenced to stay here to help others pass along, which suits us fine. For myself, with my show-biz years as a manager, agent, and jack of all trades, moneys that should have been in my clients' accounts kept popping in mine. I paid the price with an eventual jail term. Embezzlement, they called it, though I thought of it more as an extra bonus.

Our current interesting person is Roger Harrow, a Police Officer during World War Two and after, from the South Wales area of the good old UK. A little ironic maybe that Biff and I, two slightly shady characters from America's Big Apple, should be palling up with a Limey cop, but we leave the past behind when we turn up here.

Roger Harrow: I had an exemplary career with the Gwent Constabulary. Not the most exciting officer on the force, but hard working and thorough in everything I did. Slow and sure rather than crash-bang-wallop, but I made it to Chief Inspector, showing that hard work could be rewarded.

Izzy Abelman: The former Chief Inspector now, Roger.

Biff Brescia: Ex-Chief Inspector.

Roger Harrow: Well, I was once: back there, back then, and without a stain on my character. You chaps seem quite firm in the assessment that your Fourth Floor is a holding area for small-time misdemeanours, but if so then what am I doing here? Wrongdoing of any sort is anathema to me. I was a by-the-book policeman who never bent the rules in any way. I was a non-smoker, drank only in moderation, never cheated on my wife. If anyone deserved to bypass this particular grouping, then it's me. As much as I find you entertaining companions, I should not be here.

Izzy Abelman: And how many times have we heard that? Even Biff has an occasional moment of pleading innocent.

Biff Brescia: Growing up on the Lower East Side of New York, it was inevitable that I would have at least small-time mob connections, especially when I got into boxing. Frankie Carbo controlled The Garden and was unofficial Czar of the Fight Game on behalf of his Mafia overlords, and was also a hit man for Murder Inc. Argue with him and you might end up wearing a concrete overcoat.

I was a bit of a slugger at welterweight, not very scientific but something of a crowd pleaser. Working my way up through the preliminaries, I had a number of ten-round bouts without ever getting near a title shot. I knew my limitations, was never going to be a world champion, so when I was paid to lose a particular fight I made sure I lost.

And I suppose you think I was wrong, mister high-and-mighty policeman, you and the Feds. You don't know what it was like, back in the day.

Roger Harrow: As you keep telling me, that was then and this is now. A new existence, sort of…

Izzy Abelman: But there were consequences, weren't there, Biff?

Biff Brescia: And if you're referring to Barry Lee, as we both know you are, what happened to him wasn't only my fault. He was a good-looking kid and popular with the fans; flashily nimble, but not much of a hitter and a bit too fragile to mix it with the big punchers. He was being built up with very careful matchmaking and they needed him to beat someone with a reasonable reputation. All I had to do was carry him to a close ten-round decision and the judges, also in on the deal, would give him the verdict. We did it so neatly that nobody ever suspected the fight had been fixed.

Izzy Abelman: And what happened to Barry Lee?

Biff Brescia: You know what, Izzy. You've heard me tell it many times. He had a couple more-easy evenings and then they put him up against Art Grambo in a final eliminator, the winner to challenge for the title. Grambo was a nut case who would probably have been committed to an asylum if he hadn't been able to relieve his psychopathic tendencies in the boxing ring, and he wasn't the sort to listen to reason or follow instructions.

The kid was out of his depth and didn't have the sense to take a ten count and get out of there. Grambo gave him a terrible beating and when the kayo was finally administered he was rushed to hospital, still unconscious.

Roger Harrow: Did he survive?

Biff Brescia: For about three years yes, though it might

have been kinder if he hadn't. Brain damage they said, though I don't remember the technical terms, and confined to a wheelchair. Head lolling, dribbling, talking gibberish.

Roger Harrow: Nasty! But not your fault, surely.

Biff Brescia: Wasn't it? Maybe I didn't actually inflict the damage but I couldn't avoid some of the blame. If I hadn't thrown our fight, if I'd beaten him like I should and could have, then there would have been no way he would have got an eliminator against an animal like Art Grambo. It was guilt by association, and that was when I started to fall out of love with the fight game.

Roger Harrow: Have you met him since? Here in the hotel?

Biff Brescia: No.

Izzy Abelman: Though there have been times we've explored other floors, Biff would never agree to seek out Barry Lee. Not that it would have been easy since you are not encouraged to linger in any but your own allotted area.

Biff Brescia: And we had the old-fashioned idea of using stairs when it would have been much simpler to just float through walls and ceilings.

Izzy Abelman: When Frank Sinatra sang the Rogers and Hart song "There's a Small Hotel" in the film *Pal Joey*, it certainly wasn't about this place. We soon got fed up with being constantly moved on, but our overriding impression was one of a never-ending immensity. This place is huge; it might even go on forever.

What about you, Roger? Are you so absolutely certain that your whole life and career have been whiter than white?

Roger Harrow: As boring as it might be, yes I am. From my very first success, when as a rooky policeman I arrested a Valley thug, Emrys Thomas, who had bludgeoned his aunt for monetary gain, right up to my retirement. I played it straight, and in my personal life too.

~~~

Izzy Abelman: As had been the case when Biff and I tried to investigate other areas, we would be recognised as, well, sort of like trespassers. The same as we would react if an outsider turned up on our Fourth Floor, and we didn't get that sense of otherness in relation to our policeman friend. In spite of his protestations it did seem to us that Roger must have a blemish, however small, lurking in his background. This place doesn't make mistakes like that.

Biff Brescia: Izzy was the first to notice it.

Izzy Abelman: There's someone here who shouldn't be, Biff. Don't you sense it? A couple of the transients moved on an hour back and there have been no regular additions since. I think whoever it is, is over by the stairway entrance. Better check. Come on…

Biff Brescia: Lost your way, Bud? Taken a wrong turning? Got no sense of direction?

Izzy Abelman: What my friend means is: who are you and what are you doing here?

Emrys Thomas: I know moving between sections is not encouraged, but my name is Emrys Thomas and I'm searching for someone important to my previous existence.

Izzy Abelman: That's a name I've heard before. It wouldn't be Roger Harrow you are looking for, would it?

Emrys Thomas: The very same! Constable that was! I knew I was finally on the right track. Can this be him?

Roger Harrow: Murderer!

Emrys Thomas: Hear me out before you call me that!

Roger Harrow: You were heard, in a court of law, and at the end the judge put on his black cap. You had your day and you weren't believed. A murderer you were, tried and sentenced.

Emrys Thomas: An innocent man, falsely accused, but I don't blame you for that, Mister Policeman. The case against me stacked up high, and in the end the truth was buried. Humour me, gentlemen, I deserve to be heard.

You sir, tell me if you will, what is your last memory of the other place?

Izzy Abelman: A hospital bed with me attached to various machines and my ex-wife sitting near with tears in her eyes.

"I never stopped loving you, Izzy," she said. "Why did you have to be such a silly man?"

Then everything faded.

Emrys Thomas: And you also, if you don't mind.

Biff Brescia: Struggling with the wheel as my car skidded off the road, and a big tree coming up fast.

Emrys Thomas: Mister Policeman?

Roger Harrow: I'll not play your games.

Emrys Thomas: Then I'll tell you mine.

It was standing on the gallows, my head covered, a noose around my neck, hearing words that bore no relation to my situation. It was hoping that my last seconds could be stretched into limitless time. It was that short, sharp drop when the trapdoor opened.

Bad enough even for the guilty, but pure hell for someone wrongly accused.

Roger Harrow: Your own aunt: battered and robbed! The letter of the law was adhered to with scrupulous care; and don't you dare to suggest it wasn't.

Emrys Thomas: I don't! Yet still the verdict was wrong.

Roger Harrow: Liar! You staggered drunk from your house with blood-splattered clothes, straight into my arms as I pounded the beat along the row of terraced houses where you lived. Blood-stained shoeprints led from where your Aunt lay dead in the house next door.

In your bedroom we found the cudgel used and more banknotes than you could account for.

Of course you denied it. You were too drunk to properly know what you'd been doing. But the Crown Prosecutor said the evidence was sufficient, and the jury agreed.

Izzy Abelman: Hold on a minute, Roger, there is something I think you might be overlooking.

Roger Harrow: It was all done properly, according to the letter of the law.

Biff Brescia: Listen to Izzy, Mister ex-Chief Inspector. A shyster showbiz manager he might have been but very little escapes his scrutiny.

Izzy Abelman: Biff and I have been here long enough to have picked up some of the working practises that keep the whole enterprise ticking over. There are innumerable layers, or floors if we want to stick with the hotel analogy, that cover every facet of human behaviour between very good and extremely bad.

What happens to the good is shrouded in mystery; they are eventually summoned and leave, something we all aspire to. The very bad though, they are dragged to the basement; to the torment of a furnace the size of a bubbling volcano.

Roger Harrow: And your point is?

Izzy Abelman: Just this, Roger: if he had committed the crimes he was accused of, then Emrys Thomas would have gone straight to the basement, not spent all this time wandering in limbo.

Roger Harrow: Are you saying we hung an innocent man?

Emrys Thomas: Yes!

Biff Brescia: Sure looks that way.

~~~

Roger Harrow: The more I think about it, and there has been nothing else on my mind for I don't know how long, the closer I come to accepting Izzy's interpretation of events. The person guilty of such a crime would have been heading straight to the basement, and I'm sure was and is even now suffering in those terrible flames.

Here, at least, such wrongs can be rectified. Not where we all come from though. Back there the error is compounded and continued, which offends me much. The career that gave me such pride started with the hanging of an innocent man.

Emrys Thomas: I understand that you were an honest copper, Mr ex-Chief Inspector. If it's any consolation, I don't blame you in any way. If our roles had been reversed I would have made exactly the same assumptions you did. You, your superiors, the prosecutor and judge all acted in good faith. It was Tom Hopkins, the real culprit, who stitched me up. My drinking partner that evening – who made sure I ended up drunk while he remained sober.

The only police failure was in accepting that the money found in my bedroom was all that my poor aunt had hoarded away when in reality it had been a lot more, and Hopkins had the rest.

As for his comeuppance, it was as Mr Abelman suggested: he has, for many years, been burning in the furnace below. He might have got away with it previously, but not here.

Roger Harrow: So what is it you are after? What do you want to achieve? What do you want from me?

Emrys Thomas: Elsie Pugh visited me while I was on remand, awaiting trial. She was carrying my child, so she claimed, and though it had not been a regular courtship I had been thinking of doing the proper thing by her. Circumstances being as they were, I told her not to visit me again and if the trial went against me to never reveal who the baby's father really was.

Assuming Elsie was telling the truth, there could be an existing line emanating from that back-alley knee-trembler. However unlikely, I would hate them to one day discover a convicted killer as part of their family tree, especially when it wasn't true. I want the record book back there set straight. I want my name cleared.

Can you help me?

Can it be done?

Roger Harrow: If it can, and if I can help, then "yes" on both counts. I always believed in the law and any miscarriage of justice needs to be corrected. Can we assist in any way, Izzy?

Biff Brescia: If there's a loophole to be found, Izzy is the man to find it.

Izzy Abelman: Hmm! Let me give it a bit of thought.

~~~

Izzy Abelman: After much debate, and with many points of view being aired, it was decided that Emrys would assist Biff with the smooth running of the Fourth Floor while Roger and I would look at ways and means of righting the terrible wrong we were now all too aware of.

Roger Harrow: It was thought that my knowledge of police procedures coupled with Izzy's sharp eye for detail would offer the best chance for a successful outcome. Even Emrys, who had initially demanded that he carry out the investigation himself, finally saw that we were right. He could hardly have remained impartial.

So it was, I admit, with some nervousness that I joined Izzy for the trip; it being my first time going back.

Izzy Abelman: I think Roger, Chief Inspector that he had been, already had some ideas as to how we could achieve our aims. It was a strange experience, being back in the other place, seeing people living their pre-death lives. Some returnees become addicted to it; the rest of us call them White-Sheet Charlie's or Chain Rattlers, and it would seem that they never rise to the upper levels back at the hotel. Some even try to interact with those still alive, which is very much frowned upon.

We made for the Gwent Police headquarters at Croesyceiliog. I willingly allowed Roger to lead the way through the maze-like corridors. This was his territory.

Roger Harrow: Even before I retired there had been some moves towards relooking at old cases that, for whatever reasons, had become regarded as unsafe verdicts, and my suspicion that such investigations might have grown in importance proved correct. Izzy and I finally located the offices where a whole unit was dedicated to such endeavours. This was where I felt we would have the best chance of achieving our aim.

Izzy Abelman: This was why having an ex-policeman along was so necessary. If it had been Biff and I, however well we worked together, we'd have floated those endless corridors with very little to show for it.

Roger Harrow: The unit was split into a number of teams, each of which had a case under investigation.

Izzy Abelman: While the Lead Officer had a to-do list on his desk, along with files of the next half-a-dozen cases to be looked at.

Roger Harrow: Our task was to get the Emrys Thomas conviction included and to bank on modern techniques, which hadn't been available at the time, being sufficient to show his innocence.

Izzy Abelman: This was where abilities currently allied only to the condition of our present situation would be needed. *Automatic Writing*, adapted and tinkered to be compliant with a computer keyboard, produced a new list on which Emrys was number five. Putting him straight in at the top might have been too obvious, we thought.

Bringing up his case notes from the file room to be placed fifth on the Unit Leader's desk was accomplished by means of *Levitation*. Working mainly during the night, when the hustle and bustle of the day was replaced by a big reduction in personnel numbers, we still had an occasional dodgy moment. One cleaner in particular swore off alcohol after stepping from an office to see a folder floating along the corridor, apparently unaided.

Roger Harrow: Well that's all we can do, Izzy. It's a waiting game now until our case reaches the top and becomes subject to a new investigation. If we only had all these modern advances available to us back then, we'd have got it right first time.

Izzy Abelman: Spilt milk, Roger. Time to get back and tell Biff and Emrys what the situation is.

Roger Harrow: I won't be sorry to put this place behind me yet again either.

Izzy Abelman: Nor me, Roger. I have no idea why those White-Sheet Charlie's find coming back so habit forming.

~~~

Roger Harrow: We had only been back long enough to update Emrys and Biff when that which sends a shiver of anticipation through all who exist in this place occurred – the sudden appearance of Smoke. That special Smoke, twisting and swirling as it made its way through our Fourth Floor, seeking whoever it had come to elevate.

The rest of us could only watch in wonderment and awe as it finally encircled both Izzy Abelman and Biff Brescia. According to Hotel legend they alone would be hearing the glorious sounds that only exist within the amorphous entity, voices and music that combine to tell those chosen of their elevation.

I shall miss them both, Izzy and Biff, but wish them well on the next stage of their upward journey.

Emrys Thomas: Amen to that.

Roger Harrow: It's you and me now then, Emrys. I get the feeling that we are the new custodians of the Fourth Floor. Our departed friends will be a hard act to follow but I'm sure we will develop into a worthwhile team, and we will of course keep an eye on what happens in that other place as your case is relooked at. I will not be able to rest properly until your innocence has been acknowledged.

Emrys Thomas: Thanks for that, Mister ex-Chief Inspector. You and I, hey, who would have thought? This place brings out the best in us.

Roger Harrow: Just before they left us, the Smoke parted enough to give a glimpse of their faces, both Izzy and Biff.

Emrys Thomas: I saw them too.

Roger Harrow: Such happiness! One day our turn might come, but until then … come on, friend, we have work to do…

CRACKED CONCRETE

IF THE ABANDONED industrial complex had been nearer shopping facilities then Mike Hutton might have considered moving there on a permanent basis. As it was, he arrived at 9.00 a.m. and left at 5.00 p.m., Mondays to Fridays, and 9.00 a.m. to 12.00 noon on Saturdays, always riding his 750cc Suzuki motorcycle. Once he had removed the helmet, which was an obvious giveaway, the leather flying jacket and goggles made him look like a pilot, he thought: World War Two, Battle of Britain variety.

Hutton had found the complex within days of leaving his last proper employment, and the redundancy cheque they had given him meant he was under no immediate pressure to find another job. The decaying site consisted of five units, or had done, all of which he had explored before settling upon a former warehouse as his main base. The office, which he had taken over, was to the side of the roller-door entrance and exit, above both locker and mess rooms, and provided a full view of the whole building. It even had a beat-up old desk that nobody had considered worth the effort of taking when the place had closed. Hutton had brought a chair from home, which was a flat above a newsagent's shop, two turnings away from High Street back in town.

A cat colony occupied the site and he had worked hard to clear them from his chosen headquarters. The animals, for their part, seemed to accept Hutton's occupancy of that one building. An occasional cat might wander in, as if checking his tenancy, but by and large they left him alone.

AGNES CLIFTON SAT on her bed, hunched forward at an awkward angle, forearms resting on her thighs. "You were lucky to find another job so quickly," she said, a throwaway remark or one that could mask low-key probing. Hutton had found it easier to explain the regular hours of his coming and going with fictitious employment.

He grunted an uncommitted response, preferring to concentrate on the helicopters flying overhead. Her semi-detached home seemed to be below what had become a regular flight path since the skies took over as the transport system of choice for many. Street gangs, dog packs, even marauding urban foxes – all had combined to promote the ever expanding taxicopter companies.

At least it left the roads freer for people like Hutton. Trouble was always a possibility, but speed limits no longer applied and his Suzuki had so far seen him whizz clear of any bother.

Reaching out, he cupped his hand around the darkened areola of her nearest nipple. It was a Sunday morning and both, having just risen, were naked. The overhead roar of the helicopters excited him and Hutton could imagine himself thrusting into Agnes in time with the rhythm of their engines.

"It's early yet," he murmured, and they returned to the warmth of entwined bodies and rumpled quilts.

THE ELECTRICS SUPPLYING the aging complex had long

been disconnected but Hutton had reassembled a backup procedure and was able to open and shut the roller doors through a circular chain and cog system. It was both tiring and lengthy, but beneficial in improving his upper body strength. There was a concrete parking area outside, where lorries would have waited their turn to either load or unload, now cracked in places, as was the internal floor of the warehouse itself.

One warm July afternoon he had brought down his chair to sit at the entrance, sunning himself lazily and sipping lemonade. A few of the cat population were also stretched out on the concrete, napping. All was quiet and peaceful until, without warning, a fox appeared as if from nowhere. The cats scattered in a flash, bar one, slower than the others; old maybe, or infirm. Whatever the reason, the fox pounced.

Hutton was half out of his chair, thinking to try and distract or scare the predator into releasing its prey, maybe by waving his arms and shouting, but he wasn't needed. A feline army, so it seemed – meowing, spitting, snarling – raced at the fox, biting, scratching, hitting. Old Reynard soon dropped its victim, becoming more intent upon defending itself. Blood and fur flew before the fox, realising itself to be vastly outnumbered, managed to turn tail and run.

A number of cats had suffered injuries, mostly minor, though the original victim was unmoving and appeared dead, something Hutton confirmed later. He had been totally shocked by the cats' actions, but in retrospect could understand the logic. A successful kill would have marked the site as a plentiful food source for the fox and it would have returned regularly, maybe with others as well, something the cats could not countenance. Their one advantage was in having a vastly numerical superiority, and they had made the fox pay in a similar fashion to the way ants would attack and defeat a much larger beetle.

But cats weren't ants…

Hutton looked at his feline neighbours with a new respect after that.

COLIN CLIFTON HAD died when a carjacking incident went wrong two years previously. He had rushed from the house to prevent what he had spotted from a window and had been bludgeoned around the head with the crowbar his assailant had been trying to open the car door with.

He had saved the vehicle from being stolen, but at what a price…

Agnes, sterile and therefore childless, had sought employment initially as a form of therapy. An attempt to reintroduce herself into the wider world she had previously relinquished in favour of the private existence she had enjoyed with her husband, and it was while working as a departmental dogsbody that she had first met Mike Hutton, the moody oddball who was now her lover. She had dodged the cull when redundancy volunteers had been called for, and then forcibly selected, staying on as part of a reduced work force after Hutton and the others had been cut loose.

At thirty-eight she was three years older than Hutton, not enough for it to be problematic, and she sometimes considered whether or not their relationship would benefit if he were to move into her home on a permanent basis, but it was something he never suggested. He came to see her every Wednesday evening, staying the night and leaving on Thursday morning; then spending the weekends with her, from

Saturday afternoon until Monday morning. On the other nights he slept at his flat, which he showed no signs of wanting to give up.

Colin had died because of laziness, leaving his car on the driveway instead of putting it into their garage. Agnes had naturally been bitter towards the perpetrator, who had never been caught, but her husband had been to blame for putting himself in such danger in the first place. She still had moments of sad joy when she could bask in memories of their time together, but they occurred gradually less often once she got over the guilt of physical sex re-entering her life.

Hutton, for his part, was quite content with their ongoing arrangement. The newsagent he lived over had a secure yard at the rear where he was able to keep his Suzuki in safety, under a tarpaulin cover. On the nights he spent with Agnes the motorcycle was locked in her garage. He would definitely not be making the same mistake as her late husband.

His attitude was that he lived at his flat and visited his lover. Their relationship was based on little more than sex which, while admittedly good, was hardly sufficient for a lifetime's commitment. It was best to let things stay as they were, for now at least.

THE GRADUAL FRAGMENTATION of society, it seemed to Hutton when thinking of the fox incident, influenced animal behaviour as well as human. As people withdrew, becoming less and less homogeneous, their former four-legged friends had to adapt to new situations.

"They are probably a lot smarter than we give them credit for," he remarked.

"I had a spaniel once that was really clever," said

Agnes. She hadn't liked the fox story, Mike having supplied all the gory details, and preferred not to think of what went on outside her own personal bubble.

"I pay more attention to them now," continued Hutton, "and I can tell you that feral dog packs seem to be better organised and have more purpose than the yobs hanging around street corners, throwing stones at windows."

"Trudy."

"Pardon?"

"My spaniel: her name was Trudy."

Ye Gods! grumbled Hutton to himself. If it wasn't for the fact that she was so good in bed…

AFTER DISCOVERING IT, Hutton had researched the site to the best of his ability. It had been known as the Foxglove Trading Estate and the warehouse he had claimed as his own had specialised in tinned foodstuffs. There was an overhead gantry, now rusted and without power, which he would sit in sometimes while imagining what it would have been like as a busy and productive enterprise.

Of the other four units, there had been an engineering machine shop, a skip-hire company, a manufacturer of chemical pesticides, and an engine reconditioning workshop. All long gone and the place now bequeathed to him and the cats, with weeds growing from many of the cracks in the disintegrating concrete. The one place completely free from such growths was the former pesticide factory. There were cracks aplenty, as elsewhere, but without any weeds. It seemed more cold and forbidding than the other units and even the cats gave it a wide berth.

At one stage Hutton had planned to tidy the whole

site but ended up concentrating only on the warehouse he occupied. Sometimes he would map out the floor area: tinned vegetables in aisle (a), fruits in (b), meats in (c), or whatever configurations pleased him on any particular day. At other times he would just sit at his desk and ponder upon the variables of life and the unerring march towards the disintegration of society. Or contemplate more personal issues, such as his relationship with Agnes.

Hutton knew that she wanted him to move into her house permanently. She hadn't actually put it into words yet but would do at some point soon. And why wouldn't she? His staying power was of legendary proportions and multiple orgasms for the partner of his choice was a given.

She knew which side her bread was buttered on.

BIG AL, THEY called him. People used his full Christian name at their peril. Big Al Popham had never understood why his parents had called him Alvin. What was he, a bloody chipmunk? He had been away for a spell – ducking and diving, keeping his head down – but now he was back on home turf.

Squat, broad, and very powerful, a Neanderthal-looking individual, he'd run with the gangs when younger and kept up loose affiliations since because it made sense, but he preferred doing things solo. He felt best on his own, with no concerns about other people's baggage.

Street corner etiquette had prompted him to announce his return to the current Head Honcho, a spotty-faced kid Big Al could have crushed with no bother, but for the fact that these punks had it over him numerically. He would help them out whenever they had a need of genuine muscle, and for the rest of the time the territory was his to patrol.

Big Al Popham was back. Watch out, one and all.

AGNES HAD NOTICED the black and tan coloured German shepherd a few times before, usually with other dogs but occasionally alone. It was sitting on the pavement opposite her house, staring across the road, and though she had stepped back from the window she felt the animal could see her and was noting her movements.

"Damn dog," she muttered, stepping back further into the room.

What was it Mike had been rabbiting on about? Something about cats getting smarter? Ha! *Rabbits* and *cats*! She smiled to herself, proud of her little quip, but maybe he had been on to something. That dog outside could almost be said to be studying her, which smacked of intelligence. It was a breed that had always made her feel nervous. Maybe because they were so wolf-like in appearance.

Another helicopter flew overhead, the drone of its engine getting louder, then receding.

She had laughed at the news item about a man being attacked by a goat. It brought to mind cartoons she had seen of someone bending down and being struck on the backside by a goat, or a ram; anything with horns, really. It wasn't so funny, though, when it turned out the man was dead, killed by the animal.

Cows, too. Agnes could remember a number of incidents where someone had been trampled by cattle. And now this wolfish dog was watching her home. Maybe Mike was right. Maybe it was the beginning of Orwell's *Animal Farm*.

And here comes another, she thought crossly, as yet another engine roar grew, hit a peak, then faded as it passed overhead. Mike liked them. Well, he would, wouldn't he. Agnes thought he secretly pictured himself as a helicopter pilot; the romance of the air, and all that nonsense. She just wished they would fly in a different direction.

HUTTON RODE TO his Foxglove Trading Estate hideout at maximum speed and in a foul mood. The newsagent's proprietor, his landlord, had been waiting for him when he went to get his Suzuki from the yard at the back of the shop. Hashim al-Hafiz was a refugee success story, someone who came to this country, worked hard, prospered, but now had enough. There had been an attempted burglary at the shop the previous week, the fourth that year. Physical threats were commonplace and shoplifting on the increase.

Mr al-Hafiz was putting the business up for sale so would need the upstairs flat to be vacant. Hutton had been a good tenant and none of this was his fault, but life was hard. Would he please start looking for an alternative living arrangement?

The flesh impact of various crash scenarios scorched through his mind as he weaved his motorcycle through the relatively thin traffic. If he hadn't been so angry, Hutton might have imagined himself piloting a Spitfire in a Battle of Britain dogfight, a popular dreamscape when he was speeding. Why did life have to intrude? Why couldn't he be allowed to withdraw in an orderly fashion?

Hutton guessed that he would have to give serious consideration to moving in with Agnes fulltime, but he didn't really want to. Maybe he should just cut and run.

He had given thought to moving into Foxglove permanently when he first found the place. He should have been bolder, he thought now, but was a hermit's life what he wanted? The solitude would be no problem but to go without regular sex…

IT HAD BEEN one of those days at work. One of the managers, a married man with little or no concern for the sanctity of his vows, had pestered her for a date. He tried it on every now and then, ignoring the fact that she always turned him down, but it was stressful and trying.

Home at last. It wasn't one of Mike's evenings and Agnes wished she wasn't going in to an empty house but she would survive, and it was certainly a relief to get away from work.

Turning from the garage door after parking the car, she couldn't suppress an unexpected moment of fear. There on the drive, actually within the boundaries of her property, was that German shepherd. Sitting, looking at her.

"Shoo!" she called, trying to sound braver than she felt.

The dog cocked its head, still maintaining unnerving eye contact.

Agnes backed slowly towards her front door, and as she did so the animal stood and matched her speed, moving up the drive towards her. "Go away," she shouted, her voice ragged and high as she gave way to a feeling of real terror. "Go away!"

Then, just as it started to move faster in her direction, a half-house brick came flying through the air, striking the dog's muzzle. It yelped, stopped, spun around and fled, splashing blood from a gash along nose and mouth.

Agnes felt quite disorientated, even unsteady, but a firm hand gripped her elbow and held her while she recovered.

MAYBE IT WAS unwise of him to hang around here, but Big Al Popham just couldn't keep away from this particular house. He had unfinished business with it, and the bloody place owed him.

That stupid bugger, Clifton. What was his first name? Colin? Yes, that was it, Colin Clifton, dashing out and trying to play the hero. All for a piece of junk he couldn't be bothered to put into a garage. Nutter! A couple of smashes with the jemmy and his brains had been dribbling out onto the driveway.

Big Al had the initial worry as to whether the dickhead cops would link him with the killing, and when that didn't happen he still had to stay out of sight, drawing no attention to himself until the case slid onto the back burner. Two years he'd stayed away, two bloody years, until it seemed safe to assume it had been filed as unsolved and left to rot.

He wanted something in return. Fair's fair. If nothing else, he wanted that car.

It was still there, the same vehicle he had tried to steal, only now being driven by the widow woman, who locked it away properly; as did the boyfriend with his motorbike, when he visited. Big Al was keeping the place under surveillance. Sooner or later an opportunity would arise.

He was there, hiding, the day the woman had a panic attack over the big German shepherd as it trotted towards her. Without thinking he lobbed half a house brick at the beast and moved forward to support her as the animal turned tail and ran. He had no specific plan in mind, outside somehow getting hold of the garage and car keys.

Agnes Clifton, for her part, looked at her knight in shining armour and saw a powerfully built streetwise yobbo. Not too much brains, probably, but with a face that spoke of cunning and cruelty. Weak at the knees, she clung to him.

THE ONE THING she'd missed since Colin's death was a touch of the rough stuff. The fact that Mike could hump all night was marvellous, but he was not at all adventurous. The tweaked nipples and smacked bottoms were not for him, and Agnes missed that side of things. Her late husband had been full of those tricks but had little in the way of staying power. Maybe this tough looking hoodlum might be able to combine elements of Colin's rough foreplay with Mike's ability to keep going. Somehow, he looked the part.

"Thank you, thank you," she kept repeating, clinging to him as if her life depended on it.

THE BITCH IS panting for it, realised Big Al. Getting into the house was going to be easy; after that, well, one step at a time. "Let me help you to your door," he offered, keeping a firm grip on her elbow as he guided her along the path. "I'm sure the dog is gone now."

"But maybe not. It might return. I shouldn't be alone, just in case." She waved the hand holding a key. "Please stay until I steady myself. Have a cup of tea."

"Well, just for a couple of minutes I suppose."

As soon as the front door shut behind them, Agnes grabbed the man round the back of his head with one hand, pulling his face down to hers, while her other hand reached towards his groin.

"Get off, you slag," shouted Big Al, pulling away from the attempted kiss and pushing at her roughly.

"Hit me, would you!"

"That wasn't no hit. I only shoved you."

"But you want to, don't you?" Agnes smiled salaciously, moving back towards him. "Go on then, hit me good."

This was way outside Big Al's comfort zone. All he'd ever demanded was a passive partner, a woman who would merely lie there while he did the business. Nothing fancy, very straight, and nothing that even hinted at a relationship. Panic coincided with anger and the woman came at him again, with that big dirty grin on her face, so he grabbed her around the neck and started to squeeze.

COLIN AND AGNES had sometimes talked about erotic asphyxiation, the breath-control play, but it had scared him. Too many accidental deaths, he'd claimed; an Aussie singer, a British MP, and a Hollywood actor being among those who'd perished while playing the game. And it was usually regarded as a solo enterprise, though Agnes could see no reason why it couldn't be worked into a twosome.

It had been something she had often thought about, and when the man started putting pressure on her throat her first reaction was that he was willing to play the dangerous game along with her, and she reached again for his groin.

Big Al became more and more enraged, pouring all his energy into his grasping clasping hands, and by the time Agnes realised that this was no sex game it was too late. Her final struggles were both futile and pointless and ceased well before he loosened his grip and let her lifeless body slip to the floor.

THIS HAD NOT been what he was there for but he would cope, he always did. With a grim determination he searched for her car keys and a key ring which he hoped would include one for the garage. He also stuck what money he found into his pocket. It might be best not to ransack the whole house though. Too time consuming. Stepping over the dead woman he made for the front door and left the house. Being totally concerned with only his self, Big Al missed seeing the shadowy figures lying in wait as he hurried to get the car he had come for; he was still applying a personal logic that claimed it was his by right.

THE GERMAN SHEPHERD'S muzzle continued to drip blood and throbbed painfully. His howls had soon brought the rest of the pack to him and they had settled down to wait, strategically placed, determined to extract revenge.

Big Al knew nothing until they were upon him, dogs of various breeds, not all recognised by the Kennel Club; snarling, biting, intent upon his destruction. They took his legs first, bringing him to the ground, sharp canine teeth then sinking into his arms and hands. Big Al's screams were matched by the drone of a helicopter flying overhead.

Finally the big German shepherd came and stood on his chest, throwing back its head and howling at the sky before lowering its gaze, looking at the man. Big Al saw those eyes and screamed with pure terror. The German shepherd bared its fangs and went for the throat.

THE CATS HAD been edgy all day at the Foxglove

Trading Estate. Hutton too, as he wrestled with the personal problems he had building up. Five o'clock had been reached, the time he normally left, but today he was still sat at his desk, pondering. Should he go through the rigmarole of flat hunting again, or just accept the inevitable and move in with Agnes? Neither course of action really appealed.

The skinny tabby trotted in through the open roller doorway and looked up at him through the large office window that gave him such a good view of the warehouse. Once it had established eye contact with him the cat moved a few steps away and then looked back, repeating the sequence until it had gone through the doorway. It then came returned and started the whole process over again.

The cat's oddball behaviour reminded Hutton of the *Lassie* films he had seen repeated on television when he was a kid. The way the smart dog would get the message across that she wanted someone to follow her when there was trouble. He stood up from his desk, left the office, and took the steps down to the warehouse floor.

"What's the matter, gal?" he asked the tabby, smiling a little self-consciously. "Has one of the children fallen down the well?"

The cat moved off, glancing back now and then as if to make sure he was still following. Hutton tagged along, more than a little intrigued, realising he was being led towards the former pesticide plant, and what was that he could hear?

Cats, that's what!

Hissing, snarling, meowing, high pitched and low. Dozens of them, all around; advancing, retreating or holding their position, bellies to the ground or up on tiptoe. But beyond them, and probably the cause of all this agitation, he could see what appeared to be a pale green and glowing liquid oozing from the old building. Oozing, indeed, he could see as he got close enough, from the cracks in the concrete floor. And it wasn't liquid but a living mass of insects, some sorts of bugs, shining like a million miniature northern lights.

Hutton was no chemist but wondered if a phosphorus residue from the pesticide manufacturing process might have leaked onto the concrete floor, gradually seeping down as the cracks appeared, causing some sort of reaction within the burrowing insect population.

Dotted here and there within the flowing green mass, he could see ... what were they? Good God! Cats! Dead ones, corpses, skeletons. They were fighting a desperate rear-guard action, he could see now, and they were losing. As the unstoppable tidal wave of insects swept forward the engulfed cats were being eaten alive.

Hutton stepped back quickly as the realisation struck home: if they could devour cats they could eat humans too. Flesh was flesh. He backed away slowly, watching with a terrible fascination, as more and more of the disgusting creatures spewed out from the cracks that were visible through the open plant doorway.

The cats were losing, and knew it, many having already died. Suddenly it was every feline for itself as they gave up the fight, scattering in all directions to escape. No longer having an adversary to overcome, the insects poured forward ever faster and Hutton, now in full retreat himself, was cut off from the most direct path back to his warehouse, and forced to use a more roundabout route. All he was thinking of was jumping on his Suzuki and roaring away to safety but when he rounded a corner it was to see his machine surrounded by the glowing advance, and every bit of rubber and plastic had already been stripped away, leaving only the metal parts.

In a total panic now, Hutton dashed into the warehouse, looking for where he could hide, as far away as possible from this insect tsunami of hungry snapping mandibles. The office and the rooms beneath it were too accessible and the rest of the building was just an empty shell. Without giving it any thought, he clambered up the metal rungs and crouched inside the cab of the derelict overhead crane.

Peeping from above he saw the glowing mass sweep into the warehouse and he realised for the first time just how trapped he was. Too late for anything else now though; he would have to keep his head down, stay hidden, and outlast the buggers.

If only…

It was as if they knew where he was, and maybe they did. Maybe they could smell his flesh, his blood, the fear that dripped from every pore of his body. Up they climbed, from rung to rung, heading straight for him. There being nothing in the cab he could use; he took off a shoe and beat at the insects as they reached him, killing some. But there were too many.

Mike Hutton had never met Big Al Popham. He wasn't even aware of his existence, but he matched him scream for scream, as the flesh was ripped from his body. Only death brought silence.

THE SURVIVING CATS had fled, never to return. Hutton, the lone human occupant, was dead. The Foxglove Trading Estate was under new ownership.

SOLDIER: WORLD WAR 2

News of
Imminent overseas posting
Sent my mother hurrying
To Brecon
Taking me
To see my soldier father

Two and three-quarters
And on a day out
With my mother

I retained definite memories
Of playing on ceremonial canons
And eating corned beef sandwiches
But none of my father

Dad was soon fighting his way across Europe
And I couldn't even picture our last meeting

Luckily
At the war's end he came back home.

New memories started then

AT THE END OF A CHARGING RUN

Old photo from around '34
Good looking soldier
Playing football in Hong Kong

Rough and tough
Straight down the middle
Centre forward
Short back and sides
Baggy shorts
Lumpy boots and shin pads

Army team won everything
In Hong Kong that year
Won the First Division
Won the Cup
Won the Shield
And the tough Welsh centre forward
Scored the goals that did it

Years later
Wrongly prescribed treatment
Damaged his sciatic nerve
Leaving him with a
Permanent shake that got worse
As time went on
No compensation culture then

[/continued]

By 1982 dad had to be carried
Up and down stairs
Still had a handshake
That could hurt
But legs that no longer functioned

Two years later he died
But I've still got that '34 photo
Showing a relieved Chinese keeper
Watching the ball
Flash just passed the post
And a tough centre forward
Coming to a halt
At the end of a charging run

FEEDING THE PIGEONS

When my wife first started
To feed the pigeons
In Newport town centre
I went window shopping
Waited at a distance

The local council wanted a cull
So feeding them was banned
With the threat of a fine
But still my wife scattered bread

As a child she had never
Forgiven her Italian Papa
For the slaughter of a pig
She had considered her pet

She was never meant to be
A farmer's daughter

I now see this present act
Of civil disobedience
To be symbolic of her love
For all her God's creations

So when my wife
Now feeds the pigeons
In Newport town centre
I stand by her side
Proud to be her accomplice

GRIEF

With a dead son lost
To lock your hand in mine

Never have I loved you
More than now

The circled cross that shines
In morning sunlight

On our garden wall
Is a kiss from him

You are the one with faith
And I can live with that

If Jesus walks the planet
Let him offer you solace

I'll hold my tongue
Not offer any argument

I kiss you and state my love
I try to dry your tears

But these are days of darkness
Times beyond understanding

Sometimes love is not enough

AFTER THE HARVEST

GEORGE ALBERT REECE had never heard of Franz Ferdinand before the Archduke and his wife were assassinated in somewhere called Sarajevo in the June of 1914.

Neither was he aware of all the political whirlpools that had for some time been heading the European continent towards armed conflict. The world was shrinking, unknown to George, with less opportunity for Empire-building in new territories. Some countries looked at neighbours while fading powers sought alliances as a means of protection.

Manipulating the Archduke's shooting, Germany had backed Austria-Hungarian threats and demands against Serbia while Russia part-mobilised in defence of the Serbs. Great Britain and France were told by Germany to curb their Russian allies' militarism. Within days war was being declared by some, neutrality by others, and armies were on the march.

George Albert Reece knew none of this, though he had heard something about the British fleet being manoeuvred to block German access to the world's oceans. His employer, the landowner Squire Thomas, a stoutly patriotic man, was more than willing to pass on news to his farm hands.

With various armies moving on mainland Europe, the British government entered the conflict on August 4th when Germany refused to withdraw from neutral

Belgium. Unlike most of the other major powers, the British army consisted entirely of volunteers; there was no conscription.

Needing to boost numbers, Field Marshall Sir Herbert Kitchener called for 100,000 men to sign up. "Your Country Needs You" said the posters and 175,000 volunteered in the following week. Squire Thomas had encouraged the young men in his employ to be amongst them.

"We will cope, lads," he'd said. "Us older ones will keep the farms going until you return, which won't be long. A couple of months should be enough to kick the Kaiser's backside."

Twenty-eight year old George Albert Reece, full of the Squire's patriotic fervour, joined with the other farm hands offering to do their bit for King and Country. Rebecca, his flame-haired wife of only four months, had not matched his enthusiasm but had come to accept the inevitability of it all.

"Won't be long, Becky. Like Squire says, should be over by end of year at most. Got to do my duty."

"Well all right, George Reece, but you had better take care and come home in one piece. Do you hear me?"

"I hear you, my love."

And he'd taken her gently into his arms. However short the war was going to be, he would certainly miss her while he was away.

REBECCA REECE HAD, in spite of her misgivings, felt a surge of pride upon learning that her George was a Pioneer in the Royal Engineers. It all sounded grand and adventurous, but that was because she did not know the rank was that of an unskilled labour force being put together as part of an enlarged RE Regiment.

"Sounds as if he's making his mark already," said Squire Thomas, who also lacked any knowledge of new army requirements. "He'll come back with stripes on his arm, you see if he doesn't!"

Rebecca and other womenfolk helped swell the depleted farm workforce, joining with the men either too old or too young to fight. The Squire had dismissed the one employee of army age who had refused to enlist. He was a hard but fair man with his own set of standards and treated his workers a sight better than many in the area.

She missed her George though, her husband of only four months, and their love still as fresh as the crops in the fields. Even if the blasted war only lasted a week or so more, it would still be too long for them to be apart.

The key to a woman was a man. The right man, and Rebecca had chosen well. George had been attentive but not servile, ardent but not demanding, generous but not indulgent. Just a farm labourer maybe, but possessing a maturity not all men attain.

Her life would be on hold until his return.

THE SEASONS PASSED and a new year was born, but 1915 only ushered in grim and unwanted news. According to a despondent Squire Thomas, hopes for a swift conclusion to hostilities had ended with large numbers of casualties, a general stalemate on the ground, and further widening of the conflict. One of his nephews and a second cousin had already been killed in action and word arrived that David Hopkins had also fallen.

Young Dave, barely nineteen, who had travelled with George and the others to accept the King's Shilling. It all brought home the realities of modern warfare. The days of chivalry were long gone and

Rebecca was filled with fear at the possibility of her husband not coming home.

As the days multiplied and the war dragged on it affected everyone. Even Squire Thomas was more withdrawn and looking older than his years. It rested heavy on his shoulders that he had encouraged so many to join what he'd thought would be a quick and adventurous victory. At least he had no sons to go and fight though both daughters were helping to nurse the wounded.

The year ended with the government having to introduce conscription to make up for the terrible losses all the nations were suffering. This meant that even if they hadn't volunteered when they did, George and the others would have gone eventually. Which did ease the burden a little on the Squire's shoulders, though young David Hopkins would not have died when and as he did.

The bells seemed muted as they rang in 1916.

PIONEER GEORGE REECE, across the Channel, was too busy coping with atrocious conditions to worry about it being a new year. Getting through each day was effort enough and he used the thought of Becky waiting at home to spur his attempts at survival.

Life was a never-ending round of digging trenches, planting barbed wire, loading and unloading equipment. Rudimentary military training had been given but a Pioneer had more use for a spade than a rifle. And then there was the most distasteful of his duties, the removal and burial of the dead.

Oh Becky, my Becky, he would think, struggling through the lice and rat-infested muck, I will get through this somehow. I will get back to you.

Then, later, he became a Mole. A nickname given to members of Pioneer Tunnelling Units as underground warfare gained a foothold in the seemingly never-ending conflict. Both sides tried to tunnel under each other's trenches, from where they could either plant bombs or have soldiers burst up through. At times opposing diggers would accidentally meet while tunnelling and hand to hand fighting would result. Subterranean fighting that could bring walls and ceiling caving in.

Also, as if there wasn't already enough to contend with, there was the increasing threat of death or incapacitation by gas inhalation. Gas bombs could be exploded into trenches or dropped into tunnels. How many more ways could they invent to kill and maim? George wondered as the death toll mounted on both sides.

It did seem though, at times, that he led an enchanted existence. George dodged death by inches and always seemed to make the right choice. Men around him died: friends and strangers, comrades and enemies. And as yet another year drew to a bitter end, he was at least alive if nothing else. He was still on course to somehow get back home to the wife he'd left behind.

IT WAS EARLY in 1916 that the farm workers had their only sighting of a Zeppelin. An airship that was probably way off course since they were not near any of the industrial centres being targeted. Squire Thomas was said to have shaken his fists at the sky, his face dark with anger, while Rebecca herself felt an icy hand grip her heart as she watched the flying monster pass overhead.

The year dragged on and the news that filtered through, probably long after the events themselves, did little to raise the spirits. Germany failed to smash the French at Verdun but had survived on the Somme, with all armies suffering catastrophic losses.

Battle fronts in Europe.

Fighting taking place in Africa and Mesopotamia. It seemed as if most of the world was involved. Places Rebecca had never heard of before.

Then came the news she had been dreading, but never really believed she would hear: "Pioneer George Albert Reece. Missing in action. Presumed dead."

The words impaled her, through skin and flesh and bone. And a darker fear than she had ever thought possible engulfed her.

Some local women had already received similar messages. Others were hoping against hope never to. All joined to offer Rebecca what comfort and support they could, as was done for everyone in her position. Squire Thomas offered gruff condolences and promised that her place on the farm was secure. But, once the initial shock faded, her dogged resilience took them by surprise.

Rebecca refused to mourn. She had no body to weep over and no graveyard plot to tend. The words "Missing" and "Presumed" burnt their way through her skull and into her brain, giving her a hope and belief most refused to acknowledge.

Not dead, not her George. He had been all things to her, still was in memory, and would be again when he returned. Others might fall and be buried in a foreign field, but her husband was not like other men. He was out there, somewhere, maybe lost for now, but he would return. And nothing would persuade her otherwise.

"You must accept," said friends and family when she had continued to stare at the stars with a hopeful conviction that all would end well. "You must accept first before you can move on."

Move on?

The concept puzzled her.

From where? To where?

Rebecca thanked them for their concern but remained convinced that George was still alive and would be found.

THE NEWS SHE had been waiting for.

The news Rebecca had known would one day come, arrived in a letter as 1916 prepared to give way to yet another new year of continuing hard times on the home front and conflict abroad. She understood but little of the medical terminology, but that didn't matter as the one important fact sent her delirious with joy.

Pioneer George Albert Reece, previously missing, had now been found.

Alive!

He had been gassed, underground, where it had been thought there were no survivors. Unconscious and desperately ill, he'd had no identification on him so was not named until much later. George had been taken to a Medical Receiving Station at Allonville in France and had only now been moved back to Britain. The references to the seriousness of his condition were of secondary importance as she read and reread the official notification. Yes, he was ill, but if George had made it this far he would make it the rest of the way.

Suddenly Rebecca could stand the shaded loneliness of her little cottage no longer. She needed to feel fresh air on her face, see the fields and feel the breeze. Hear the sounds of life. No longer a person apart, she burst into the open, eager to share her wonderful news.

GEORGE'S TUNNELLING CREW had burst through into an enemy excavation and weary men grappled in an unexpected and unwanted subterranean battle. In these situations you used your fists or whatever came to hand. George killed one German with his spade. Nearly decapitating the man as he swung the thing in blind panic, and during the scuffles that followed his identification discs were torn from the twine around his neck.

The gas bomb was dropped into the British tunnel, but since the wall had been breached it snaked through into the German one as well. As they had been fighting one another, nobody realised the danger until it was upon them and suddenly they were all gasping, burning, struggling for their very lives. Mostly, they lost.

By the time the horrific spectacle was discovered it was assumed there were no survivors. In such a confined space the gas had succeeded, killing British and Germans alike. It was with disbelief that one of the would-be rescuers noticed a barely perceptible chest movement on one of the fallen Pioneers. Unconscious, barely alive, and without any identification, George was lifted free and stretchered away. Later they transported him to Allonville, where his tenacity in clinging to such a tiny thread of life astounded all the staff.

With the limited means at their disposal, those at the Medical Receiving Station could do little more than pump him full of morphine. At least that way he was spared the agony of his burning throat and lungs, but it also meant he continued to have no name.

Knowing there was nothing they could really do there, it was decided to risk the journey and send him back to England. To a Manor House in rural Somerset that had been converted to a hospital for returning servicemen. For the very worst cases. It was there, during periods of induced awakening, that his hoarsely whispered name and details were finally acquired, and a letter was sent to his wife.

IT WAS WITH a joyful nervousness that Rebecca had set out for her first-ever train journey. Squire Thomas himself had driven her to the station in his horse-drawn carriage.

"You give George my best regards," he'd told her. "The man is a hero and he'll always have a place in my employ. You tell him that, Rebecca."

And then she had swopped the horse-drawn carriage for one pulled by a large and steaming locomotive. A noisy contraption that would carry her all the way to Somerset. All the way to see her George.

The miles sped by, the chugging train noises lulling her into a dreamy contemplation of what was to come. This was indeed a day of wonder. First the ride with the Squire, then her first-ever time in a train, and a car to meet her when she finally dismounted at the small Somerset station.

It was an army staff car and the driver, though courteous, was just that, so could tell her nothing about her husband. Impatient, now that seeing him was getting ever nearer, Rebecca could do no more than look at the passing countryside and count each fleeting second. And then, finally, they arrived.

Major Tomkins, who was waiting at the hospital, seemed young to Rebecca for such a rank. Though probably, she guessed, promotions were quicker during wartime. Yet his eyes were old, and there was a weariness about him.

"I must warn you, Mrs Reece," he told her after the formal greetings were over, "before you see your husband. He presents a wasted figure. A shadow of the man you remember…"

His voice tailed into silence and though his words held pity his expression was one no doctor should ever lay bare. A look of despair, and Rebecca felt her body grow chill. She sensed that something was terribly wrong. This was not how their reconciliation should be. This was not how she had imagined it.

"But he will recover, won't he?" she whispered as, for the first time, tears filled her eyes.

Tomkins offered her a handkerchief. A conventional gesture but providing an opportunity to retrieve his bland professional mask.

"We are quite confident," he replied, "but you must realise just how fortunate he is to be alive at all. Pioneer Reece was the only survivor from that particular event, and I don't suppose we'll ever really know why he didn't die with the others."

"Maybe George wanted to live more than them."

The major's smile was lacking in humour. "Will-power alone would be a poor defence against gas in an enclosed space. If it had been a disabling chemical such as mustard or tear gas, then others might have made it too. But it was almost certainly a more lethal agent, phosgene or chlorine at a guess, and an absolute killer under those circumstances."

"But be that as it may, sir," pointed out Rebecca,

"George did survive."

THE WALK BETWEEN the major's office and the ward had been short and Tomkins paused before entering. "Your husband is unconscious at the moment. We keep him in that condition for much of the time and thought it would be best for your first visit. Try not to let his appearance distress you too much. I'm sure it will improve, given time."

Such a caution should have prepared her for the worst, and Rebecca thought it had. But no, nothing could have forewarned her for the unmoving corpse-like figure lying in the hospital bed. Shining silvered needles stapled his arms at wrist and elbow. Bubbles frothing pink at one incision, before spattering the skin with tiny droplets of blood.

His face was hideous. It had the look of a strangled man.

She wanted to run, to hide. Do anything but stand and stare any longer, and was at least grateful that he was unable to witness the horrifying dismay she could not conceal.

The major, sensing Rebecca's distress, stepped forward, gripping her elbow in case she should fall. "Facts have to be faced," he said. "Your husband's condition is such that he will never regain his physical wellbeing. We have managed to stabilise the damage done to him but no more than that. There is no magic cure. No tablet or potion. No way to be the man he was."

Like a sleepwalker stepping into uncharted territory, she allowed Tomkins to guide her back to his office and sipped dutifully at a cup of tea he got a ward orderly to bring.

"I never imagined..." she started to say but lapsed into silence.

"This has been a great shock for you. I understand that."

"But surely..." She had to have some sort of hope. "Surely time and care will bring about some improvements, however limited."

"There is something," admitted the army doctor, "but first I must make you aware of Pioneer Reece's situation. He is now an invalid and will remain so. The severity of his condition means he will be bedridden for the rest of his days."

Seeing the growing panic in her face he continued quickly.

"But there is something that might help. Not a cure, but a form of assistance."

Rebecca started to speak but he held up a hand to stop her. "Let me finish, Mrs Reece, and listen carefully to what I am going to suggest. While most of this old manor has been converted into a hospital, it does also house an experimental department working in the area of artificial aids. This mostly involves lost limbs, and great strides have been made in providing much improved substitute arms and legs. But they are always up for a challenge and the captain in charge thinks they can offer some small promise of help regarding mobility in your husband's case."

Rebecca grabbed at his words. "Can they make him walk?"

"Well ... sort of." Tomkins cleared his throat. "As I understand it, they are proposing to build him into a metal frame which would enclose his torso and legs, thus supporting him for limited movement. The frame would be screwed through the flesh and into bone, meaning it could never be removed.

"It would not, and I must stress this, it would not enable him to enjoy a full and everyday existence. But even only limited movement is to be preferred when the alternative is to be permanently bedridden."

And Rebecca had agreed, wholeheartedly. "In sickness and in health" she had promised. She would nurse and care for him and honour their love, but would also be grateful for any help that was offered.

It not being his area of expertise, Major Tomkins had his doubts but kept them to himself. "I am sure you will both be able to..." he paused a moment, searching for the words to tell this tragic woman that her husband would be more than just a freak. There were none. "...adjust," he said finally.

GEORGE HIMSELF HAD been hoarsely optimistic when she had finally spoken with him the next day. It was difficult for him to dredge up words from his damaged lungs and throat. Like her, he was pinning his hopes on whatever support a manufactured frame would offer his wasted body. For all the terribleness of his appearance, he was still her George, and Rebecca did her best to reassure him of that fact.

"We will cope, Becky," he'd whispered.

"Course we will, George. Of course we will."

She had left the hospital then. Left Somerset and returned to their little cottage to prepare for his homecoming. There were people to tell, and to warn, about his condition. And a bed had to be placed downstairs since they had warned her that steps would be beyond his range of movements.

George was never going to work again. That was certain. "No matter," Squire Thomas told her. "We know how to care for our heroes. You and George need have no worries about that."

FOR ALL HER happiness at having him home, Rebecca couldn't suppress a shudder as she watched the orderlies stagger into the cottage, heaving sighs of relief as they relinquished their burden.

The captain accompanying them was an outstanding talent in his field, and an unpleasant man. *And* not *but*, for that would suggest some measure of excuse where none existed, which not even his acknowledged ability could justify. He seemed to regard all lower ranks with contempt. This did not make him unique, just unpleasant.

"Pioneer Reece posed many technical problems," he said. "Problems which needed to be overcome."

"But he's so big," said Rebecca, almost to herself. "So heavy."

George had been sedated for the long ambulance journey from the hospital. Soon he would awake and after a final medical check she would be alone with him. For all the love she felt, the thought did scare her a little. It would almost be like looking after a child.

Sourly, the captain agreed. "But consider what we have achieved," he said. "Even when the body is weak, the brain continues its active life. We have harnessed his useless flesh into a powerful exoskeleton. It may be somewhat cumbersome, but it will allow him some movement again. It will restore a certain degree of mobility.

"Otherwise…" he shrugged. "He would have been bedridden and probably hospitalised for the rest of his life."

Yes I know, thought Rebecca, and I am grateful. But

at the back of her mind she could not suppress a tremor of disquiet.

"You must always treat him as a *normal* human being." The captain stressed the word, and she glanced surreptitiously at the silent figure bulked beneath the red blanket.

Treat him as a *normal* human being!

Later, when George was awake and the medical team had left, he spoke of his hopes. "I will learn, with your help. Soon this frame will become as much a part of me as my own flesh and blood. We will both have to adjust, my love, but there'll be nothing we won't be able to meet and overcome, together."

AT FIRST HE said he loved her, that they were still man and wife, and all that meant would always hold true. But when she continued to refuse he became angry and bitter, accusing her of going with other men and even naming Squire Thomas.

In his imagination George saw her in the throes of sex, her eyes half-closed, head thrown back, spreading her legs wide as someone else's penis plunged deep into her.

The thought filled him with revulsion ... yet excited him.

Later, as his frustration grew, he began pleading with her. "Let me," he begged in a little-boy voice. "I need you. Please."

Rebecca shook her head. "No," she replied quietly, averting her eyes. "I can't."

"Please!"

"No."

There was a long silence, as if a thick velvet curtain had descended between them.

"Damn you!" he shouted, suddenly and without warning, as loudly as his poor body would allow, startling Rebecca with his vehemence. "Damn you to hell and back! I want you … now!" George began to sob. "Please…"

It was the final supplication. If she refused him now then all that had existed before was gone forever.

"YES," SHE WHISPERED, hardly believing that the word had finally been said.

REBECCA'S EYES OPENED wide, then shut tight as the crushing weight bore down upon her, and she cried out against the violence of his need. There was a searing agony which seemed to wrench her apart the harder he thrust, until she felt that she could endure the pain no longer.

Until she screamed for it to end.

Until, finally, it was ended.

SHE LOOKED DOWN at herself: at the angry yellow bruises where his armoured fingers clutched her breasts, at the red wheals covering her body where the metal ribcage crushed her, at her thighs streaked with dried blood.

I wish he had died in that tunnel, she thought while remembering Major Tomkins telling her how fortunate George was to be alive at all.

I wish he'd die now, added Rebecca silently, bringing to mind the captain's vigorous entreaty: "You must treat him like a *normal* human being."

And the words began to hammer back and forth inside her skull, echoing until her head seemed to reverberate with the sound. Until it seemed that it would burst.

A *normal* human being.

Normal?

NORMAL...!

OUTSIDE IN THE fields the crops had been harvested. All that was left were broken stalks to be either ploughed back into the earth or used to feed the animals.

Inside their cottage a cold fear gripped Rebecca as she wondered: how soon would it be before George wanted her again?

OINK

"Is this seat taken?" The tone was deep and hoarse, a smoker's voice of too-many-cigarettes, and other bad habits.

Carl muttered that it wasn't, turning away as the newcomer sat down. He was beginning to wonder why he had thought a midnight showing of *The Rocky Horror Picture Show* might be fun. The cinema was barely half full and only a smattering had attempted fancy dress, Carl not being one of them. Bloody idiots! This wasn't New York or London.

He hoped the guy wouldn't turn out to be a talker. With all the empty seats on offer he could have sat where he liked and not necessarily next to anyone. Oh God! Even worse! What if he were a touch freak? One hand, wrongly placed, and Carl would smash the fucker. Maybe! Well he would think about it but probably do nothing more than change his seat. He would do that.

The on-screen adverts ended only to be replaced with What's On, Coming Soon and Future Attractions. "Why are we waiting?" chanted a group boasting heavy makeup and red corsets, obviously bored with waiting for the film.

"Be quiet," barked the man in the next seat. Carl cringed, hoping there would be no trouble but the chorus did die away.

It was all Karen's fault anyway. He would not have

been here at all if she hadn't ended their relationship. Carl could see it from her point of view though; they were both thirty, had been going out for five years, and she wanted the security of a marriage.

"You fear commitment," she had told him, not without justification.

The breakup had driven home what a lonely person he had become. Most of Carl's old friends were either married, some for a second or third time, or in a settled partnership. Those that weren't, though, were no longer the good companions they had once been. It was not that Karen had been the big love of his life, though he had liked her well enough. Carl did miss having someone to do things with; and also the regular sex, however mechanical it had become.

So here he was, alone in a cinema to see the late-night showing of a cult classic he had no special interest in. He could hum a couple of the tunes; "Time Warp" in particular was difficult to get out of your head whenever you remembered it, but would he have considered buying a ticket if he had still been with Karen? Most definitely not!

"About time," said his neighbour as the last trailer ended, and Carl turned towards him for the first time.

"What the…!"

Surprised, Carl saw that he was sitting next to a pig! Or at least someone wearing a pig's head, and by God it looked real. He tried to list the *Rocky Horror* characters, those he could remember: Doctor Frank-n-Furter, Brad and Janet, Riff Raff, Eddie. There were none that related to pork, so why choose a fancy dress that had nothing to do with the film?

"Why are you wearing a pig's head?" he felt compelled to ask.

"Pardon?"

"It's *The Rocky Horror Picture Show*. There are no pigs in it. It seems a pointless disguise."

"Disguise?"

"Fancy dress! Role playing!" Carl couldn't help but notice that the mouth moved very realistically when the man spoke, and that a nervous twitch alongside the snout suggested flesh rather than plastic. "You look like a pig," he finished, lamely.

"I am no pig," said the man crossly. "I am a boar, sir, a wild boar."

Carl had been leaning towards him, looking hard, but the head seemed so real he pulled back, feeling quite disturbed. Was he sat next to a madman?

"To be specific," the man continued, "I am a Ussuri boar, which you can tell by my markings. Namely, the white bands that extend from the corners of my mouth to my ears."

"The film is starting," said Carl weakly.

"Hronk, hronk," commented the man, and they both turned their faces to the screen.

The few who had turned up in costume did try to recite the dialogue and sing the songs in sync with the soundtrack but it was a ragged effort and soon fizzled out. Carl had been relieved when the man in the pig's head had not joined in with the verbal's, and even more so when he had got up and left before the film ended.

What a strange guy! Why come at all if you were not going to watch the whole thing?

MAKING HIS WAY through the neon-lit and chilly cinema car park, Carl made a mental note to avoid midnight film shows in the future. At least it was the early hours of a Sunday morning so he would be able to sleep on undisturbed once he got home.

His Ford Fiesta was parked in a shadowy corner and he noticed nothing untoward until his headlights picked out a figure lying motionless between two vehicles opposite his. Getting back out of the car, Carl went to investigate.

Horrified! He took an involuntary step back. The man was obviously dead, lying on his back with his chest not only open but pulled apart, all the way down to his stomach. Ribs were showing and organs had been disturbed. It was a gory mess and Carl froze, not knowing what to do.

"Quick! Get back in your car!"

Turning as if in slow motion, Carl saw that the speaker was the man from the cinema. The one with the pig's head, which he was still wearing.

"What…?" he started to say, but the other moved to stand between him and the dead man, blocking his view.

"Nothing can be done here and you don't want to be involved in anything like this. Come on now, move!"

Carl allowed himself to be guided back to his own vehicle, more than willing to be moved away from such a terrible sight. He slumped at the wheel while the heavily built pig-headed man clambered into the passenger seat. "Drive, my friend," he said hoarsely. "You can give me a lift."

"But that man, the body … we should call the police…"

"Let someone else have the hassle."

Carl realised that though he felt icy cold, sweat was running freely down his face. What the man suggested was persuasive and did make a nasty sort of sense. Whoever phoned this in, it would make little difference to either the corpse or the authorities. He started the car as if in a dream, or nightmare, and before he knew it both the cinema and grisly car park scene had receded from sight, if not from mind.

"Good man," said his passenger.

When he felt far enough away to be clear of any connection with what they had left behind, and had not heard any sirens of chasing police cars, Carl pulled over and stopped. "Where do you want to be taken?" he asked, looking hard at the other, taking in the wrinkled snout, upturned tusks, deep set eyes, and facial tic.

"This will do fine. I'll get out here."

Carl plucked up the courage to ask what had become a growing suspicion. "It's not a false head is it? It's not fancy dress?"

"Of course not! I told you, I'm a boar, a wild boar. I can trace my ancestry back to the far eastern Ussuri district of Russia though I myself am British by birth."

Heaving himself out of the passenger seat he closed the door before crossing the road and disappearing into a side street. The trouble for Carl was that he was starting to believe him.

THE CINEMA CAR park murder was the town's sole topic of conversation once the news got out. Carl's original intention had been to ignore the police request for all who had attended the midnight showing of *The Rocky Horror Picture Show* to contact them, but he had mentioned buying the ticket to work colleagues and his parents knew he had gone to see it.

"Our Carl was there at the pictures Saturday night, Father."

"I know, Mother."

"Just think, our boy so close to a murder scene."

"I know, Mother."

"Another cup of tea?"

"Yes please. Two sugars, Mother."

"I should know how many by now, Father."

They lived in a world of their own, but they and others knew he had been to the cinema that night so Carl had trooped along to help the police with their inquiries. Luckily the constable tasked with taking his statement was getting bored with the repetitive nature of the job.

Yes, he had arrived at the cinema just before the show started.

Yes, he had stayed until the end and had been alone.

Yes, he had gone straight to his car and had driven away.

No, he had not seen anything suspicious.

Carl had marked on a map of the area just where he claimed his car to have been parked, making it appear to have been nearer the exit and not opposite where the body had been located. Doing that had been scary, but the constable's disinterest had been reassuring.

In spite of strong media interest and intense local concern, an early conclusion to the investigation proved a forlorn hope. The victim's wife and her lover were held briefly but quickly released when their alibis held up. Rumour had it that the police were baffled, and that imminent arrests were unlikely.

KAREN WAS NOT blind to her own shortcomings. Her eyes were a little large and circular, giving an impression of permanent surprise; while her nose, though straight, was longer than needed. A strict diet and regular exercise had got rid of teenage plumpness and kept her slim and trim ever since. But now, having reached thirty, the temptation to backslide was growing stronger.

Her sleek lines were starting to fill a little with a hint of the fuller body to come.

Karen didn't want much out of life: a semi-detached, two children, a husband in regular employment. She'd thought Carl would be the one and had wasted five years on him. Not even an engagement ring!

The best thing about her was the raven black hair that shone with a brilliant sheen as it framed her face. She kept it simple in a Lana Turner sort of film noir vamp style, with a plain top and pencil skirt. Not many appreciated where she was coming from, fashion-wise, but Karen had always loved those old black and white films.

Anyway, with Carl gone she cast her net to see what other potential husband material might be waiting for her to hook, but it was not promising. Derek, from work, had taken her on a couple of dates but he was only after one thing and walking down the aisle was not on his agenda. Carl made one half-hearted attempt to win her back but had only been offering a continuation of their previous five years. Karen wanted promises that would be kept, dates set in stone, a ring on her finger.

"Derek is being most persistent," she had lied, hoping to spark off a jealous reaction. "He wants us to get engaged but I have asked for more time to think about it."

Carl had stormed off, not sure why he felt so angry, nor knowing what he might do about it. Karen though, thought it a good sign, convincing herself he would soon be back with a more positive attitude. Maybe even a proposal.

CARL WAS PISSED off. Yes, he would like to get back with Karen, but not at any price. And why was this Derek guy sticking his oar in, making things awkward? Carl thought he had met him last Christmas at Karen's office booze-up; a dago looking tosspot if Carl remembered him correctly, though Derek was an English sounding name.

Having managed to get away from work early he parked where he could see them coming out from Karen's place of employment. He saw her exchange a couple of words with the man he recognised as being his rival before they headed in opposite directions. At least they were not going home together.

"So that's the fucker!"

Startled, Carl had not even realised the pig-headed man had got into the car. James Stewart with his invisible friend in *Harvey* and Jake Gyllenhaal with Frank in *Donnie Darko* had both been given large rabbits to be their oddball companions. But that was Hollywood. This was reality, and he had been lumbered with a man-sized pig!

"What?"

"Him!" the pig, or boar, or whatever it was, grunted, nodding in the general direction of the people opposite. "The guy who is trying to muscle in on Karen."

"Yes, but—"

"No *buts* Carl, this dude has to be dealt with."

Trancelike, he eased his car into the traffic, following Derek to where his car was parked, and slotting in behind when his Bentley R Type sports saloon drove away.

"A reconditioned 1953 model, probably his pride and joy," muttered the pig in an exasperated tone, "and you drive a Ford Fiesta. No wonder Karen is fluttering her eyelashes in his direction."

"Nothing wrong with a sensible car."

"Nothing that an Aston Martin wouldn't put right."

Carl could think of no suitable retort so said nothing more. Who did this bloody pig think he was, anyway? Those big celluloid rabbits had names, Harvey and Frank, but this unwelcome lump of pork had not even had the good manners to introduce itself.

"My name is Oswald, and I don't like being referred to as a pig. I've told you before, I am a wild boar."

Was his passenger a mind reader too? "And I am—"

"Yes, yes," interrupted Oswald. "You are Carl, he's Derek, she's Karen, and we seem to have reached our destination."

Carl pulled over, making a quick stop, and they watched as Derek parked on a driveway before leaving his Bentley and entering the house.

"Shall we do it now or later?"

"Do what?" asked Carl.

Oswald snorted, in another show of exasperation. "Warn him off," he said.

"That wasn't what..." Carl started to say but stopped. He'd had no clear reason for either spying on Derek or following him home. It had just been spur-of-the-moment stuff, but maybe some sort of confrontation was an inevitable outcome. Either that or give up on Karen completely. "A friendly word might be in order," he decided.

Oswald snorted again. "An unfriendly word might work better," he said. "Come on!"

Carl followed the wild boar over the road and up the drive to the front door. Oswald rang the bell then stood to one side forcing Carl to do the talking.

The door opened and there stood Derek. "Yes?" he

asked.

"Can I have a word?"

"Do I know you? Wait a minute, you're Karen's ex, aren't you? We met at an office booze-up. I don't remember your name though. Sorry."

Carl was already regretting being there. This wasn't such a good idea after all.

"You're not playing the broken-hearted ex, are you?" asked Derek, adding a short laugh. "It's only been a couple of dates and I didn't even get to first base. Me and her are history, already."

"History!" shouted Carl. "What about you wanting to get engaged?" And that was when a charging Oswald pushed him to one side.

HEAD LOWERED, OSWALD'S snout thudded into Derek at belly button height, his left tusk ripping through cloth, skin, and flesh. Through the door and into the hall they went, down in a heap, the boar on top. Derek's initial scream gurgled to nothing as the tusk tore him open from stomach to chest.

Carl lurched forward on rubbery legs, barely able to comprehend what was happening. Leaning in the doorway he looked down at where Oswald's snout was snuffling into the open chest cavity like a sow digging for truffles. It took him a moment or two to realise that the high-pitched whine he could hear was coming from his own throat.

Derek, his eyes and mouth gaping wide in a final expression of pure terror, was obviously dead. Blood, spurting from his partially eaten heart and severed arteries, covered Oswald and even splashed as far as Carl.

"What have you done?"

The pig-thing interrupted its feeding frenzy long enough to turn its head towards the man in the doorway. "Get out, Carl," he growled.

"But—"

"Get out!" repeated Oswald, his voice getting louder. "Out! Out! Out!"

Carl took a backward step, hypnotised by the droplets of Derek's blood that sprayed from Oswald's mouth with each snarled syllable. Then he turned away, running blindly from the house, ignoring beeping traffic in his dash across the road to clamber into his car. He just needed to get away, as quickly as possible.

MEN!

Karen picked half-heartedly at a limp salad wishing it were steak and chips, but her mind was really full of what had taken place the previous evening. She had seen him hanging around before; well you could hardly miss a man wearing a pig's head, but this time he had knocked on her door and her mind had spun out of control.

It might have been the power and strength locked into the bulk of his physical appearance, or the potent mix of damp fields, masculine sweat and farmyard odours; a heady combination that swamped her senses. Whatever it was, it worked at the most intoxicating level, where action was paramount.

At first Karen thought it might have been Derek unwilling to take no for an answer, but their physiques didn't match and she didn't think it was his style either. Next she thought of Carl, but comparing him to this raging Casanova was like matching chalk and cheese, and this guy was tasty Gorgonzola. But in no time at all his identity ceased to matter and the sex was both brutal and glorious.

Pushing away the barely touched food, Karen experienced an oddly exciting mix of shame and pleasure as she remembered the speed with which she had capitulated to his unspoken demands. And that had been strange too, the way he had matched his piggy disguise by only communicating in squeals and grunts. In fact the only world he had spoken had been when leaving, when she had asked him who he was.

"Oswald," he had replied, and then he was gone.

CARL HAD TURNED up at her flat, wild-eyed and covered in blood. "Are you hurt?" had been Karen's first reaction, thinking maybe he had been in a car accident or something. First old piggy-head and now a blood-stained ex. It was just as well her flatmate Julie was visiting family for a few days.

"No." It turned out Carl had no actual injuries, which beggared the question: whose blood was splattered all over him?

"It was Oswald, not me!" insisted Carl.

Karen was startled to hear that name again. "You'd better come in and clean yourself," she said. "Then you can tell me just what has happened. This Oswald you mentioned, is he the one who wears a pig's head?"

Carl took a jerky step backwards. "Oswald! Do you know him?"

"I know of him," Karen replied carefully. It might be better to hold back on the details.

"He's not a pig," said Carl, moving further back away from her door. "He's a wild boar of Russian stock, and it was all down to him. I would never have followed Derek on my own."

"Derek!" A nasty suspicion was growing in Karen's

mind. "You had better tell me, Carl. You! Derek! Oswald! What's been going on between you all, and why does he go around wearing that grotesque rubber head, whatever sort of animal it is?"

"Haven't you realised? Carl backed away another couple of steps. "It's not a mask! It's not false! Oswald is a boar. A wild boar! And the blood is Derek's."

"Carl! Come back!" she shouted. He couldn't make such monstrous allegations without explaining them, but he was running fast back towards his car.

"DID YOU SEE him, Father?"

"See who, Mother?"

"Our Carl, in the hall."

"Not from here, Mother."

"Pushed past me. Rushed up the stairs."

"In a hurry was he, Mother?"

"I should say, and covered in blood."

"Blood, Mother?"

"Either that or tomato sauce, Father."

"Has our Carl taken up amateur dramatics?"

"Who knows? Cup of tea, Father?"

ONCE IN HIS bedroom, Carl pushed over a chest of drawers to block the door. All of them, his parents, Karen, Oswald – oh yes, especially Oswald – could just leave him alone. None of it was his fault. Oswald had obviously killed the man in the cinema car park, and had definitely done for Derek. But who would believe that the murderer was a wild boar? Nobody, that's who!

Carl's big problem was in having been at X-marks-the-spot for both killings, even witnessing Derek's gory end, and two plus two could sometimes make five. Yet none of it was down to him. Karen could take her share of the blame though. If she hadn't kept pressing for a ring on her finger they would never have split up and he wouldn't have gone to that particular film show.

And his parents: them too! It would have been better had he never been born, though how he had was a mystery in itself. Carl found it hard to imagine his parents carrying out the necessary act of conception. Maybe he had been adopted, snapped up from a Russian orphanage, more than likely in the Ussuri region. His ancestors would have been solid Russian peasantry, maybe with a touch of bacon in their DNA.

Oswald was the guilty one but he would get away with it while Carl took the blame. It was the way his life had gone from the moment of his birth.

THE POLICE SIRENS had been faint at first, growing louder until however many cars they had sent pulled up outside the house. Carl heard the front door being knocked, and the muted conversation that followed. He heard the footsteps coming up the stairs.

There was a knock on his bedroom door. "It's the police, Carl," called a voice. "Can we come in and talk to you?"

Even as a football supporter he'd been a loser. Neither Manchester teams had caught his imagination. No Chelsea or Arsenal paraphernalia covered his walls. Liverpool did not exist for him. Carl turned to look at the reflection in his Newport County mirror – and was pleased with what he saw.

The deep-set eyes, pointy ears, wrinkled snout, patterned bristles and upturned tusks. He was, without doubt, the handsomest of wild boars.

Someone tried the doorknob but it bumped against

the chest of drawers. "Come on, Carl," said the voice. "We know you're in there and we only want to talk."

Yeah, yeah! The first one in, thought Carl with a malicious glee, gets gored.

"Oink!" he said aloud. "Oink bloody oink…"

OH BABYLON

I GUESS BEING black and named Marvin Bone, so therefore called Boney by the other kids, it was sort of inevitable that I would dig into the back catalogue of that old German-based disco group. I, after all, was M. Bone, and they were Boney M. I loved all their stuff, but "Rivers of Babylon" was my favourite. One of the biggest selling UK singles ever, so the record books say.

Being big as well as black, and not the quickest pupil in the class, my future prospects seemed limited by both my situation and my inclinations. On the one hand, a life of crime beckoned – muscle being an always useful commodity. On the other, the possibility of a sporting career – something the young me excelled at in general. I still hold the area school-age shotput record, to this day.

Paul Mulligan could have been an academic success. He had the brains. Could have passed exams, gone to university, qualified as whatever he wanted; skinny little white-arsed honky rebel. Trouble was, he only had eyes for the gangs. School, when he bothered to turn up, was just an amusement.

Some of the kids took the piss out of me, often with a racial element, and I usually flattened them. When Paul Mulligan took the piss I generally saw the joke and laughed along with it. His barbs were never about my colour. In that strange way of opposites attracting, we got along okay.

I SOMETIMES WONDERED if I was named after Marvin Hagler, Marvellous Marvin Hagler, one-time Middle-weight Champion of the World. According to my Mum, my father chose the name and I couldn't ask him since he did a runner before my first birthday. I hoped it was after Hagler though, because I was well into boxing myself.

Marvin's fight with Tommy "Hitman" Hearns was short, brutal, and an absolute epic, which he won. He was either dumb or too cocky when he lost to Sugar Ray Leonard, letting them talk him down from fifteen rounds to twelve. Sugar Ray, after a good first half, was tiring towards the end while Hagler was coming on strong. Another three rounds and he might well have been the winner.

I won some schoolboy titles and joined the local Amateur Boxing Club, moving through the weights as I grew into the heavies. I wasn't very scientific but was able to bludgeon my way to building up a reasonable record with a good percentage of wins against my name.

Paul Mulligan, meanwhile, had worked his way through the small-time hoodlum ranks. He aimed to make his mark and move up with the big boys, and in our neck of the woods that meant Olly Roxborough. Our local Big Cheese, with legit business interests as well as all the illegal ones. He dabbled in boxing as a small-hall promoter and manager, owning a gym which was situated over a pub, which he also owned.

"Don't go with Roxborough," was the advice given to any budding talent at my Amateur Club. "None of his fighters have good careers." But when I came to Roxborough's attention he had my old school friend whispering in his ear, and it was Paul who made the approach.

"They say he don't look after his boys," I said.

"I can't comment on the past," said Paul, dismissing it with an expressive shrug, "but I'm on board now and I'll make sure that everyone gets a fair crack, especially my old mucker."

"My trainer says I should be okay to go for the ABA's in a year or two."

"Why wait? You might get injured, you might get beat. Then it's a couple of years wasted. Turn pro now, Marvin. Get some money in your pocket. I'll make sure Olly Roxborough treats you right."

I listened to him then, just as I had at Merton Hill Comprehensive. I should have remembered that Paul often got me into trouble back in our schooldays.

IF I EVER asked about my father, Mum would usually laugh and say he had been a Haitian Warlock. I guess she wasn't too cut up at his vanishing act since I had a succession of "uncles" and even a step-dad or two. She was a survivor, my mother, and always made sure there was someone able to put food on our plates.

But a Haitian Warlock?

More chance of my dad being from Birmingham, and if he had been from Haiti he would've been a Voodoo Priest rather than a Warlock. I knew that much. I might have been slow in the classroom but that didn't mean stupid. Things would click into place eventually but by the time they did the teacher had already moved on to something else.

SO I SIGNED a contract with Olly Roxborough and embarked upon a boxing career. My new home-from-home, the gym over the pub, was Spartan in comparison to my old Amateur Club, but it did have Bob Jenkinson as Head Trainer. Old, yes, with a walnut face and not much hair left, but still trim at not much more than the featherweight limit. He had briefly held the British Title, though his best remembered fight was losing an all-out battle against Baby Mendoza, before the Spaniard went on to win one of the World Belts.

Those were the best of times, my early pro career; working and learning under Bob's tutelage while putting together an unbeaten run of twelve fights. Six and then eight rounds on paper but none of them went the distance. One was stopped because the guy was badly cut; on three occasions the ref stepped in to save a helpless opponent from further punishment; and the other eight were straight kayos.

"Don't run before you can walk," Bob would council me in husky tones that were maybe an early warning of the throat cancer that would put him down for the full count only a few years later. "The bums and no-hopers are okay for your learning curve but you aren't ready for the big boys yet."

I look out at the rain, now, coming down in sheets, like the world is going to flood. Is there a new Noah somewhere? Building a new Ark? Could be that we humans are not worth saving though...

Twelve straight inside-the-distance wins and I had become something of a local celebrity, making the sporting pages of the press. Even the nationals were tipping me as a prospect of note, building me up as a future champion.

"Easy does it, Marvin," warned Bob Jenkinson. "The papers will knock you down as quick as they build you up."

"You could be British Champion tomorrow,"

claimed my pal Paul. "None of them could stand up to your punching power."

"I look at your muscles and I go weak," said Tiffany Burrows, and I flipped the record so Boney M were singing "Brown Girl in the Ring".

Tiffany was a mixed-race beauty and an aspiring model. Like I keep stressing: slow but not stupid. I knew she would never have glanced in my direction if I'd been stacking shelves in a supermarket. Tiffany wanted to go places and was willing to hitch a lift with anyone who could help, and being seen on the arm of British boxing's new heavyweight hope wouldn't hurt. I knew it but didn't care. Me, with a girl like Tiffany! It was barely credible.

"You dog!" laughed Paul. "You lucky, lucky dog!"

"Don't let your love-life interfere with training," snapped Bob Jenkinson.

"Come here, baby," purred Tiffany.

Then Olly Roxborough, local villain and my promoter/manager, announced my first ten rounder, a final eliminator against Alan "Pitbull" Pope, the winner to challenge for the British title. My trainer was not pleased. It was the first time I had seen anyone stand up to Mr Roxborough, but Bob Jenkinson insisted on having his say. Basically, he did not think I was ready to mix it with likes of Pope, a roughhouse slugger and former champion who was looking to get his title back.

The boss left it to Paul Mulligan to put the trainer in his place. Did Bob like his job looking after the Roxborough stable of fighters? Did he want to keep that job? If he did, then it was time to button up and concentrate on keeping them in good shape. Match-making was not his concern.

As for myself, with an unbeaten dozen stretching out

behind me and Tiffany making me feel like a king, my attitude was: you line 'em up and I'll knock 'em down. I was going to the top; my girl was certain of it.

It's Biblical, this rainfall. Been pouring down for weeks and there have been news reports of flooding all over the country. No-one could remember the last time our river had burst its banks. I look out with my one good eye, and it's like seeing a shimmering curtain of wet.

I trained hard for the eliminator, skipping and punching to the rhythms of Boney M; though maybe I should have concentrated more on the biblical lyrics of "Rivers of Babylon" rather than the Tiffany-linked "Brown Girl in the Ring". Bob Jenkinson tried to give me a crash course in defensive strategies. I listened to him, out of respect, but I was confident that my punching power would get the job done.

"Pope has a good chin. He takes punishment well," said Bob.

Not punching like mine, I thought.

"And he's got a big overarm right hand."

I've got a left and a right, and a knockout in both.

"They don't call him 'Pitbull' for nothing. If he spots a weakness he's all over it like a rash and doesn't let go."

Weakness! What weakness?

Was I overconfident? Well it's no good climbing into the ring if you don't think you can win. You see the worry lines and nervous expressions on boxers who know they are on a hiding to nothing. You see their hesitant actions as they are manoeuvred into positions that the other guy dictates.

"How are you feeling, Marvin?"

"Just fine, Mr Roxborough, fine and dandy."

"Good lad. Win this one and you'll be going for the

title."

Two fights and I would be British Champion, with European and maybe World title fights to come. It all spread out before me, and Tiffany was part and parcel of the whole thing, maybe even as Mrs Bone. But first I had to get passed the Pitbull.

My thirteenth bout! Unlucky for some but I wasn't superstitious. Maybe I should have been.

Bone versus Pope was a contender for "Fight of the Year".

No, it wasn't a fight, it was more like a war. He might have been nearing the veteran stage but he still had ambitions. I had youth but he had experience.

We went at each-other straight from the opening bell, both of us determined to land the killer blows that would win us the fight. Never mind fancy footwork and building up the points, neither of us planned on it going to the scorecards.

Was Pitbull a dirty fighter? Of course he was, but clever with it. He knew how to do the majority of the rough stuff on the blind side where the referee couldn't see it. I was too raw and when I retaliated I would be pulled up and warned.

For three rounds we went toe-to-toe. His chin was as good as Bob had said, but so was mine, and we hit one another with punches strong enough to stun a bull. The crowd was going wild.

"Where's your defence?" Bob was snapping into my ear between rounds. "He's suckering you into his sort of fight. Stand off him and move. Make him work." But all I was thinking of was landing the big one and seeing Pitbull flat on his back.

Halfway through the fourth I threw a big right hook, timed to perfection and as hard as I could. Sensing what was coming, Pope leant towards me as he tried to duck and I hit the top of his shaven skull. The hurt that shot up my arm told me that the damage was serious. Pitbull was staggered, but his skull was thick and he grabbed me into a clinch while his head cleared. I dug a gentle right into his ribs and nearly cried out with the pain. It turned out later that I had broken bones in my wrist, but all I knew at the time was that I would be throwing no more big right handers that night.

Backing off I tried to switch from slugger to orthodox, keeping him at bay with straight lefts. Suddenly I was wishing I had paid more attention to Bob's attempts at improving my defence. The bell was a welcome relief but there was little Bob could do during the interval. I admitted to having hurt my hand but played down the full extent of the damage. Bob wanted to retire me there and then but I insisted on a few rounds more to see if I could nail him with a big left.

Alan Pope was canny enough to realise something was wrong and upped the pressure, giving me no respite as he stormed forward. Over the next four rounds he gradually dismantled me, handing out quite a beating in the process. A more experienced individual would either have gone down and taken the ten count, or have retired hurt as Bob wanted; but I kept demanding one round more, hoping against hope that I could still land a knockout.

Come the ninth and Pope was concentrating on a cut on my left eyebrow. He backed me onto the ropes and while the referee tried to break up our mauling he thumbed me hard in the already bloodied eye. I dropped to my knees, Bob threw in the towel, and the referee stopped the contest. Pitbull had won on a technical knockout.

My wrist healed fine, no problem. But the eye, oh man, my left eye. Detached retina, burst blood vessels, and goodness knew what else. I came out with twenty-five percent vision, and lucky to have that, which ended my boxing career. One-eyed fighters don't cut it.

I'm stuck here, now, in Paul's house, looking at the deluge with my one good eye.

I DON'T THINK Pitbull tried to blind me deliberately. He was probably after the cut, hoping to worsen it enough to cause a stoppage, and his thumb slipped down into the eye. Though the ref missed it, television cameras caught the incident quite clearly. The British Boxing Board of Control withheld Pope's purse money, eventually declared the fight "No Contest", and offered me a rematch, but the full extent of my injury made that impossible.

In the end another heavyweight was nominated to replace me in the eliminator and was easily defeated. Pitbull went on the challenge for the title but a cagey champion kept him at bay for a decisive points victory. As for me, my license was revoked; Marvin Bone, ex-boxer.

Tiffany came to see me twice in hospital, then her visits tailed off. Paul dropped by occasionally. He was sorry the way things had worked out but when I was ready I could become one of Bob Jenkinson's assistant trainers at the gym. The old guy seemed to be ailing, he said, so eventually the Head Trainer position would be up for grabs.

His last visit hit me as hard as any of Alan Pope's punches. "Someone's going to tell you, so I guess it had better be me," said Paul, my friend since schooldays. "Tiffany has moved into my place. We are an item, now."

Oh, Babylon! The river that splits you rises to swallow you whole. Babylon! Babylon! Was it you who sinned so badly, or am I mixing it with Sodom and Gomorrah? Either way, destruction was the cure.

I'd thought Tiffany was Boney M's "Brown Girl in the Ring", my magnificent mulatto. But no, she turned out to be the Whore of Babylon. God would punish her one day, of that I was sure.

And still the rains pour down.

A man has to eat, and all I really knew was boxing so when the doctors finished with me I joined the staff at Roxborough's gym, under the direction of Bob Jenkinson. The boss would drop in now and then, talk to Bob and usually pat me on the back: "Always a job for you here, Marvin."

Paul Mulligan rarely showed his face. He had moved up and no longer concerned himself with the boxing side of things. Word had it that he was Olly Roxborough's right hand man now. On the odd occasion he had to visit the gym we both behaved as if we were strangers, staying as far apart as possible. He pulled a few strings and got Tiffany some catalogue assignments. Her coffee-coloured skin looked sensational in snowy white underwear. Well I thought so anyway. Bitch!

WITHOUT GOING INTO it too deeply, I have always considered myself a Christian, especially the Old Testament variety. An eye for an eye, tooth for a tooth, and I saw nothing wrong with mixing in any other belief system that offered a possible answer. After all, my Mum had always named my father as a Haitian Warlock, whatever that might have meant.

So I fashioned an eight-inch Voodoo Doll and scrawled the name PAUL across its body with an indelible marker. I stuck needles and nails into it and tried to send damaging thoughts in his direction. Maybe this would be the prompt God needed to bring down His wrath and lay it at the sinner's door. Not long after I started doing this, Paul accompanied Olly Roxborough on a visit to the gym and I overheard him complaining of bad indigestion that he couldn't seem to get rid of.

Indigestion! Or black magic? Could that little figure back in my apartment be working?

Bob Jenkinson's health continued to deteriorate and by the time he got himself checked out the throat cancer was terminal and the Sisters of Mercy were soon caring for him as the end approached. I didn't get the Head Trainer position – there were others better qualified than me but I remained on the team.

The last time I saw him he was as talkative as ever, though obviously with great difficulty. "Come close so you can hear me, Marvin," he instructed hoarsely.

"Be cool, Bob," I said. "Don't strain yourself."

"Shut up and listen. There's things I should have told you before. You knew at the time that I wasn't happy when they matched you with Alan Pope."

"And you were right."

"You put up a marvellous show of pure guts, Marvin."

"Marvellous Marvin," I said with a chuckle, trying to keep it light.

"But it was three or four fights too early. The papers had built you up though, looking for a new young hope, and even the bookies were taken in by your twelve straight wins. You were the betting favourite and there were good odds on offer if you wanted to back the old Pitbull."

"What are you saying, Bob?"

"Olly Roxborough, for all his faults, knows a bit about the fight game. He knew you were still too raw and inexperienced for a roughhouse nutter like Pope."

"So?" I asked, beginning to suspect where this was leading.

"So your pal Mulligan spread the bets out and about. A bit here, a bit there, until Olly had laid out really big money, and all on Pope to win."

"Are you sure about this?"

"I wouldn't be telling you otherwise. Nobody knew how it would end, mind. You were supposed to just take a beating and then Olly would look to get your career back on track again. Nobody foresaw the injuries you would suffer, or the 'No Contest' verdict."

"If I hadn't broken my bloody wrist I would've beaten him."

"You might well have, Marvin, you might well have…"

Bob's voice was barely a whisper and I could see how much the conversation had taken out of him. "At least all bets were cancelled, spoiling their plans. Ask the nurse to come, please, Marvin. Me! Addicted to morphine. Who would have thought it?"

He died the following week.

I kept what Bob told me to myself. I'd been warned that Olly Roxborough didn't look after his boys. I'd been told that his boxers didn't have good careers. My mistake had been in thinking that Paul Mulligan would look after me; I couldn't plead ignorance.

I turned up at the gym and did my job. I was polite to Mr Roxborough when the occasion arose. My continued blanking of Paul was put down to the Tiffany situation, which was partly right. I made a second doll and wrote OLLY on it. I stuck pins in them both, and when the boss man complained of rheumatic pains I smiled to myself. God moved in mysterious ways and if He wanted to use a bit of Voodoo help, that was fine by me.

OH, DIDN'T IT rain, children. Forty days and forty nights! It seemed longer this time. I bumped into Tiffany in the High Street and she was brazen enough to stop and talk.

"Want a coffee?" she asked.

Anything to get out of that non-stop rain so we dodged into a nearby café.

"I'm sorry the way things turned out, Marvin."

I just grunted.

"I know you must think me shallow and mercenary, and maybe I am, but I'm also ambitious – you knew that – and I need a partner who can match those ambitions; maybe even help them. We had some good times though, didn't we?"

"Sure, good times," I agreed.

"Maybe the timing wasn't good but I had to move on. I wasn't cut out for the dutiful little woman looking after her injured man."

"I guess not."

Tiffany finished her coffee. "I'm glad we've had this little chat," she said. "Paul tells me the two of you don't speak, like a pair of kids. You really should shake hands and start afresh."

"Maybe one day," I mumbled, "but not yet."

"Bye-bye, Marvin."

I stayed in the café, playing with my empty mug and

watched as she put up her umbrella and strode out into the rain: statuesque, regal, the Whore of Babylon. But had I detected a tinge of regret in her manner? Could it be that, deep down where she didn't fully realise it herself, she wished that she was still with me?

My apartment, which I could ill afford now on Assistant Trainer wages, was on the fourth floor. Whatever the flooding situation, which seemed destined to reach our corner sooner or later, I would be okay. Paul, however, was looking a bit dodgy. Moving up, he had bought a detached residence in a new housing project. Nice place, well suited to someone getting on, but it nestled in a substantial dip. He obviously hadn't considered the possibility that God's punishment might again be by water.

I had heard him mouthing off, that last time he'd come to the gym, when the subject of potential flooding came up. "I'll not leave my property unguarded for the looters," he'd declared. "I'm well prepared for a long stay."

Cocky bastard!

That evening I let his Voodoo Doll lie in a bowl and turned on the tap. The waters were building up and Babylon would sink beneath the waves. I imagined a little stream of bubbles leaving the doll's mouth and racing to the surface. Drown, Mulligan, fill your lungs with the Lord's holy water.

But what about Tiffany?

Was she a whore or just deluded? In spite of all that had happened I couldn't erase the memories of my hands on her perfect skin, back when she lay beside me. Was I right in suspecting that she still harboured feelings in my direction? Did I want her to drown too?

Things went from bad to worse right across the

country. A State of Emergency was declared and the Army was belatedly put on sand-bagging duties, but not even Governments can control the weather and there were no dry spells in the forecast. Locally, the river was swollen with all the excess liquid pouring into it, and the next high tide was awaited with horror. People living in the low parts of town had been advised to evacuate their homes, but I knew my one-time friend had said he wouldn't do it.

It came to me, then, what I had to do. It wasn't about Paul anymore, or about me. It was about Tiffany, trapped in a house that was likely to be flooded. It was about that beautiful brown-skinned girl waiting to be rescued; waiting for me to rescue her.

She would be so grateful, and would see Paul for the treacherous rat he really was. "Take me home, Marvin," she would whisper, throwing her arms around my neck. "Take me away from this terrible man."

Drenched from the moment I stepped outside, I ran all the way to his part of town. The wind howled and the rain beat down. Sodden, I hammered at his front door. Paul opened it and I pushed him aside before his surprise could be translated into speech. "Tiffany?" I called. "Where are you, girl? I'm going to take you to safety."

"She's safe here," retorted Paul.

"When it floods?"

"Sure, up in the attic. It won't reach that high. She's up there now, making it cosy. We've got plenty of food and bottled water, and whatever else I could carry up. Your knight in shining armour act is wasted here."

I just stood there, clenching and unclenching my hands. Not sure what to say or do.

"It's about time you stopped carrying a torch for her.

Tiffany is mine! End of story."

"It's not just about her though, is it?" I snarled, anger rising through me.

"What else?"

"How about me being overmatched against Pope, just so you and Roxborough could bet against me, expecting me to lose!"

"It was just business, Marvin. You weren't supposed to be so badly injured."

"What's going on?" asked a new voice.

We both turned towards Tiffany as she entered the room. "I heard voices," she said.

"Marvin has come to rescue you from the floods, and from me."

"My apartment will be safer than this house," I explained, trying to ignore the sarcasm in Mulligan's voice.

"Don't be silly, Marvin," she said. "Paul is my blue-eyed soul boy and he's going to manage my modelling career. This house will be just fine."

"Get back up the attic, Tiff. High tide is nearly upon us. I'll join you shortly."

"Yes, Paul," she said, ignoring me completely.

"You've got your answer, Marvin," he said after she had left the room.

"We were such good friends, Paul, all through our school years. Why did it go wrong?"

He laughed, nastily. "I was the runt, easy to beat, but who was going to touch me when the hardest kid around was my pal? We were never really friends, Marvin, but you were useful."

Two things happened next, in quick succession. Firstly, I hit him with all the pent-up rage that had been building within me, and Paul dropped like a lead weight. Secondly, there was a terrific roar which could only mean that our river had burst its banks and was reaching out to submerge the town. I heard Tiffany scream, up above me in the attic. Then the tidal wave struck the house; flowing, surrounding, finding its way into the ground floor.

Stepping forward as the water swirled at knee height and rising, I placed a foot on Paul's unconscious body. In a repeat of the scene I had played out with the Voodoo Doll I watched real air bubbles rise from his mouth. I didn't remove my foot until those bubbles had stopped.

Wading through the water, which had by then reached over my waist, I went looking for the stairs. Up higher would be the means to reach the attic. What was it Paul had said? Food, bottled water, all they would need for a long stay? Well he wouldn't need it any longer – but I was still alive.

Glancing down, as I stand here now, it looks as if the downstairs rooms are almost totally submerged. Above me Tiffany is in the attic, crying. "Paul?" she keeps calling. "Paul? What's happening? Where are you…?"

I grip the sides of the metal ladder and place my foot on the first rung. The Whore of Babylon waits above me and when I join her I will pull up the ladder and close the trap door. We will be snug and safe until the Lord's vengeance starts to subside, though I think it will be a long wait.

I start to climb the ladder…

TALKING TO THE ALIEN

Faceless
Invisible
But we can sense them

We smell breath
Exhaled in subtle differences

And sweat
With hints of interplanetary byways

Once acknowledged
We can sometimes see beyond disguise
And we can talk

Skins are a problem
The alien tells me
But won't let me witness the weekly ritual
Of shedding and disposal

I have come to a pub on the edge of town
Where he is seen as an eccentric
Who sits alone and sups a quiet pint

Beer
He says
The only thing that makes life bearable
On this God-forsaken world

[/continued]

Boxed in
On a compulsory fact-finding mission
That seems more like a prison sentence
Beer is the only thing he'll miss

Talking to the alien
Can be heavy

INVADER

World is corrupt
Poisoned beyond
Redemption

World is dead
Lifeless
We did our job

Mother Ship gone
Land Force lost
All dead

My orbiting scout
Alone

The one survivor

No food
Water
Not much air

We did our job
They did theirs
I'll not digress

Message ends…

ESCAPE FROM PRISON WORLD

Q-Man the brains
Greenies the muscle
And I'm the fly-boy needed to exit
We've got a deal

But first I'm going to kill Mason Jones

Others yearn to smash the faceless
Droid bastards who guard us
But I just want to see goody-goody Mason
In a pool of blood

Q-Man nods
Greenies flex tough
Time is a-coming
Breakout time

Mason gets his … soon

PROBE

Astronaut A
Experienced specific stigmata
Blood loss during Eucharistic
Rites and rituals

Astronaut B
Enacted polymorphic role-play
While examining the boundaries
Of psychodrama theatricals

Astronaut C
Was caught in a repetitive
Neural instability during
Interrupted sleep patterns

Astronaut D
Developed a death-wish
Hatred towards
A, B and C

The Probe only had one Astronaut

VENGEANCE

THE PALE-PINK bathrobe she had been wearing when answering the door was crumpled on the hallway floor between two large and slightly ostentatious Japanese-styled umbrella holders. "Take me, Peter!" she demanded, pulling at his clothes. "Take me here! Take me now!"

"Easy girl," he muttered, kicking off his slip-on shoes while she kissed his neck, blew in his ear, and heaved his t-shirt up and over his head.

"No, not easy, I want it hard!"

Was she hot, or was she HOT! But someone had to keep their feet on the ground, even bare ones. "You're sure your husband is out for the day?"

"Of course I am."

He was now as naked as her.

"He thinks that silly office couldn't run without him. Never takes time off," she continued, pulling him down to the floor. "Makes do with a pub lunch so we can eat together in the evening."

The hallway boasted highly polished laminate flooring which, while fully admirable in itself, was not Peter's favourite surface for the sort of Sex Olympics Pauline obviously had in mind. "Wouldn't we be better in the bedroom?" he suggested hopefully but knew he was on a loser when she adopted her spoilt girl pout.

"For all Ben's size," she said, knowing full well he didn't like to be reminded just how big her husband was, "he treats me like a piece of porcelain. He's so bloody gentle! This time I want it rough and tough. I want you to have me here on this hard-wooden floor with no consideration whatsoever for my comfort or wellbeing. You understand, sweetie?"

"Sure." He didn't go quite so far as to shrug. "I guess..."

"Sweetie Peetie...?"

Knowing his liking for old blues singers, Pauling often called him after Peetie Wheatstraw, a badass singer/pianist who called himself "The Devil's Son-in-Law". Usually when she wanted to get round him for something.

"Please..."

Well she was naked, he was naked, and the hall radiator was turned on. Also, it was what he was there for. Peter was a twenty-two year old self-styled Big City Playboy, Newport variety, working his way from a deprived childhood towards the better things in life. Pauline was a bored thirty-eight, married to older businessman Ben who, yes, was called Big, because that was what he was.

When he played Pauline carefully, like an expert fisherman casting for a big catch, she could be a quite generous and understanding lady. Peter had left his car home this morning, with the intention of telling her how he couldn't afford the repairs needed to pass a non-existent MOT. So he pushed her roughly by the shoulders, forcing her flat on her back. "Okay," he drawled, reaching out and flicking both her nipples in turn. "You're my bitch-girl, and don't you forget it."

"Ohh, Peter," she moaned, and that was when the front door burst open.

"I knew it!" shouted an angry voice. "I just fuckin'

knew it!"

Pauline scrambled away from Peter and scurried to the far side of the hall, muttering between sobs that it wasn't her fault. She pressed the knuckles of her left hand to her mouth.

Glancing over his shoulder from where he lay, Ben really did look big, and angry; big, angry, and looking for trouble. Peter started to crawl to where his clothes lay scattered but Ben pinned him with a heavy foot to the centre of his back, which hurt!

"Oh no, boyo," hissed the wronged husband theatrically. "You're going nowhere."

Peter had experienced narrow squeaks before. Of course he had. Big City Playboys took their chances and knew the score, but he had never been caught quite like this. Then Ben removed his foot and he rolled quickly onto his side, correctly guessing that a good kicking was on the menu.

The first kick was aimed at Peter's stomach and when it landed he grabbed Ben's foot and hung on before he could kick a second time.

Ben pulled.

Peter held on tightly.

Ben pulled harder.

Peter let go.

Ben staggered back, losing his footing and shouting obscenities as he fell into the coat rack. Peter grabbed the nearest item of clothing and was up and running before Ben could recover. Through the front door, he went, out into the cold day and onto the road. Still as naked as the day he was born.

"Come back ... you bastard!" he could hear Ben shouting.

"Good morning ma'am," said Peter, passing an

extremely surprised lady out walking her pet Pekinese.

He finally stopped running when it seemed reasonable to assume he was not being chased and when there was nobody near to take in his nakedness. Peter held up the single item of clothing he had managed to escape with: Pauline's pale pink bathrobe. Luckily she boasted a quite statuesque figure so, even though a little tight, he was able to double-knot the belt and successfully cover the physical embarrassment of total nudity. Though what it might be doing for his psychological wellbeing was another matter entirely.

A number of years back, when Newport was still only a town, all this would have been totally unthinkable. At least now, the freer attitudes of a cosmopolitan city meant that even exotic creeds and beliefs could be clasped in a metropolitan embrace. Peter knew he was a Big City Playboy but if anyone, seeing him like this, thought it possible he might be a Big City Gay Boy, well he could live with that.

"Good morning," he said with a nod, passing an elderly couple and feeling happy in the state of bonded citizenship he shared with them.

"Poofter!" shouted the old woman at his fast receding pale-pink back.

There were always exceptions, he thought sadly. It was at that moment a mobile phone in the bathrobe pocket started to ring. Taking it out, Peter stared at the shiny red object, the jangly ring-tones of a fifties pop hit doing little to calm his startled sensibilities. He lifted it slowly to his ear.

"Okay, you slime-ball gigolo," thundered Ben's voice. "Pauline has put me in the picture, so I'm up to speed with how parasites like you prey upon ladies of a certain age, and I've got all your details."

There was a pause but Peter thought it best to remain silent.

"I've got your wallet in my hand," continued the angry husband. "I know your name, Peter Mark Cunningham, and your address. I even know your National Insurance Number. I've got you taped, buttoned down, in a hole with no way out. I'm not finished with you yet, Peter Mark Cunningham, not by a long way."

Peter slipped the phone back into the bathrobe's pocket. He was beginning to wonder whether or not this might be a good time to ditch the flat and move back in with his parents for a spell. Changing his address would therefore be no problem. Even changing his name would not be too much hassle. He wasn't sure about his National Insurance Number though.

Parents, always there and ready to help; that little welcoming light shining in the window of their hearts. But maybe he had better not turn up dressed only in a woman's pale-pink bathrobe. Not in the Pill area, Newport's old Dockland. And not with his workshy father still clinging to an old-time hard-man status that no longer had any meaning, nor with his mother almost permanently under the influence of antidepressants and cheap plonk.

Maybe it wasn't such a good idea after all.

Just ahead maybe half a dozen eight- to ten-year olds, who should have been in school, loitered on a corner sharing cigarettes.

"Hey! Look at 'im!"

"Why are you dressed like that, mister?"

"He's a nut, that's why."

"He's a tranny."

"No, trannies wear wigs and false boobs."

"Well he's half a tranny and all nut."

"That's for sure."

Peter held his head high, quickening his pace to get passed and away from them. This was no way for a Big City Playboy to be spoken to, not by these kids, nor Ben on the phone, but he kept his dignity intact, as much as circumstances would allow.

"Take no notice, babycake. The cheeky little devils give me a much worse time than that."

Peter had not noticed, till then, that he had company. The newcomer was slim, sleek, and tidy. Not a hair out of place. Dressed a little flamboyantly for Peter's taste, and with just a hint of – oh dear – makeup.

"There is definitely something, hmm, theatrical about you," suggested the newcomer.

Peter stopped and looked him straight in his delicately shadowed eyes. "There is a perfectly reasonable explanation for my present predicament," he said, "and it in no way involves my sexual orientation."

"What a pity," said the other. "You have such beautifully defined cheekbones."

"Look," declared Peter, "as a citizen of the world, I defend your right to be whatever you want. This home of ours, this Gateway City to Wales, holds tolerance to its municipal bosom. All I ask is that you offer the same privilege to me."

"Are you sure you're not gay?"

"Piss off!" Peter turned sharply and strode away. There were other things now becoming more important to his situation.

He would soon reach Stow Hill, leaving these quieter residential streets behind. There would be the St. Woolas Hospital and Cathedral to pass. Then the steep drop down to the city centre, and that meant people.

Maybe even a lot of them, and him still dressed in a pale-pink lady's bathrobe. Also, there was the question of Big Ben lurking in the background.

In the short term he could still change his address and name. Even see what could be done about his National Insurance Number. If things started to look really bad he might consider relocating to Cardiff.

Cardiff?

Well, only as a last resort.

Turning a corner, which brought Stow Hill into sight, Peter was astonished to see that the main thoroughfare he was making for was completely filled with black men wearing what appeared to be tribal costumes and carrying spears and shields. Some wore ostrich-feather headdresses, and all of them were moving towards the Newport city centre.

Whatever the occasion, some sort of festival he supposed, though not one he had heard about, it could be to his advantage. He could join the throng, be part of whatever the celebration was and hopefully drawing less attention to himself.

Peter even allowed himself a smile as he hurried to join the throng. He was still smiling when the long spear, an assegai, struck him in the chest. Peter was dead before he hit the pavement. His body gave a single spasm, the pale-pink bathrobe turning a dark red as the blood poured from the terrible wound.

Peter was not the first to die that day, and he would not be the last.

THE ZULU HORDES came pouring down Stow Hill in much the same way as the Chartists had in 1839; this time there were no Redcoats with muskets waiting in the Westgate Hotel. There was no longer even a

Westgate Hotel itself. Yet another retrogressive step, according to Simon's grandmother, and further proof that Newport had been a really nice town turned into a crap city.

"Why are some of them wearing ostrich feathers?" asked Belinda.

"Chieftains," guessed Simon, trying to sound as if he really knew. He gripped her elbow as a couple of assegais thudded into the boarded-up former Burtons shop front. Guiding her swiftly passed the jewellers – she would only start looking at engagement rings – they ducked into Phones 4U.

"What's going on?" he asked a cowering sales assistant.

"It's all over Wales," she replied hysterically. "Zulu's everywhere. Invading! Killing! There's bound to be atrocities."

"Atrocities?" echoed Belinda, turning it into a question, which was ignored.

"What about resistance?" demanded Simon. "Has the army been mobilised?"

The shop girl shook her head. "All the networks are down now," she explained. "No way to find any more."

Newport's only problems since becoming a city had been economical, but this was something else. A council meeting would certainly be called. Even Cardiff Bay would be a hive of activity, realised Simon. He was sure the First Minister would be rallying the nation.

Outside, the Zulus were chanting, shouting, waving their assegais and cowhide shields, killing any locals they came across. Simon noticed that one word was being repeated a lot: "Dialedd". It was strange that invading Zulus should be chanting the Welsh word for vengeance. Strange, and rather scary.

The three of them: Simon, Belinda and the salesgirl, crouched behind a counter while a sea of black bodies ebbed and flowed passed the Phones 4 U shop front. Cries of fear and terror intermingled with the shouts and chants of the African invaders. Then the shop door burst open and a Zulu warrior charged in. Simon and Belinda held their breath and tried not to move but it was too much for the salesgirl. She leapt to her feet and made a dash for the door.

With a triumphant whoop, the Zulu hit the girl across the head with the wooden shaft of his ixwa, a short stabbing assegai as opposed to the longer throwing variety. Dropping both his shield and weapon he set about removing the stunned girl's clothing.

"Ah…" whispered Belinda quietly to herself "… atrocities!"

Rising, before Simon could stop her, she lifted a large display stand and crashed it down on the Zulu's head, probably killing him outright. To make sure though, as the screaming girl disentangled herself from beneath her would-be attacker, Belinda picked up the discarded ixwa and plunged it into his back.

Simon looked at his girlfriend with a new and sudden respect.

It seemed quieter outside the shop now, the invaders seemingly working their way down Commercial Street. "What's going on, Simon?" asked Belinda.

"Well it might sound daft, but the only thing I can think of is that this is the Zulu Nation's revenge for Rorke's Drift."

"Rorke's what?"

"A mission station in southern Africa where 150 British and Colonial Troops held out against three- to four-thousand Zulus in 1879."

"Eighteen – fucking – seventy-nine?"

"I know!" Simon shrugged. "But why else are they here, and shouting vengeance in Welsh?"

"I saw it on the television," broke in the salesgirl, now on her feet and dressing. "It was an old film, with Michael Caine talking posh."

"That's right, and I'll bet most of the Zulus have seen that film as well. The regiment concerned, though based at Brecon, were not primarily Welsh, recruiting heavily from the Midlands. The film wrongly named them the South Wales Borderers, which they weren't called until a couple of years later."

Simon was in full lecture mode now. "Of the known nationalities comprising the 24th Regiment of Foot at the battle, forty-nine were English and thirty-two were Welsh. If they want true vengeance, maybe they would be better off invading Birmingham."

"For God's sake, Simon! People are being speared to death on the streets of Newport, and probably throughout the rest of Wales, and you're giving us a bloody history lesson!"

Well someone had to evaluate cause and effect, thought Simon peevishly, but decided not to make an issue of it. "It looks quiet out there now," he said instead. "Maybe we should make a dash for it."

"I'm not," said the Phone 4U girl quickly. "I'm going to stay here until I know it really is safe to leave,"

"Belinda?"

"I'm game."

You most certainly are, my dear, thought Simon, picturing again how she had dealt with the Zulu attacker. Slowly and carefully he opened the shop door. There were bodies in both directions, mostly Newport residents; people who had been shopping or just passing through the city centre, totally unprepared for what was to come. Only a few Zulu warriors lay among the dead.

It seemed that the invading force had split into three at the bottom of Stow Hill; attacking along High Street, Commercial Street and Bridge Street, which meant that the Civic Centre was most certainly captured by now. Skinner Street looked untouched to the left so Simon guided Belinda in that direction, turning into Dock Street when they reached it.

"I don't suppose they are still running," she said, nodding towards the Bus Station entrance.

Simon just shook his head. He could see smoke rising from beyond some of the buildings and the sounds and clamour of fighting could be heard. "Maybe we should have stayed in the Phones 4U shop," he muttered, worried that any corner turned might lead them into the conflict. "This way will only lead us into Commercial Street and they have definitely gone that way. We'd better go back and look for somewhere to hide. It was stupid of me to suggest coming into the open."

With Simon holding his girlfriend's arm tightly, they started to retrace their steps. "I do love you, Belinda," he said as they hurried back along Dock Street but before she could comment a group of men came running from the Bus Station.

"What's happening?" asked Simon.

"They're in there," panted a man wearing a bus driver's uniform.

"Butchering people hiding in the buses," said another, "killing them with those bloody spears."

"Behind you!" shouted Belinda

Coming out behind the men were about a dozen

chanting Zulu warriors. "Dial! Dial!" they repeated over and over again.

"Split up," called Simon, desperately hoping that it might confuse their attackers if they went in different directions. Instead they merely bumped into each other as panic took over.

Was this really it? Simon wondered. Was the last thing he would ever hear going to be that single Welsh word? Hadn't they learnt any more of the language? Then Belinda grabbed hold of him as a dark shadow suddenly covered the Sun. "What's happening?" she asked, pointing.

The chasing Zulus had halted, looking up. "Dabulamanzi kampande!" exclaimed one, and they all threw themselves face down on the ground.

Simon, Belinda, and the others, turned slowly to see what on earth could have spooked them in this way. There before them, distant yet near, was the huge and monstrous figure of a Zulu warrior chieftain, standing an unbelievable sixty metres up into the sky. He/it/ whatever towered, probably over the whole of Wales. Simon had recognised the name. Prince Dabulamanzi, the rashly aggressive half-brother of the Zulu King, had led the failed attack on the Rorke's Drift Station. But that was in 1879! This can't be happening, he thought wildly, but if it was a vision or a dream it was one they were all sharing.

"KILL DIMOND Y RHAI SY'N DAL I WRITH-WYNEBU." boomed the huge Zulu in a voice that carried far. "Kill only those who still oppose," said Simon in a quick translation from the Welsh. "YN CYNNIG CAETHIWED I'R GWEDDILL," continued the apparition. "Offer servitude to the rest," muttered Simon.

"What's going on?" asked Belinda. "I don't understand."

"DIAL YN FY!" declared the new conqueror.

"Vengeance is mine," whispered Simon. Dropping to his knees and pulling Belinda with him.

The new First Minister waved his gigantic assegai up into the clouds. "DABULAMANZI KAMPANDE!" he declared, for all to hear. "TYWYSOG CYMRU!"

"Prince of Wales," repeated Simon in English, as he bowed his head to the pavement.

The other men followed his lead. Belinda too, crying quietly with a mixture of anger, fear, and the frustration of not knowing what was to come.

Oh, we are fucked now, thought Simon bitterly. Well and truly, shafted to the hilt.

SINGING SAD SONGS

I'M SURE I read somewhere that Anna Mae Bullock used to pester Ike Turner to let her sing a song or two with his Kings of Rhythm band. He eventually said yes, changed her name to Tina Turner, and the rest is history.

A veteran pianist I knew, who'd spent his semi-pro days playing the nightspots and jazz clubs of South Wales, told me Tommy Woodward from Treforest could be a right nuisance. Wherever there was music being played he would try to talk himself on stage for a couple of numbers. That was before he became Tom Jones of course.

Not all wannabe stories have such successful endings. For every one that makes it to the big time, there are dozens, hundreds, who fail. One such was Penny Marshall. God, what a pain in the arse she could be. Every bit as pushy as Anna Mae Bullock and Tommy Woodward, but without the talent that saw them grow into Tina Turner and Tom Jones.

It wasn't that she couldn't sing at all. Penny was okay, but that was it, she was just okay. Nothing special. No better or worse than countless others; all lacking that individual spark to make them stand out.

We all have heroes. Hers was Billie Holiday, loving the brittle heartbreak, especially in her later work. Some critics said it was a sign of failing vocal ability, but for Penny the tiny imperfections were flawless examples of human frailty transformed into sound.

For me it is the Zen Buddhist Monk and poet, Philip Glenn Whalen, a key figure in the San Francisco renaissance during the fifties. Close to The Beats and a good friend of Jack Kerouac, he took part in the landmark Six Gallery readings in 1955 – the event which boasted the first public airing of Allen Ginsberg's famous "Howl" poem.

His beliefs and poetry were inspirations I tried to incorporate into my own lifestyle. I wasn't a Buddhist in the sense of officially belonging to a particular persuasion, but did find myself drawn to the Zen principles of being for the benefit of others.

I did try to help Penny, firstly because it was what a Zen Monk should do for anyone, and secondly because I was irresistibly drawn to her, in spite of bad attitudes.

But then Penny Marshall died.

So much for my puny help.

I WROTE POETRY because it satisfied an inner need, but I earn my daily bread as a guitarist. I've turned down many an invitation to join existing or new bands, including some household names; you'd be surprised, but it was never about fame. I was content being the go-to guy for TTI Records (Top Tunes International), a well-considered independent outfit that made a good fist at operating under the shadow of the majors. I was the unnamed guitarist on a good eighty percent of their output, and that was the way I liked it.

Everyone called me Monk, either because of my Buddhist leanings or because they thought it was my real name, and that was fine. Doug Gibson, head honcho at TTI, often tried to talk me into joining the production team but I had no ambition to progress beyond being a well-respected session musician. The only one who ever came close to upsetting the natural equilibrium of my life was that underperforming overambitious girl. She wasn't unattractive but no ravishing beauty either, with a bad-tempered streak plain for all to see.

Penny was always hanging around, trying to get people to listen to her latest demo. She was one of a number of hopefuls who were occasionally used to provide backing vocals, but she was never content with that. Penny dreamt of being out front, in the spotlight, with her name on the record.

"Give it a listen, Monk," she would ask, pressing yet another tape into my hand. "Just imagine how much better it would sound with some of your hot licks behind the voice. Fat Gibbo would listen to it properly if you told him it was good."

"Don't let Doug hear you calling him fat," I warned her. "He'd have you chased off the premises."

"Sod him," she said, waving a dismissive hand. "You're the power behind the throne, everyone knows that. Half of TTI's records would be nothing without your guitar, and you know I'm good. You know I deserve a shot."

And the angry flash of her blue-green eyes were more than enough to have me thinking thoughts that were in no way compatible with being a monk. But the fact that I fancied her did not blind me to her vocal limitations. Penny was a trier though, switching genres in a never-ending search for the one that would suit her voice. At different times she dipped into country, rockabilly, disco, hip-hop, reggae, lover's rock, and on one disastrous occasion even tried her hand at rap. Give her an A for effort.

It was only the rigorous self-control of all Buddhist adherents that enabled me to keep my feelings for her in check. She had any number of boyfriends during when I knew her and at the time of her death had been in some sort of relationship with an alcoholic drummer who had been booted out of a local band after missing one gig too many. If I had been stupid enough to declare my feelings she would either have told me to get lost or decided I might help her get a record deal if she bedded me, and that would have been worse than being turned down.

"Are you gay?" she asked me once. "You're about the only man here at TTI who hasn't hit on me, apart from the couple we all know play for the other side."

I didn't even dignify her question with an answer.

WHAT SHE WANTED, why she pestered me maybe more than others, was for me to take her latest demo and put my guitar behind her voice. "You know Doug won't let anyone use the studio for private work," I would tell her. It was my standard excuse. True, as it happened, so at least I was able to refuse without the added discomfort of having to lie.

Wearing a succession of low-necked tops, she would point her barely concealed breasts in my direction like a pair of fully loaded bazookas. I sometimes wondered if she suspected how I felt and did her best to break my resolve. The cow!

The news of her death skewered me like a blow to the solar plexus, and for a while even my faith was not of much help. I phoned in sick and pulled the plug on a couple of sessions I was due to play that week. Whether Doug would cancel them or get in another guitarist I didn't know, or care.

I stayed in my flat, hardly moving from the bed, and thought about her. I pictured her flashing eyes, high cheekbones, the angry set of her mouth. I tried to picture her white and unmoving, like marble, but couldn't. I tried to picture her dead but couldn't do that either. In my imagination her auburn hair glinted with sun-kissed highlights. I don't know why. I rarely saw her in that sort of outdoor setting. Maybe never.

A few days later Doug called me. He was checking with all TTI key holders.

"You didn't come in last night, did you Monk?"

"Hell no, I haven't shifted from my sickbed since I phoned in."

"I didn't think it would be you, but some bugger's been here." He sounded really pissed off.

"What's up, Doug?" I asked. Something was obviously bothering him.

"Someone came in last night and did a demolition job on the place," he told me. "Office computers, studio equipment, all smashed, and no sign of a break in. Whoever did it must have had keys, and even locked up after they'd finished."

"Have you called the police?"

"Of course I have. The place is a crime scene at the moment. They will want to speak to all key holders at some stage, so be prepared for plod to pay a visit."

"Should I come in?" I asked. "I'm feeling a bit better now."

"No point," said Doug. "Nothing can be done here while the investigation is ongoing."

I made him promise to keep me updated and he ended the call. What a bummer, I thought. Stealing the gear I could understand, though not condone, but to just destroy it. Did someone hate TTI, or Doug himself, that much? It didn't bear thinking of.

Oh, Penny girl, this is a crazy world at times. Maybe your overdose was a simple answer to all of life's problems. Your answer anyway, whether accidental or deliberate, but you should have stuck it out, tried to be braver.

I WAS INTERVIEWED in my turn, along with the other key holders, but nobody was ever arrested or charged. Doug Gibson negotiated with his insurers, replaced the vandalised equipment, and life at TTI returned to normal. I continued to miss Penny being around the place. Maybe I always would. I still had the final demo tape she had forced me to take the very last time I saw her. It gathered dust in my flat now. I hadn't played it and had no intention of ever doing so.

"You're a glum-faced sod these days, Monk," the boss told me. "I think you're pining over that red-haired wannabe who topped herself. You were always chatting with her."

"She had a name you know," I snapped. "Penny Marshall – and it might have been an accidental overdose. There was no suicide note."

"Touchy!" responded Doug.

THINGS DRIFTED ALONG, then I returned to my flat one evening to find my four kitchen chairs up on the table, and I had not put them there. The flat had been locked and only I had a key. As can be guessed, I was shaken; there was no obvious explanation. Chairs don't move of their own accord.

I said nothing about it to anyone, especially not at TTI. Enough people there thought I was a bit of an oddball because of my Buddhism, so I didn't think it wise to give them floating furniture to add to the list of my whacky ways. Then it happened there too.

Doug blew his top, big time. Every small piece of equipment was balanced on something larger, microphones on keyboards and amplifiers, that sort of thing. He was steaming.

Once again there was no forced entry and the place was locked. It was annoyingly silly, completely pointless, and did nothing but cause unnecessary tensions. Doug withdrew key holder privileges and employed a night watchman. He started getting quotes for the installation of security cameras.

"At least nothing was damaged this time," I offered.

"Small mercies, Monk," said Doug. "On two occasions now someone has invaded these premises, and that in itself is a cause for alarm. If it continues in spite of the changes I've made then I don't know what the outcome will be."

Maybe I should have told him that it had happened to me as well, but I hesitated and in the end I didn't. A bit head-in-the-sand I suppose, hoping it would stop without any action on my part. Not that I suppose talking about it would have done any good really.

Away from the studio, in the privacy of the flat, I increased my time spent chanting, hoping that contemplative reflection might at least calm my mind, but it didn't help. I still missed seeing Penny hanging around the TTI headquarters, and I continued to feel ill at ease over what had happened there and at my flat. But life continued, as it must.

I WAS TIDYING up after laying down some choppy guitar leads over the staccato chords on tracks by Larry Rich & The Poor Boys, who Doug was hoping would be the next big thing in reggae. It was quite late and Ted, the night watchman, was snoozing in his cubbyhole waiting for me to leave so he could lock up behind me and settle down for the night.

"Won't be long, Ted," I called, catching a movement out of the corner of my eye.

"Ted?" I asked again when he didn't answer.

Still nothing!

I was by the mixing desk, standing in a pool of light while the rest of the studio was bathed in gloom. "Is that you Ted?" I tried again when glimpsing movement at the far wall.

"All I ever wanted was my name on a CD cover," said a voice that seemed to somehow surround me. Was it in front, behind, somewhere to the side? A voice I felt I could very nearly recognise.

Penny? But that was impossible.

"That's not funny!" I said angrily.

"You never did have a sense of humour, Monk."

The mimic, whoever it might be, was good. It was nearly spot on but missed by adding a degree of coldness Penny never managed to achieve. Her moods were more likely to overflow as molten lava rather than ice.

"Show yourself!" I demanded, trying to sound calmer than I felt, and whoever it was did start to move slowly in my direction.

It was a colourless figure that gradually emerged from the dim background, reminding me of a black-and-white negative. It seemed to float rather than walk, and I found myself able to breathe only in short gasps as the enormity of what I was starting to believe struck home.

Yes, it was Penny, but a different version to the one I'd known in life. This one was gaunt of face, thin of body, as if suffering from a wasting disease. It was all I could do to suppress a sob. There were so many conflicting emotions spinning through my mind and I had little control over which should gain ascendancy.

I'd always had a theoretical belief in the spirit world. It was, after all, part of Buddhist doctrine: the recently dead moving between planes, the pear-shaped Hungry Ghosts, the preparation for eventual reincarnation. But I had accepted such things blindly, without any meaningful experience … until now.

"Monk…" The word echoed around my head.

"It was you, wasn't it?" I asked. "Here and at my flat?"

Doug, and everyone else, had assumed the intruder to be either someone with a grievance or a complete nutter. Nobody had considered that it might be a poltergeist.

"Of course it was," revealed her whispery confirmation. "The first was just an angry reaction, but the second one here and the one at your flat, were attempts at gaining attention. If someone had put two-and-two together and come up with ghost then you might have held a séance and I could have contacted you that way. It saps spiritual energy to appear to the living, but you forced my hand."

"Why me?" I demanded. "Why not your boyfriend?"

"Leroy? He was just another passing phase. You're the one, Monk, because I still want the same thing. Play the last tape I gave you and add your guitar. Tell that fat bastard Gibbo that it should be released. It's good, Monk. I finally cracked it."

"You gonna be long?" asked Ted as he entered the studio, keen to see the back of me.

Penny disappeared, gone in a flash, the instant we

were interrupted.

"All wrapped up," I replied and moved towards the door.

AS SOON AS I got home I played Penny's final demo tape, the one I had decided not to listen to; and long before the end I was weeping, my broken heart in pieces.

It was good; no, better than that, it showed a talent hitherto unsuspected.

Sod's law, isn't it, to have finally clicked when it was too late.

It was longer than her usual demos: ten songs, all associated with her heroine, Billie Holiday. Penny had ditched her sometimes foolish search for commercial success and was finally singing from the heart. Yes, the Lady Day influences were there for all to hear, but there was enough of Penny Marshall in the mix to lift it beyond being only a copy.

The ten songs were: "God Bless the Child", "Summertime", "Trav'lin' Light", "The Man I Love", "Gloomy Sunday", "T'ain't Nobody's Business if I Do", "Crazy He Calls Me", "Mean to Me", "Good Morning Heartache" and "These Foolish Things". I played the tape again and again, with the musician in me gradually taking control. I was soon working out how best to let my guitar complement her voice.

"Well…?"

Startled, I turned to face the diminished version that was the spectral Penny and tried to find the right words. "You did it, girl," I said finally, completely failing to do justice to what I had heard. "I can't wait to start putting a musical accompaniment to your voice."

BEING SOMEONE WHO could get a tune out of anything capable of making a noise, I was at least competent on a number of instruments, and wrote some interesting trio arrangements to add to the vocal tracks. It was slow going because Doug kept me busy with TTI work, but I was in no rush, and Penny had forever.

She didn't visit me all the time because it really was hard to maintain a visual link with the living. "It's not like gliding from realm to realm like an ice skater," she told me. "It's draining, digging deep into any reserves of mental energy you might have accumulated."

On another occasion she told me that her death had been neither totally accidental or suicide, but an ill-considered mixture of both. Yes, she had invoked thoughts of ending her life, and had never been careful about the amount of substances, harmful or otherwise, she had bombarded her body with. She had not specifically intended to die that day and taking enough to kill her had not been entirely an accident.

"Oh, Penny, why didn't you share these thoughts with me before you died?"

"Come to you, Monk? I couldn't even get you to help with my demos."

Which was fair comment, I suppose. Though I refrained from pointing out that none of the other tapes she had forced me to take had shown any of the potential so evident in her Billie Holiday tribute.

Another time, I questioned her about the transition from life to death. "It was like awakening from a long and deep sleep," she told me. There had been a faraway background buzz of murmuring and she hadn't wanted to open her eyes. Then a voice had whispered in her ear, calling her *daughter*, and had helped her overcome any initial panic. "My first reaction was to feel sick, sour-tasting bile rising to my throat, which was strange really, since I no longer had a stomach, or a throat, or any other bodily bits and pieces."

I wasn't sure whether this comforted or worried me.

WHILE WORKING ON the demo tape I sometimes questioned my own motives. I guess guilt was the overriding factor. I should have helped her before she died, and I should have made my feelings known, whatever her reaction might have been.

When alive, Penny had wanted all the trappings that went with stardom: fame, money, adulation. Now however, in some sort of role reversal, I was the one supplying the ambition. I suppose I was hoping for the sort of posthumous success that the little-known Eva Cassidy had enjoyed after her death. Penny, however, seemed to have little interest in what would happen after I had finished my side of our shared project. Maybe ghosts lacked that get-up-and-go element in their makeup; or was there less pressure when you had eternity.

Finally, having done as good a job as I was capable of, I didn't wait for her agreement and took the demo to Doug. We sat together in his office, listening to Penny putting her heart and soul into her sad-song tribute to Billie Holiday.

"I think you were a bit biased in your opinion," he said, when the last number finished.

Biased? Was he joking? I counted to ten.

"I understand why, my friend," he continued. "Undeclared love must be even worse than unrequited."

All I wanted was for him to acknowledge how good the demo was, not indulge in nonsensical claptrap, but he wasn't finished yet.

"I've been there, Monk. Remember when I fell for the lead singer of the Hurly Burly Boys? What a mess I was in then, though that was the unrequited variety. If anything, I declared my feelings too loud and too often, but I experienced real hurt, and then they turned down the deal I'd offered them and signed with Gee Whiz Records instead. Bastards!"

Though he was a tough negotiator and knew the music business inside out, Doug had his failings. Number one of which was a weakness for pretty-faced Boy Band lead-singers; not that I could see any connection between that and Penny's demo.

"Are you saying," I asked, trying to mask my surprise, "that I overegged how good the tape was?"

"Like I said, Monk, I understand why. Yes, the Lady Day material means she is singing better songs than on most of the stuff she begged me to listen to in the past, but her vocals are no better, not even with the classy accompaniment you have added."

Had he suddenly developed cloth ears? Did he have a personal grudge against Penny that I knew nothing about? If this was Doug's genuine opinion I would take the demo elsewhere. Give someone else the chance to issue it. "We'll have to agree to disagree then," I said, moving to retrieve the tape.

"Hold on a minute," said Doug. "Play it again and try to point out to me what it is you think I am missing, because on that first listen I heard nothing out of the ordinary."

Only too happy to comply, I sat back down as a short keyboard introduction led into "God Bless the Child". Unlike previous demos, Penny's voice responded to material that was close to her heart. "Can't you hear the subtleties of her phrasing?" I asked, bewildered that it could be missed.

"I'm sorry, Monk. It's her usual unimaginative delivery. She keeps in tune but there's no dynamics."

It was as if we were listening to different singers.

"Her depth of feeling?" I suggested. "Her vocal dexterity?"

"Plodding," said Doug.

"Summertime" came and went, thrilling me and boring him, but when the third track started it was like a slap across my face. "Trav'lin' Light" was as dull as Doug claimed. It was as if someone had flicked a switch, and the rest of the tape was the same.

I muttered a vague apology and got out of there as quickly as I could.

HER EYES WERE hollow, cheeks sucked in, mouth a gash – though the bloodless lips were turned up in a gloating parody of a smile. It seemed every time she let herself be seen, her appearance had worsened.

"It was payback time," she replied when I'd asked her to explain the demo's duality.

"Payback for what?" I demanded.

"For all the times you chickened out of helping me. For as long as I controlled it, you heard the vocal tracks the way you wanted them to sound. Doug heard them as they really were, and finally you did as well."

"Just getting your own back for me not playing guitar on your demos?"

"You thought you were so much better than me, with your high-and-mighty Buddhist ways and in-demand guitar playing…"

"Not true," I said trying but failing to interrupt.

"…Fat Doug might have listened better if you had

helped me. He might have given me a chance then. Everything might have worked out."

This was ridiculous, heartbreakingly so. Penny seemed to be blaming me for her life twisting and turning into avenues that eventually led to her death. "But I loved you," I said, finally admitting it to her.

"Love? Hah! You were just a source of amusement. Behind your back we called you Wee Georgie Harrison, with your beard and platitudes."

"Doug did finally hear you with my accompaniment, just as you wanted," I said, striking back, "and he still turned you down. Whatever the setting he doesn't think you're good enough."

"And he'll suffer too. I haven't finished with you yet, Monk, but Doug will have his share as well…"

"Just you…" I started, but it was a waste of time. She was gone.

Two days later, returning home, I had to slosh through water to turn off a tap that was running into an overflowing bath. Not what I needed at the end of an arduous recording session that had been continually interrupted by unexplained technical faults. I suspected Penny but each instance could have had more earthly reasons. I was edgy with other TTI employees, wondering which of them laughed behind my back and called me Wee Georgie Harrison. Not that I objected to being compared with the former Beatle, it was the demeaning tone I didn't like. It wasn't meant as a compliment.

What followed had to be down to Penny. The Welsh four-piece post-grunge group, Tree Axe, refused to complete a session and said they would never return to the TTI studio again, claiming to have heard unearthly whispering and seen a shadowy figure. Doug decided it was drugs, alcohol, or a mixture of both, and even thought of suing them for breach of contract. In the end he hired another studio for them to complete their album.

I felt sure the vendetta against Doug and I would continue and maybe even become more extreme. Something needed to be done, and my involvement meant it was down to me; I looked up the Buddhist ways of dealing with unruly or evil spirits.

The first method was a non-starter, involving as it did a Phurba, a ritual dagger used by a tantric practitioner to release a troubled spirit from suffering and guide it to an improved rebirth. Whereas I could accept Penny as lingering between realms, she seemed nasty by design rather than troubled, and there was no way I could get hold of a ritual dagger anyway.

Next up was a Spirit Trap, which seemed much more promising. A spindle-like contraption wound with coloured yarns, the series of interlocking threads being able to ensnare the ghost, and the whole thing was then burnt. Hanging in a tree or on a mountain top were the suggested sites but I felt the TTI studio would suffice, being one of the only two places dead Penny had appeared, and I didn't fancy setting something alight in my flat.

Fire, of course, though looked upon as an enemy in our close-packed maze-like human habitations, is a cleansing agent in the natural world, encouraging regeneration. So it would be in the burning of an evil ghost, the cauterisation of a diseased spirit. Or so I was willing to believe.

WE WERE BACK to key holders at TTI, night watchman

Ted having quit without notice, loudly claiming the place to be haunted. "Sozzled old fool!" decided an angry Doug. I knew better but having a key again suited me.

Ghosts, I had discovered earlier when reaching out to Penny, are not for touching. She had backed away from my hand, telling me to keep my distance, and maybe that was something I could us to my advantage.

Letting myself in to the deserted night-time TTI studio, I placed the Spirit Trap in amongst the various speakers and regular recording paraphernalia, hoping that she wasn't secretly spying on me, as she sometimes did.

"Penny?" I called. "Listen! Doug turning you down needn't be the end of it. The guy at Gee Whizz Records owes me a favour and I am sure he would give your demo a full and proper consideration."

"Don't you get it, Monk? I no longer care," she relied, shimmering into view. "I wanted it so badly when alive. You wouldn't help me then."

"I did try to help you, Penny, on a person to person level."

"Bollocks, Monk! The only help I wanted was with my demos but you refused, and you're paying for it now."

"But I loved you," I said, holding out my hands and taking a step towards her.

"Keep away," she hissed, moving backwards.

I took steps to the left, she moved to the right.

I moved to the right, she floated to the left.

"Stop it, Monk!"

But I kept going, this way then that, manoeuvring her into position until she stood immediately in front of the Spirit Trap. Backing away to avoid my stretched-out hands, she fell right into the contraption. It had worked and Penny was held fast, caught amongst the coloured threads.

It had been my intention to take the Spirit Trap away from the TTI building, to burn it in the open, but it seemed so flimsy I was afraid it might fall apart if manhandled too much. I couldn't risk Penny being freed. I moved it near to the door though, so I could get out quickly if need be.

I could see movement within the trap, probably Penny trying to get out, and my hands were shaking as I squirted lighter fuel over it, over myself and the surrounding floor area as well. I didn't want to be doing any of this, and I wasn't sure it would work. Could you really kill a ghost? I flicked on my lighter and flames shot up and about with a speed that panicked me. Without warning, not only the Spirit Trap but all around it was burning and crackling as the fire spread. My clothes too, and there was nothing I could do to stop it. The more I tried to beat out the flames the faster they spread.

Everything was ablaze as fire ran riot all around me while I screamed as I burned, filling my lungs with evil-smelling smoke. As I dropped, falling into a merciful unconsciousness, there was no knowing which finally applied the fatal thrust, whether I died by fire or smoke. Not that it mattered or that I cared...

IT SEEMED THAT I had been asleep for a long, long time, and I was content to remain so. The last thing I wanted to do was wake up. The low buzz of background voices was like a lullaby, encouraging me to fight against waking, but eventually a kindly voice whispered in my ear, calling me *son*, and helping me accept the reality of my situation.

I opened my eyes and was relieved that the fire and smoke were gone. I could still smell it, though, and taste it in my mouth and throat; which was odd since I no longer had a nose, mouth, throat, or any other body parts. There had been so much more I had wanted to do with my life, but ambition was for the living. All I could think of for the moment was to join the ghostly chorus that seemed to be welcoming me.

I opened the mouth that I didn't really have and was soon singing sad songs…

MUM'S THE WORD

ALAN CHESTERFIELD GREW up with the pomp-rock of Meat Loaf and the shock-rock of Alice Cooper. "My name is Chesterfield, baby. Smoke me…" had been his largely unsuccessful chat-up line back when he had need of one. He had not used either line or name in quite a while now.

Marvin Lee Aday had become Meat Loaf.

Vincent Damon Furnier switched to Alice Cooper

Alan Douglas Chesterfield turned himself into Muthu Mayhem.

He had paired the almost operatic excess of Meat Loaf's Jim Steinman period with the spectacular theatricals of an Alice Cooper stage show, touring the world with an extravaganza based upon his debut CD *The Last Public Hanging*. Magic and illusion, fantasy and horror, all blended within the epic structure of his hi-octane music and culminating with the Muthu himself being strung up on stage.

A worldwide hit, it played to packed audiences everywhere and the CD went to number one in every country. Not even the unfortunate suicides and/or accidental deaths of a number of teenagers trying to emulate his onstage demise could stop the juggernaut from rolling on and on. But *The Last Public Hanging* had finally run its course and his record company executives were eager for a follow-up.

For Alan Chesterfield the millions already banked,

while welcome beyond his most extravagant dreams, were not sufficient to sustain his inner self. It was the fame and adulation that fuelled his personal need, and he was well aware of the dangerous second album syndrome. Many singers had followed a smash hit record with one that had bombed. As had actors with films and authors with books, and such people sometimes never recovered from the blip, becoming mere footnotes in One-Hit-Wonders quiz questions.

It was not a fate that could be contemplated for the Muthu, but he was confident that *Curse of the Spider Priest*, an Ancient Egypt exploitation, would do the business all over again. "Song & Dance: Nile Style" would be the first download offered from the CD, and the stage-show finale would be his mummification. And this time a third element might be added. Talks were at an advanced stage for a cinematic tie-in.

THE ENDLESS SAND and blowing dust depressed her. The hot wind and searing daytime heat left her limp and dejected. With Europe bracing itself for the almost certain outbreak of war, Agnes Liston-Jones felt that a digging season in South Saqqara was the last place she wanted to be. But she was a dutiful wife and Robert badly wanted this last try for archaeological fame and glory.

First discovered by Karl Richard Lepsius in the nineteenth century, the small pyramid had been excavated earlier in the thirties by Gustave Jequier, who had beaten Liston-Jones to the punch in acquiring permission for the dig. But Robert was convinced the site held more than only the burial place of Pharaoh Qakare Ibi, third ruler of the eighth dynasty; something about a high priest, if Agnes remembered rightly. All she wanted to do was get back to England before war was declared. Egypt would still be there when it was all done and dusted. When that Hitler chap had been put in his place. They could come back then, if Robert still wanted to.

BOZ CRABBE HAD hightailed it over to the UK for talks with Muthu Mayhem's people. He was a writer/director in the Ed Woods tradition of low-budget film making and the prospect of a substantial investment in one of his projects had him drooling. Most of his work went straight to DVD but *Spit in the Mad God's Eye* had somehow gained a theatrical release and won the previous year's Platinum Pig's Bladder award for worst film. Not that Crabbe minded; any-publicity-is-good-publicity was his motto, and it had got him a little newspaper coverage when he announced *Revenge of the Vampire Mummy* as his next production. And that, in turn, had led to interest from the singer's management team.

"It was Muthu himself who came up with the idea," said one of the suits. "The CD and stage show will both be called *Curse of the Spider Priest*, but you can stick with your original title and storyline for the film. What Muthu suggests is that you write his character, Amsunaton, the Spider Priest, into your script and let him play the part. In return we will cover the costs of you filming over here, where you can make use of the best technical and special effects people in the business."

"I've already signed a contract for Gwen Young-blood to play Nefertiti," said Crabbe, naming the Bronx songstress whose singing career was in terminal freefall. A contract he would break if necessary.

"The rest of the cast is in your hands, Mr Crabbe. Muthu Mayhem's name alone will guarantee success. What we would like is for you to produce a roughly drafted script. One that Muthu can consider, and maybe put a little input into. How does that sound?"

Boz didn't like the "input" bit but he did like the crinkle of dollar bills, or whatever the British equivalent was. Pounds or Euros, he wasn't sure, but it didn't matter. And he could keep Gwen on board. "That sounds fine to me," he said in response.

ROBERT HAD GONE to fetch supplies and hopefully an English language newspaper. Their radio had been on the blink and Agnes was desperate for news from back home. For all of Mr Chamberlain's assurances, she was not optimistic that hostilities could be avoided.

In theory, during Robert's absence she was in charge of the site. But in practise she left it to Fenuku, their Egyptian foreman, while she stayed in the shade. And it was he who came running to her, all excited and jabbering.

"Calm down, Fenuku," she told him. "You know I cannot understand a word when you talk fast like that." In all probability it would be some minor altercation between the labourers. Something the foreman should be able to settle without involving her.

"You come, Missy. You come, pleeese!"

Fenuku tugged at her sleeve in his excitement, reminding Agnes of a dusky Charlie Chaplin as he hopped, bow-legged, from one foot to another.

"What is it then?" she asked, allowing him to guide her towards where the men had been digging but were now standing around and talking amongst themselves.

"We find!" babbled Fenuku. "Where the Mister? He right! He right! We find…!"

Agnes looked down into the large hole, sloping into a shadow that contrasted darkly with the harsh sunlight she stood in. As she peered, her eyes growing accustomed to the gloom, she saw that they had reached the bedrock, and carved into it were steps leading downwards.

So Robert had been right. South Saqqara did have more secrets to reveal.

The spluttering engine of their old truck interrupted her thoughts. "Here the Mister!" shouted Fenuku. "We find, boss, like you say. We find! We find!"

Robert ran from the truck and stood beside her. "I knew it!" he shouted triumphantly. "I bloody well knew it!"

BOZ CRABBE HAD been surprised to find out that Muthu Mayhem was a total Ed Woods geek, knowing all his films and even their original titles. Crabbe knew them too but was savvy enough to play second fiddle to the man with the money.

"*Grave Robbers from Outer Space* is a favourite," said Muthu.

"Don't know that one," lied Crabbe.

"They changed *Grave Robbers* to *Plan 9*. Did it all the time." Muthu was on a roll. "*Night of the Ghouls* was originally *Revenge of the Dead*. *Bride of the Monster* was *Bride of the Atom*. *Glen or Glenda* was *I Changed My Sex*."

"Well fancy that," said Crabbe.

"Did you know," continued Muthu, "that the Reverend Steve Galindo of Seminole, Oklahoma, founded the Church of Ed Woods in 1994. They celebrate Woodmas Day every 10th of October, Ed's birthday."

"Hey! You're a walking Ed Woods encyclopaedia." And just as well too, thought Boz, giving silent thanks to all those know-nothing critics who had likened his work to that of the late filmmaker. This Limey singer, being a fan, had long wondered just what Woods might have done with a big budget movie, and throwing money at a Crabbe Production was as near to getting an answer as possible.

Was it just luck that they had come up with Egyptian themes at the same time? Or had fate intervened? Kismet, baby, thought Crabbe, pure kismet.

AGNES WAS GENUINELY pleased for her husband. Robert had always lagged behind the biggest names in world archaeology but now it looked as if he would become one of them. It was not a big site, this find, but maybe an important one. The stone steps led into a corridor which, in turn, led to a sealed chamber. Not a big one, and containing little in the way of treasure, which was maybe why it had never been looted. Just a sarcophagus, eating utensils, and what appeared to be some religious tracts.

The corridor walls were decorated with hieroglyphics, which Robert was intent upon deciphering. He had picked up earlier hints that a high priest might have been entombed in the area. Something missed by others. Now, if possible, he wanted proof of identity before announcing his find to the world.

"I thought it might be Ibi's high priest, buried near his Pharaoh," explained a jubilant Robert after yet another day spent poring over the painted messages. "But it seems that the fellow, Khepadet by name, not only died before Ibi but was executed on his order. I haven't been able to work out why yet, but it does appear that this high priest was a wrong 'un." Agnes couldn't explain it, but a cold shiver ran through her body at the moment her husband put a name to the mummified remains that lay within the sarcophagus.

IN THE SAME way Ed Woods had befriended and given work to an aging and faded Bela Lugosi, so Boz Crabbe usually found a part for Henry Sheldon, a veteran of the British stage whose promising Hollywood career had disintegrated in booze-orientated disgrace. For years he had got by playing butler roles on American television, but even that had dried up.

Sheldon had originally been going to play a high priest in *Revenge of the Vampire Mummy*. Then all of a sudden they were shifted from a dingy Los Angeles backlot to a state of the art studio in London, and money seemed to be no object. This English rock and roller had taken over his role and he had been switched to playing Nefertiti's father, the aging Pharaoh. A smaller part but with an increase in pay. The only drawback from Sheldon's point of view was in having to share more scenes with Gwen Youngblood.

Boz Crabbe soon realised he had made an error of judgement in lending Gwen the books *Stanislazski in Focus* by Sharon Carnicke and *A Dream of Passion* by Lee Strasberg. He had signed her for the film for two reasons. First was the fact that she had done no acting before so was cheap. Secondly, he hoped that her one hit record from three years previously might drum up some sort of publicity.

Gwen herself had recently been dropped by her record company and was hoping that either an acting career might blossom or that a film appearance would kick-start interest in her singing. To her credit, whatever she attempted she threw herself into wholeheartedly, and if that included bedding the director, so be it.

She read the two books Boz lent her from cover to cover, immersing herself in the Method School of acting. Suddenly she was as self-obsessed as Marilyn Monroe and as opinionated as Marlon Brando. Unfortunately, she was not as talented as either.

Henry Sheldon, sweating uncomfortably in his Pharaoh regalia and badly in need of a large G&T, waited irritably.

"But Gwen, honey!" Crabbe was trying to be patient.

"All you've got to do is cross the room, kneel before the throne, and say 'But father, I love him'."

"So you keep telling me, but what's my motivation? What does the throne represent to the inner me? Why would Nefertiti demean herself in such a way?"

"Just do it for me, sweetheart…" implored Crabbe.

"It's called acting," snapped a cross Henry Sheldon. "Just follow the bloody script."

KHEPADET! AGNES COULD not blot the word from her mind. From the moment Robert first mentioned the name it haunted her. She couldn't wait to get away from this place, from this executed high priest. To return home to England, whatever mess Europe might be heading towards.

Robert was too engrossed in the corridor hieroglyphics to pay any attention to her worries. Being left, therefore, to her own devices meant Agnes was growing quite disorientated by the ghostly whispers that echoed through her head. It sometimes seemed as if this Khepadet was calling to her. Which was mad, she knew. He had been dead for, what was it? Thousands of years! Agnes wasn't sure. However long it was though, dead was dead. But still the whispers persisted.

MUTHU MAYHEM, MUCH to Crabbe's relief, turned out to be more than competent in the role of Amsunaton the Spider Priest. Henry Sheldon, he knew, would be fine as long as they could keep him sober, and the British TV star they had signed to play the romantic lead was really good. Crabbe's only problem was with Gwen and her total immersion in Method Acting. She wanted to be *motivated*, her new favourite word. She wanted to know about her character's place in Ancient Egypt.

The Muthu guy was having problems as well, it transpired. He wasn't happy with the way his planned stage show was coming together. The songs, naturally, were fine, and he knew the special effects people would do their usual good job, but something was lacking. It did not seem authentic enough.

"Know what I mean, Boz? It's all in the detail, or should be, but isn't."

"You with your show is like Gwen with Nefertiti. Trouble is, neither of us has sufficient background knowledge. If only one of us was an Egyptian, hey!"

Muthu was on it like a shot. "What we both need is an expert," he decided, "and I know just the guy. John Liston-Jones, grandson of a minor pre-war arch-aeological boffin. He works for one of the museums and has written books on Ancient Egypt. I read some when researching factual stuff before writing my songs."

"Sounds good, Muthu." Boz was properly en-thusiastic. "He might be the answer to our prayers."

"He can sort out the historical elements that might need fine tuning in my stage show and keep you up to speed with whatever Miss Youngblood wants to know. I'm sure he'll be open to a bit of well-paid consultancy work. I'll get my people onto it."

IT WAS GETTING *stronger now and Agnes felt unable to resist. They would be locking me up back home, she told herself, recognising the absurdity of her feelings, but not being able to control them. There was an evil in this place. Calling her, summoning, demanding her compliance.*

"I'm ill, Robert. You must get me to a doctor."

"Not right now, old thing. It's the heat getting you down I expect," said her husband. "I'm starting to crack more of the code in the corridor. It's something about Khepadet and Ibi's favourite wife."

This only made her feel more troubled than ever. "I cannot stop here any longer," she said, her voice trembling. "I must get help."

"And you shall, dear, I promise. Just a few days more, that's all I need. Then we can go and tell the world just what it is I have discovered."

AS FAR AS knowing anything about Ancient Egypt was concerned, these people were total dullards, realised John Liston-Jones, but for what he was being paid he would play along. He had a vague recollection of seeing Gwen Youngblood on television some years before, probably the video of her one and only hit. An attractive girl, but none too bright. Luckily neither of the projects he had been hired to advise needed to be spot on in historical detail. Even so, Nefertiti speaking with a broad Bronx accent was an unintentional comedy he could have done without.

Liston-Jones led a quiet academic existence and these show business people were from another world. He had inherited a family interest in Egyptology, maybe because of the strange events surrounding his grandfather at South Saqqara just before the Second World War. His father had actually visited the site, though only as a tourist, just before his tragic accident. Nobody had been able to explain why his car had not followed the bend in the road.

Maybe now, funded by the money from this consultancy, John could take unpaid leave from the museum and finance an actual dig at the site of his grandfather's strange disappearance. There would probably be nothing to find but it would satisfy a longstanding ambition to see for himself.

WHATEVER IT WAS, *the call simply had to be answered.*

Agnes was hardly aware of her own actions, with nothing existing outside the wordless whispering that filled her mind. She left the tent, half-running until she reached the pit dug by the labour gang, most of who had been paid up and were gone now. Robert was down there, with Fenuku and the few remaining workers, struggling to complete the translation that would confirm the importance of his find. Without knowing why, she scrambled down the slope and then the roughly hewn steps, unprepared and uncaring.

The blood and carnage that greeted Agnes in the corridor would normally have caused her to swoon with terror. Her darling Robert, poor little Fenuku, the last workers: all slain, ripped and torn into grotesque caricatures. But she didn't even notice, merely picked her way passed the mutilated bodies as if they were not there.

Her shoes squelched in blood and she nearly tripped on a severed arm, but Agnes staggered along the corridor, blind to everything in her rush to get to the burial chamber. And when she did enter it, the creaking door slammed shut.

REFINED. SCHOLARLY. EDUCATED. He was totally unlike the men she normally came into contact with, and he had not made a move on her, not yet anyway. Gwen was really in awe of this John Liston-Jones guy.

"Neferneferuaten Nefertiti was the Great Royal Wife to the Pharaoh Akhenaten," he had said, showing her pictures of the bust held in a Berlin museum. When he'd said he had photographs of Nefertiti's bust, Gwen thought he meant breasts and had expected nudies.

He was telling her now about the cult of Aten which Akhenaten and Nefertiti had tried to impose on the Egyptian people, a single god instead of many. It was supposed to be background information to enable Gwen to better understand the character she was playing so that filming could continue without her constant interruptions.

Partly in awe and partly falling for him, she listened carefully but understood little of what he was saying. Gwen might not have known George Bernard Shaw's *Pygmalion*, but she had seen *My Fair Lady*. Casting herself in the Eliza Doolittle role she was seeing the clipped toned John Liston-Jones as her personal Professor Henry Higgins.

IF THE REALITY *of the situation had been apparent, Agnes would have been screaming with absolute terror. Whatever had summoned her headlong rush to reach this place, it still held sway over her as she stood there. For one brief moment surprise sparked in her mind as she saw a vaguely smoke-like figure seemingly rise from the sarcophagus, but then it was squashed. She felt no sense of what was happening as her clothing fell off and she was laid flat upon the hard rock floor.*

Her husband had been a gentle lover and the only one she had known, but never would again. His savagely torn body lay mercifully out of sight and beyond her understanding. She knew nothing either of the ghoulish shape that plunged deep within her, easing the dripping pockets of dust-filled need that centuries of enforced abstention had created within his trapped being. Plunging that continued until, for the time being at least, the entity could rest again.

When Agnes regained consciousness she was lying on the sand, her naked body covered with a smelly blanket, with the Egyptian who had found her trying to trickle a little water into her mouth. She was delirious, with no memory of what had taken place, and could offer no explanation.

The site was flat, blowing sand and dust, with no apparent digging or excavating having been carried out. Fenuku and the labour force had vanished, as had her husband. Nobody knew where, and Agnes's memory of recent weeks had been wiped away.

FILMING HAD BEEN going quite smoothly and Boz Crabbe was quietly confident that this was going to be his cinematic breakthrough into the big time. Muthu Mayhem and Gwen Youngblood would bring in their particular fans. Well, Muthu would anyway, and others would come because of his undeserved reputation. But they would be shocked, all of them, because *Revenge of the Vampire Mummy* was going to be a box office hit. There might not be any Oscar nominations but commercial success was his first priority. Art could come later.

The only downer on the horizon at the moment was Gwen's suddenly lukewarm bedroom performances. She had been such an enthusiastic participant up until now. It was a shame but Crabbe could see that the girl was falling for John Liston-Jones, who he had helped bring onto the set to educate her. It was *Born Yesterday* all over again, with him in the Broderick Crawford role. Not that he really minded, but if he had to lose out did it have to be to a wimp with a double-barrelled name!

Never mind all that though; tomorrow was going to be a tough schedule. They were going to film the attempted rape, when Amsunaton, the Spider Priest, kills the old Pharaoh and attacks Nefertiti, only to be killed in his turn by Bek, the young Captain of the Guard. This was near the end of the film, with only the mummification and the royal wedding to follow.

Danny, the TV actor brought in the play Bek, had the potential to be huge, and Crabbe had already signed him to a five-picture deal. As for his fading relationship with Gwen, there would be starlets and wannabes aplenty fighting to take her place when the film broke big. Even his four ex-wives would come crawling out of the woodwork, but they could get lost.

Tomorrow was going to be a big day at the studio.

IN SPITE OF *a substantial reward being offered, the Egyptian police found no trace of Robert Liston-Jones. The few sightings that were reported all turned out to be mistaken identity or dead ends. Agnes, for all that she so dearly wanted to help, simply couldn't. She could not even explain why they had been at the site for so long without digging a single spade of sand.*

The investigating officer was mightily relieved when the lady was deemed fit enough to travel. Out of sight, out of mind, he hoped. With the wife back in England, maybe he could file this as unsolved and get on with cases he could find an answer to.

Agnes, for her part, not long after arriving home discovered she was pregnant.

JOHN LISTON-JONES had spent the previous evening offering advice to the producers of Muthu Mayhem's stage show. Today he was a guest at the studio to watch the filming of what that idiot Crabbe obviously considered a pivotal moment in his masterpiece. Neither enterprise had anything to do with historical accuracy. Some of his suggestions had been incorporated into set designs and costumes but his main function seemed to be directed at satisfying Gwen Youngblood's thirst for knowledge. At least she did seem genuinely interested in the real Nefertiti, unlike the version she played in the film, which bore no relation to reality.

Today, for instance, this non-existent Amsunaton character was going to attack her after killing her father. Then she would be saved by a Captain of the Guard, who she would later marry. Utter bilge, every bit of it, but for the sort of money they were paying him he would stand there and smile.

UNDER THE BURNING sun at South Saqqara, beneath the hot surface sand, something stirred. Down at the hidden bedrock, where carved steps led to a corpse-strewn corridor: the mangled remains of those who had unwittingly released the evil that lurked within the sealed burial chamber.

Within that cursed room, in the sarcophagus, Khepadet's mummy tormented itself with memories of many women, including Ibi's favourite wife, and dreamt of more to come. Whispers were starting to fill the space where he lay, occasionally becoming words that could be heard, if anyone had been there to hear them.

"Son of the son," murmured the thing. Then "Son of the son," again. "The time comes, shortly."

BOZ CRABBE BOSSED the studio like a five-star General. This was the big showdown and everything had to go just right. Amsunaton, now the mad vampire, would decapitate the Pharaoh and drink blood from the severed head, before attacking and trying to have his way with Nefertiti. Then the handsome young Bek would come storming in to save the day, killing the vampire by plunging a ceremonial snake carving into its heart.

Crabbe nodded to himself. He had to admit it, these Limey special-effects people really were the business. The blood and gore was going to be spectacular.

Muthu Mayhem was in costume and having final touches of makeup applied. He had often been described as decadent and tubercular, an image carefully developed, but he was paler than ever for the part he was playing. It had gone well, this filming lark. To such an extent he was seriously considering acting as a long-term career move.

Henry Sheldon, on the other hand, was contemplating a career coming to a close. Though if Boz was right and this load of tripe did put bums on seats, maybe some more character parts might come his way, but he knew better than to count on it. For now, however, all he was really thinking about was the private-members club he frequented when in London, a place that sold large gins and catered for unusual tastes. And the sooner he could get this stupid costume off the better.

I am a palm tree in an oasis in an Egyptian desert, thought Gwen Youngblood, holding her arms out and letting them sway in an imagined breeze. She held the pose for a minute, then sat down. One of her favourite anecdotes was of Marlon Brando in an acting class told to imagine they were chickens about to be bombed. The rest of the class scurried about, clucking wildly, while Brando merely settled in a corner and laid an egg. When asked why he had not joined in the general panic he replied that he was a chicken, and what did they know about bombs!

Gwen would often try to picture herself being that smart. "Cluck," she would say under her breath. "Cluck, cluck," and strain out an egg, wondering all the time how she could bring such insights into her performance as Nefertiti.

John had been so helpful though the background information he provided was secondary to the dark brown eyes he looked at her with. If he didn't hit on her soon she would have to make the first move.

Meanwhile, the object of her desire felt the beginning of a migraine coming on and was wishing he had turned down the invitation to watch today's filming. There was a fuzziness mixed with the dull ache, not his usual headache at all. Linton-Jones wished fervently that he could be home, lying in a darkened room with a cold compress on his forehead.

"THE TIME, IT comes," whispered whatever it was that lay in the sarcophagus, reaching out in a manner that paid no attention to distance. "Son of my son. Open your heart and mind to the possibilities laid bare before you."

The stale air in the chamber swirled in ever increasing circles. Pockets of movement where none should have been possible.

"Damn you, Ibi! You are dust but I still exist."

The whisper was growing in strength.

PEOPLE WERE RUNNING around like headless chickens. That silly Boz Crabbe was shouting orders. The oddball old actor playing the Pharaoh was taking his place on the set. Gwen, in costume, looked around until she saw him, then waved. John managed a half-hearted gesture in response; thankful he was sitting too far back for her to join him.

Oh dear! Some sort of kerfuffle? No, it was just Mamma Mayhem, or whatever it was he called himself, deciding he needed a toilet break. Off he went, the rags he wore flapping, while Crabbe took out his annoyance on the second assistant cameraman, who was waiting to carry out his clapperboard duties.

John's head pain grew suddenly worse, getting so strong he felt in total anguish and feared he might vomit at any moment. Standing on unsteady legs, he staggered off in the direction of the men's room.

"SO IT STARTS," said the swirling smoke in a voice now more than a whisper. Through the rock it floated, and the sand, out

into the pitiless sun. "Now, seed of my seed," it commanded, encircling the globe at the speed of thought. "Now!"

MUTHU MAYHEM WAS back, standing in position and ready to make his entrance. "Right, if everyone is quite prepared," growled Crabbe, nodding at the second assistant cameraman.

"Quiet on set," called the man. "Scene twenty-seven, take one," and the clapperboard clicked together.

"Action!" instructed Boz Crabbe.

Old pro that he was, Henry Sheldon went immediately into actor mode as the camera turned. Holding himself erect and regal, he entered via an alcove and crossed towards his throne. Turning sharply at the sound of dragged footsteps he saw that the damned fool of a Muthu had come in early, but since Boz had not called "Cut" he carried on with the scene.

"Amsunaton!" he exclaimed loudly. "I thought you dead, thrice-fold."

Damnation, thought Sheldon when Mayhem missed his cue but continued towards him without speaking. "Cursed Spider," he called, covering the lapse. "Vengeful Vampire. I'll kill you myself, and this time let it be permanent."

The monster had reached him now, lifting a hand which boasted long fingernails that looked more like razor-sharp steel than anything else. The hand flashed, slashed, and Sheldon's severed head fell to the floor.

"What the…!" gasped the cameraman.

"Keep turning," shouted Crabbe. He wasn't sure what was going on, or how it was being done, but it would be brilliant footage.

Gwen entered right on cue as the vampire drank from the dead Pharaoh's head. It looked even more realistic than it had in rehearsals. "Father!" she cried. "What have you done, vile beast?"

Instead of replying, as per the script, the creature dropped the head and loped over to where she stood, knocking her to the ground. Before she could fully comprehend what was happening, her costume had been torn off and the Amsunaton figure was standing over her, in an obvious state of arousal.

Managing to drag her gaze upwards, Gwen looked at the creature's face. Feeling totally bewildered she saw that it wasn't Muthu looking down at her through all the makeup. It was John Liston-Jones!

"Go get him, Danny," muttered Crabbe to the actor playing Bek, giving him a little push. But instead of being the hero the man became the next victim when the thing grabbed the carved wooden snake from his fear-weakened grasp and plunged it into his heart instead.

Blood was spurting. Gwen was screaming. Studio employees were scrambling in a mad dash for the exits. Boz Crabbe, bug-eyed and manic, lurched onto the set. "What are you doing to my film?" he yelled, before dying alongside his dreams when the monstrous being lifted him into the air and broke him in two.

Khepadet threw the two halves of Crabbe's torn corpse aside, turning back to Gwen, looking at her through his uncomprehending grandson's eyes. At least he had not had to summon this one. Tearing away some of the rags he wore, to make his movements freer, he dropped to the floor, sinking into her.

BY THE TIME the police marksmen entered the studio, weapons at the ready, Gwen Youngblood was still screaming but John Liston-Jones was standing away from her. What on earth was happening? He kept asking himself.

The old man playing the Pharaoh, decapitated.

Boz Crabbe somehow torn in half.

The young actor Danny, also lifeless. A wooden snake protruding from his heart.

Also, though at this moment unknown and unseen, Muthu Mayhem was dead in the gents.

John looked down at the blood-soaked rags he was wearing, then up at the policemen who were slowly edging their way towards him. "What's happening?" he shouted before starting a shambling run towards them.

A number of shots rang out, three bullets thudding home. John Liston-Jones was dead before he hit the floor.

Gwen, the only survivor, screamed in tandem with wailing sirens as more police cars pulled up outside. If this didn't boost her career, nothing would. She continued to lie there, waiting to be rescued. Though she was surrounded by dead people, deep in her womb a new life was already forming.

WAH-WAH

In a genre renowned for the claiming
Of unproven relationships
Earl Zebedee Hooker really was
The younger cousin of the more famous
John Lee Hooker

Born in Clarksdale, Mississippi
A birthplace that Hooker shared with
The likes of Son House and Ike Turner
Muddy Waters and Howlin' Wolf
Lived there a spell
And Bessie Smith tragically died there

Earl was an acknowledged master of
The slide guitar and wah-wah blues
Paving the way for the likes of
Jimi Hendrix and Jeff Beck

A misspent youth saw him run with
Chicago street gangs
A careful man with a dollar
Renowned for his reluctance to pay
The members of his bands

He died young
Finally losing his battle against tuberculosis
Being remembered mainly
As a musician's musician
Still known to have been enormously influential

SUCH TWISTS OF FATE

Hard bop player Lee Morgan
Was hired by Dizzy Gillespie at 18
And Dizzy knew a thing or two
About jazz trumpeters
A year on and he was part of
Coltrane's *Blue Train* sessions
Later joining Art Blakey's
Jazz Messengers
Before recording with Benny Golson
And leading his own group
He even had a crossover hit
With *The Sidewinder*
But his development as a
Soloist, band leader and composer
Was cut tragically short
When his long-term girl friend
Shot him after an argument
At Slug's Saloon, a New York club
Where his band had been playing
His injuries might not have been fatal
But the ambulance was delayed
By bad-driving conditions following snow
And Lee bled to death
On such twists of fate do we live or die

NO VALENTINES FOR
THE JAMES DEAN OF JAZZ

Chet Baker burst upon the scene
In the piano-less quartet
He formed with Gerry Mulligan
Cool jazz was "in" and
His looks and swoon-era vocals
Seemed to guarantee stardom
But his personality was as fragile
As his poignant and emotionally charged
Trumpet playing
Whatever the question
Heroin was the answer
Drifting in and out of drug-deluded decades
Baker resurfaced at odd moments
Like a jazz mercenary
  Have trumpet
  Will play
  Where's the money
Folding stuff always needed for the next fix
Yet there were still occasions
When the music was sublime
Which only emphasised what had been lost
Chet Baker
Sweet and sour
From jazz idol to ravaged junky
What a waste

THE SECOND MRS ARMSTRONG

Lil Hardin ranked with
Such as Jelly Roll Morton
Among the greats
Of early jazz piano

Playing with King Oliver
She tutored the unsophisticated Louis
Becoming ambitious on his behalf
    Hot Fives
    Hot Sevens
    Solo stardom
She was the gal who guided
While he just wanted to play

Their friendship lasted
Surviving divorce
And she herself died
After performing at
A Louis tribute concert

Amen sister

LOCUST DAY

THE BOTTLE STOOD out of arm's reach on the dressing table. Half full or half empty – it didn't really matter – he would still have to fetch it for himself. He swore softly. It was that kind of night. Even more, it was fast becoming that kind of existence. Carla, Tibori, the whining bastards he collected from…

Carla stirred irritably at his side, interrupting his train of thought but failing to substitute a more pleasant one. That's right, he thought, move away … but be careful to keep your legs together…

"…or you might catch cold," he finished aloud.

"Che cosa?" she murmured, voice muffled.

"Nothing, baby, just nothing."

Sinclair looked around the room, laughing quietly but without humour as he caught a triple view of himself in Carla's wall-length mirrors. She had a thing about mirrors and up until a week ago he had understood why. She loved to watch herself becoming more and more aroused as his expert fingers played her like a violin, until her eyes could no longer focus. The thought brought a quick hard pain to his groin.

Heaving himself from the bed, he scooped up the bottle and drank without the benefit of a tumbler, gulping the liquor fiercely so that it spilled over his chin and trickled down his bare chest. Might as well behave like trash if you're going to be treated like it.

If the old saying was true – that before you have it you could eat it, then after you've had it you wish you had – then Sinclair's problem was in wondering where his next meal was coming from. He gazed again at his reflection, appraising himself almost as if he were seeing a total stranger.

He studied the blond hair and European features inherited from his mother, and how they clashed with the dark pigmentation his father had donated. "Momma, Poppa, how *did* you manage it?" He could have been the only one-man black-and-white stag show. "I should be a star." Shrugging, he swung himself from the bed and onto his feet. At least he could use it to empty his bladder, seeing she had become so damned fussy.

Through one of the mirrors he could see that Carla's outline had taken on a few taut angles, and the disapproval so evident beneath the sheets stung him as sharply as the raw whiskey had in his throat. His frustration plus her intransigence tipped some balance within him, bringing both a feeling of emptiness and acute resentment bubbling to the surface of his mind. He hesitated for a moment; then, slowly and deliberately, raised the bottle and hurled it at her image in the silvered glass.

The crash drew the first active response from Carla that night.

Screaming obscenities, she flew from the bed towards Sinclair, hammering at his chest and attempting to rake her nails down his face. He caught her wrists, grinning insolently, and although she struggled frenziedly he handled her almost without effort. Sinclair twisted her arms behind her with one hand, steadily raising them upwards, forcing her chin down onto her chest. The words she tried to spit out were lost at her teeth and dribbled away in hysterical spittle as she began to choke.

Backing her to the end of the bed, he dropped her onto it, letting her go.

"You black bastard!"

"Shove it, Carla…" His mood must have shown on his face.

"Hit me then," she sneered up at him. "Hit me! It's what you want."

"What I want you've been refusing."

She almost bounced off the bed and stood breathing hard, her fists clenched. They stared at each other like two fighters waiting for the bell. Christ, he thought, noticing that her nipples were hard and her nostrils flared, she's getting off on this. She wants to be knocked around! But he just couldn't be bothered.

"Send the bill for that," he said, waving a hand at the shattered mirror. "…care of Tibori."

He reached for his clothes but Carla turned, viciously, as if to claw at him again. Sinclair sighed once, almost apologetically, but not quite – it was more the deprecation of someone brushing aside a troublesome fly – then backhanded her sharply, just once. She collapsed in a leggy heap and remained that way while he finished dressing.

Before he left Sinclair went over to where she lay, moaning in a quiet sing-song fashion. He looked down, lifting her chin on the toe of his shoe. "Time you learned, girl. You don't put the freeze on your friends, especially when they are picking up the tabs. Dig?"

Carla looked up at him, reaching out a hand. "Art…?" she whispered.

Sinclair shook his head and turned away. "Ciao,

Carla."

He walked out, leaving her, and with considerable restraint he closed the door very gently behind him.

People, thought Sinclair as he took the lift down to street level, you could never really tell about them. Especially women. Take Carla: at first … really something; then, without warning, the frigid bit. Man, that had been some putdown. Shaking his head ruefully, he stepped into the foyer and strode out from the apartment block.

It was raining, hard, a swirling unremitting downpour that blew every-which-way to drench shirts and soak jackets. Rome in February, he thought. "You can bloody keep it…" Turning up the collar of his light evening outfit, he started down the street. Once on the main drag he could dry off in a bar before calling a taxi.

As he neared them, Sinclair's attention was drawn to the few bedraggled shapes that lay in the dark strip by the corner of the apartment block, just inside the shadows cast by the lights of the living city. You could find a million or more in exactly similar circumstances in any metropolitan area: vagrants … tramps … bums … who clustered nightly about the fringes, awaiting any morsel of plunder that might come their way. At least nobody tried to mug him on this occasion. Perhaps the rain was discouraging even the *Birichinos*. He could handle anything they could offer, but it was usually messy and tiresome.

It's a hard world, he thought as he walked through the rain, but you're a hard guy, Sinclair… You'll make out. Then, finally, he hit the nightlife.

The street was brightly lit, but the weather gave even that a dreary aspect. The buildings seemed to crouch and draw inward out of the wind. The flashing signs were wet smears, sadly reflecting their melancholic neon onto the dripping pavements.

Sinclair turned into the brightest portal he encountered. The name DONDOLIO glittered inter-mittently above lurid representations of the resident strippers. "See our Lesbian Show, citizens of the world… The Best!" invited a recorded voice, repeating the invitation in a number of languages.

The best? Well, he would see. It was on his list to check out this dive anyway – the place was new and required assessing for Tibori Angstrom's cut.

A fat-mouth at the entrance regarded him shiftily. "Your membership card, Signore?"

"*I* need to be a member?"

With a nastiness he quite enjoyed, Sinclair stood before him, savouring the heavy's puzzled expression. He knew the man was groping for the link Sinclair's black skin and blond hair warned him existed; he needn't have sweated … help was at hand.

"Signor Sinclair. *Mister* Sinclair … I most humbly apologise," wheedled a sly sounding voice as a fat figure rolled up behind them and whispered urgently in the doorman's ear. The man looked up sharply, a high colour showing suddenly on his cheeks.

"Mr Sinclair, I didn't realise…"

But Sinclair was gone, ushered rapidly into the belly of the club by the ebullient maître d.

"This way, sir. This way. Your first visit, am I right? Of course I am. I am Franco. I'm sure you will find my little establishment to your liking…"

The garrulous whine tailed off into silence as Sinclair held up his hand. "Sure, Franco, sure. Now, if you would get this dried I might even begin to agree with you."

Franco disappeared, clutching the soaking jacket and waving a waiter to the table. Sinclair was feeling better already, enjoying the power of his position. How they envied him, these mice. In their eyes he had it made.

Had it made?

Chief Collector for the Rome kickback. Sounded good, but in reality little more than an errand boy – and he was fed up to his back teeth with the whole situation. But he'd had enough of making like a loser tonight. What he needed now was to feel a winner again.

The waiter, having been instructed to look after this special guest, stepped forward eagerly when Sinclair beckoned. He smiled inwardly and ordered a Budweiser, but the waiter just looked at him blankly.

"Budweiser…? You know … beer?"

The waiter shook his head. "No beer, sir."

"Okay, Seagram's then. Lots of crushed ice and squeeze a wedge of lime."

The drink arrived and Sinclair sipped it as he looked around. Nearly every table was occupied, and he noted a more-than-usual sprinkling of women. Most, apart from the hostesses counting drinks, had curious and almost expectant expressions. Waiting for the floorshow, he realised. Waiting to be turned on.

The show, as it turned out, was an approximation of the old nursery rhyme: when it was good it was very, very good, but when it was bad it was lousy.

It started bad.

A slack-chested stripper languidly removed what little she had started with, swung her hips a few times and vanished. It was about as sexy as striped pyjamas. But then the red lights dimmed, leaving only the bandstand and part of the floor brightly lit, while the audience remained in shadow. A musical chord blared, and the lights were extinguished completely.

"Presenta ... Les Bico!" echoed a disembodied voice.

From the darkness came a sudden single throb of a tumba drum, and the freezing glare of a spotlight threw a white circular glory about the two lesbians. They stood unmoving in close embrace, curve hugging curve, for what seemed an eternity. Both were quite young and completely au naturel.

The drum thudded again and the girls sprang apart. The taller, a blonde, swayed in ever-tightening circles around the other, who faced the audience with one arm across her breasts and the other hand shielding her crotch like a shy virgin. Then the blonde paused, her hands and lips caressing the other's skin, before she sank to the floor, kneeling before her partner.

The atmosphere was electric.

Sinclair glanced around, taking in the hush that had descended on the club, cloaking it with an apparent lust. Franco could be on a winner here, he judged, estimating that Tibori's cut would be better than peanuts. Back on stage the girls' madly contorted bodies spoke of conquest and submission, of sensuality and desire, so that even someone like him – seen it all, done it all, what's new then baby – felt the moment creeping into the darker recesses of his mind.

Then, without warning, the drums exploded into a pulsating intoxication of sound and the spotlight flashed red, the performer's satiny torsos glistening crimson in its glow. The rhythm pounded ever faster, boom-boom-boom, threaded with a sharp and tormenting staccato beat. The girls writhed like angry snakes, responding to the rising crescendo, twisting faster and faster until ... the tom toms stopped, the lights went out, and it was over. The audience sat transfixed for a long moment, then burst into wild applause.

Sinclair found himself curiously aroused, sufficiently so to get Franco to invite the younger of the two girls to his table. Her name was Yvette. Her skin was flawless and her hair, cut short, was black like desire, though there was a tired look about her eyes.

They drank in silence at first, with him feeling oddly tongue-tied. Speaking with a lesbian was, in a strange way, almost like speaking with a nun; both lived an existence from which men were excluded. Both, indeed, had *rejected* the world of men, and in doing so had proclaimed their complete emancipation; faith and flesh … the only true liberationists.

"Your act was very good," he said finally.

"It was no act," she responded with a faint smile. "It was the real thing."

"Like in Coke."

She was probably too young to remember the old advert, he realised, which struck him as funny. Yvette joined in, laughing because he was, even if she didn't get the joke, and they both relaxed, feeling more at ease in each other's company. They had though, become the centre of attention. People at other tables were staring openly at them, craning their necks to get a better view of the odd couple.

"Shall we leave?" Sinclair suggested as he became aware of this unwanted curiosity.

She agreed readily; once his now-dry jacket had been returned they left the club. Franco saw them off, making knowing looks in Yvette's direction. Sinclair was never drunk enough to be taken in by such tactics. He knew full well that Franco hoped Yvette might, in some way, ameliorate Angstrom's fix. Sinclair quickly disillusioned him.

"I'll send a couple of men with our accountant, Franco. You will of course cooperate?"

"Most assuredly, Mr Sinclair. You have my word."

"Keep it that way and we'll get along fine, really fine. Is that my cab?"

They kept the same transport all night. The driver had nowhere else to go and Sinclair's money was better than most. Their last call was at a dive near the river, a place you could locate quite easily through smell alone – a potent mix of smoke, lust, stale perfume and hash.

High atmosphere for lowlife, thought Sinclair. He could take his liquor but maybe best not mixed with exhaled pot. Too much, sweetheart! He stood up and would have fallen if the girl had not held him tightly around the waist.

"You're drunk!" she exclaimed.

They both laughed and she continued supporting him towards the exit, but a vague figure appeared in front of them, blocking their path. "Art! I thought it was you: Art Sinclair. You've really been laying one on tonight."

The voice moved around him and a face appeared close to his. "Don't say you don't remember me," it said.

Bollux? Pollux? Caster and Bollux...? His mind wandered.

"Pollard, old boy. Alan Pollard."

The name did a zig-zag tour before Sinclair drunkenly tagged it to a memory. A reviewer and columnist with the British music press, Pollard had sometimes been helpful back in his London club days. The guy was probably in town to cover the forthcoming jazz festival.

"Alan Pollard," he said with a broad smile. "Sure thing."

Yvette tugged at his waist. "Come on, Artie, let's get out of here…"

But Pollard wouldn't be put off. "Max has been asking, Art. Said he couldn't find you anyplace."

Sinclair heard that okay, slicing right through his pleasant drunken fog, dispersing it. But Yvette was still trying to pull him away, afraid that she might lose a guy willing to spend big … for nothing. He pushed her off and she lost her footing, sitting on the floor rather suddenly. Everyone able to look saw she was minus her panties; Sinclair the exception: he was looking intently at Pollard.

"What about Max? Why should Kaufmann want me?"

"No idea, Art, but if *Max* is looking, then *Cully* is asking."

"What's the connection?"

"He works for Cully now."

Max Kaufmann had no liking for Sinclair, none at all, not since Art had caught him with his sticky fingers in Angstrom's cash box and tossed him out. And now he was working for Cully Homeyard. Sinclair grunted noncommittally. The reason why Kauffmann left the organisation was a secret known only to the pair of them. Who knew when a favour might be needed or pressure applied? You had to play the angles.

"Well, well, old Maxie," said Sinclair. "Thanks, Al." He patted Pollard's shoulder and waved towards the bar. "Whatever my friend wants, on my personal account," he told the barman. "Have a bottle on me, Al, and keep in touch. You know where I am, I guess."

Despite her protests he put Yvette in the cab and sent

her home, hailing another to take him back to his flat, which he hadn't been near while staying with Carla. Playtime was over for now.

The Tibori Angstrom organisation was a very sophisticated setup with fingers in many pies and interests in most of the major European cities. When Angstrom's step-son heard that an old enemy was not only in town but asking, it just had to be taken seriously.

But was Pollard giving it to him straight, wondered Sinclair as he entered his apartment block. The answer was yes, and Kaufmann sure was keen to find him.

He was propped in Sinclair's doorway: fast asleep.

-2-

JAB, JAB, LEFT hook. Move to the right.

Straight left, right cross. Move to the left.

Chin down and crouch. Throw two-hand clusters at body height.

Mikey Dandridge, "The Cardiff Kid", was shadow boxing. When his trainer signalled he would switch to the big bag, alternating between the two disciplines and sparring a few rounds later.

The Cardiff Kid? Hah! He hadn't been back to Cardiff in years and was certainly no longer a kid. They still used it though. Good publicity. His headlining days might well be in the past but the nickname helped remind people of what he had been, back in the day.

A former world champion, that's what!

Even Dandridge had to admit though, that luck had played a part. Winning the Welsh area middleweight title had been an important first step. Then, bypassing the British title, he had grabbed the European crown by defeating the French champion in Paris, which had given him an automatic world ranking. A couple of

American journeymen conspired to make him look better than he probably was, and a Las Vegas date with Rico Incente was signed, sealed and delivered.

Incente had been around for years, one of those typically tough Mexican fighters. Not one of the all-time greats, but a highly respected performer. At one stage he had held three of the internationally recognised belts, but age was beginning to catch up with him and it was only his remaining WBO title he put on the line in Vegas.

Mikey Dandridge was lucky enough to be the challenger on the occasion an old champion had that one fight too many. Almost anybody would have beaten Rico Incente that night and The Cardiff Kid stayed on his toes and danced his way to an unanimous points win. Mikey was the new WBO Middleweight Champion of the World.

Right time, right place.

He was an honest enough fighter who always gave of his best, but he wasn't really of world-title class. A couple of carefully selected voluntary defences enabled him stay as champion but his limitations were exposed when he could no longer ignore the WBO's officially nominated challenger; he was beaten in seven rounds by a methodical Russian whose name he had trouble pronouncing.

Thinking it to be a weaker division, Dandridge moved up to the light heavyweights. He did become British champion but failed in a crack at the European title, and his hopes for another world title shot faded to nothing.

That was all over ten years ago now, and he was still doing it. Dandridge had picked up some good purse money and with sensible investment could have set himself up for later in life, but he had always enjoyed the highlife and as the cash came in he spent it.

Having bulked up as training became something of a chore, he now campaigned as a cruiserweight, and even took the occasional bout up with the heavies. The Cardiff Kid knew his place in the scheme of things. His days as the headliner were long over. Now he was merely an opponent, and opponents were generally expected to lose. He was a trial horse for young and up-and-coming hopefuls, and a win over a former world champion would look good on their records. Not that Dandridge lost every time out. He gave as good an account of himself as he possibly could and sometimes his experience was too much for the raw youngsters he was usually matched with. And when they did beat him, he made them work for it.

Between fights he sometimes did consultancy work for personal security firms and hit the casinos as often as his bank balance would allow.

Having switched to the big bag, Mikey Dandridge thumped home punches with unexpected venom. "Hey!" called Leonard Stein, his manager/trainer/friend these past five or six years. "Save it for fight night."

His original manager had dumped him as soon as the titles had been lost. A few other trainers came and went before he hooked up with Stein, a boxing man who recognised all that was wrong with the sport but who nevertheless could not resist the gladiatorial combat of two well matched contestants.

Dandridge had won his last fight on a third-round stoppage when his opponent had suffered a nasty cut over the left eye. The fact that the up-and-coming Dartford lad would probably have won had he not sustained the damage meant little. A win was a win and it had made him a suitable fall-guy in the next stage of Faustino Bacca's rise to the top. A flamboyant Italian with film star looks, his career was being carefully stage-managed to make him look better than he actually was.

Stein had studied film of Bacca's last few fights and was convinced that Dandridge could pull off an upset in Milan. "He's made for you, Mikey. He keeps his right hand low and throws looping lefts. You step inside the hook and his defence is non-existent, and I don't think he's got too good a chin. Some pretty ordinary punchers have staggered him, though to be fair he's always come back to win so far. But you are a step up, and this lad is not as good as his publicity."

He doesn't have to be, thought Mikey Dandridge, taking out his frustrations on the big bag, not with the big moneymen in his corner…

-3-

GREY HAIRED NOW: bespectacled and with the beginnings of a mid-fifties paunch, but still with an aura of calculation and power. Tibori Angstrom ruled his organisation with an iron fist. He had killed his first man while still in his teens and had willingly removed anyone who had stood in his way during his relentless rise through the criminal ranks, yet he could have his heart strings tugged by a violin concerto. A man of many contradictions.

Women had been on a par with possessions, to be used or discarded according to his mood, until the day he'd met Margaret Sinclair and her half-caste son Arthur. Her partner, Folarin Okeke, had been a major player in the Nigerian underworld. Emerging from the university confraternities system of campus cults, he had participated in the Cheetham Hillbillies turf war with the Gooch Close Gang. Later he was sent to London to smooth out the British end of various drug deals, and there Okeke had met the statuesque beauty who had tempted him to make his temporary visit more permanent.

Though they never actually married – Okeke had wives back in Nigeria – they lived in splendid harmony and had a child together. Margaret kept their relationship completely separate from his business dealings, which she knew to be shady though not of its full extent. That only became apparent to her after his murder, a shooting that had all the hallmarks of a professional assassination.

His body was shipped back to Nigeria for burial in Abuja but a memorial service was held in London. Okeke's connections were such that the gathering included many of Africa and Europe's leading gang-land figures, probably including whoever had insti-gated his killing, and it was here that Angstrom first set eyes on Margaret Sinclair.

It was love at first sight, something he was totally unprepared for. Angstrom had never met a woman like her before, and never would again. He had realised, however, that her late partner's memorial service was hardly the time or place to instigate a courtship, but he had her kept under surveillance and when she eventually showed signs of recovering from her initial grief he engineered a friendship which he patiently allowed to blossom into a love that led to a blissfully happy marriage.

It had come as a terrible shock to Angstrom that all his wealth and power was as nothing when confronted with the cancer that took Margaret from him. Some things could not be bought. Now, still in thrall to the memory of his one love, he allowed her son greater leeway than anyone else on the planet.

Arthur wanted an open-ended leave of absence from his syndicate duties in Rome. Cully Homeyard, a former employer, friend, and all-time living legend, was in some sort of bother and was asking for help.

"The King of Rock and Roll is in trouble again. He jerks like a paranoid puppet. Moans like a caterwauling feline on heat. Dishonours the good name of music every time he opens his mouth; and has not got the good sense to accept his luck and behave."

Sinclair shrugged. "Cully is a nice guy, nothing at all like his public image, which is a mighty big problem for him. He has to give the impression of living a life of wild extremes. It's what the fans expect."

"Fans! Image!" Angstrom snorted derisively. "Last time it was blackmail, wasn't it?"

Homeyard, on a Christianity kick at the time, had hired Notre-Dame Cathedral in Paris for an evening of private contemplation and worship. In spite of strict security someone had obtained photographs of him kneeling at the altar, his head bowed and hands clasped in prayer. The mythology of his lifestyle was so deeply engrained it might well have damaged his career substantially if the pictures had been released, and blackmailers could not be trusted to be satisfied with a single payment.

Art smiled at the memory. That had been some caper, and he had been instrumental in bringing it to a satisfactory conclusion. Well, satisfactory for Cully, that was.

"Yes," he agreed with his step-father. "I don't know what it is this time, only that he wants to see me urgently."

Angstrom appeared deep in thought though in reality his mind was already made up. "It might be to my advantage for you to be in London at this time," he said slowly. "A boxer I have an interest in, Faustino Bacca, has a fight against Dandridge coming up soon."

"Mikey Dandridge, former middleweight champion, now campaigning at cruiserweight," interjected Sinclair.

"You know your boxing."

"I know that Bacca doesn't take a punch too well and that for all his veteran status Dandridge still takes the game seriously. I wouldn't put money on your boy."

Angstrom grimaced. "Exactly! Which is why I bought up the Britisher's gambling debts – which will be torn up, plus earning him a generous bonus, when he loses the fight."

"The fix is in?"

"Yes, but a sixth sense tells me this Dandridge, though he has agreed, isn't happy about it. While you are over there you can check him out for me. Make sure there are no unforeseen problems."

"Of course," agreed Sinclair.

"And there is a slight connection…"

"Connection?"

"Dandridge gave security advice to Homeyard once."

Sinclair silently acknowledged the old man's thoroughness. He had his finger on all the pulses.

-4-

TAKE THE SEXUAL energy of early Elvis, the glorious excess of Little Richard, add a smidgeon of Springsteen's gravitas. Mix together, break the mould, and you have the onstage persona of Cully Homeyard. Born Colin Hill in a small Somerset village, in private he was still as nerdy and needy as he had been back then.

A fact kept well buried beneath layers of security. Back when Sinclair had been on the payroll one of his functions had been to trash hotel rooms and organise the general level of mayhem expected from the Rock 'n' Roll Superstar.

"Good God, Cully! You look bloody awful!"

Even though he was expected, it had taken an age for Sinclair to pass through all the rigmarole surrounding the biggest cash generator in the music business. Now, finally allowed to enter the private apartment at the top of the tower block owned entirely by the Homeyard Corporation, he was both surprised and shocked at the man's drawn and haggard appearance; especially his eyes, which twitched and flitted nervously. Haunted, was the single-word description that seemed best suited.

"You always did cut through the bullshit," said Homeyard coming across to hug Sinclair like a long-lost brother.

"One of my failings, Cully, but you really don't look well. Are you seeing a doctor?"

"It's not that sort of ailment, Art."

"Oh?"

"Later, okay? Let's catch up a bit first. Pour yourself a drink and tell me all about Rome."

Cully was not a fully-fledged teetotaller; he did like a shandy, though with more lemonade than beer. All at odds with a publicity machine that claimed he downed a full bottle of vodka at a single sitting. But he did keep a well-stocked bar for visitors.

As he had in the old days, while they talked Sinclair marvelled again at the dual personality syndrome that allowed such a quiet and unassuming person to become the wildest man on the planet while performing. There was a greater undercurrent of unease about him now, Sinclair noted while they spoke, that he hadn't possessed in the old days, not even during the Notre-Dame episode. The man seemed unwilling to move on from generalities and chitchat; Sinclair finally decided enough was enough.

"Cully, my man, you sent for me. You must have had a reason, and if it's my help you need then just say the word."

Homeyard stood and paced nervously. "Storm in a teacup, Art. I guess I panicked and overreacted," he said, a shade too quickly.

"You've been on edge from the moment I walked in. Something's up!"

"Well yes, I do have a problem, and you were the first person I thought of but I'm no longer sure that your particular expertise would provide the answer. I'm sorry if I have dragged you away from anything important, and for nothing."

"I was due a break from Italy, and it's always good to see you Cully. You know that. As to your problem, let me be the judge. I might be more help that you give me credit for."

The other thought about that. "Can you stay in London for a few days?"

"Certainly. I've got an errand to run for Tibori, but I'll hang around for as long as you need me."

"Good man, Art. Look, let me sort things out in my own mind first. Come and see me in three days and I'll tell you all about it. Okay?"

"If that's the way you want to do it."

"I'll get Max to ease you through all the lower-level bureaucracy."

"How is Maxie fitting in with you?" asked Sinclair,

remembering his own problem with the man.

"Fine: good worker, pleasant enough fellow. I've no complaints." He pressed a buzzer to summon the man.

"Good," said Sinclair, and promised to return in three days.

Max Kaufmann obviously had something on his mind as they rode a lift down to street level. "Did you, er…" he started, but stopped. "What I mean is…"

"Spit it out, Max," said Sinclair. "You want to know if I mentioned your sticky fingers to Cully, is that it?"

The man nodded, looking grim. "I like my job here and I like Mr Homeyard himself," he said. "I learnt my lesson back in Rome. I play everything straight now. No more funny business."

"That's good to hear, Max," said Sinclair, "because Cully speaks highly of you. No, I said nothing about the past and will only do so if you make me."

The lift eased to a stop. "Keep your eyes open, Max. Your boss is in some sort of bother but isn't ready to confide in me yet. You see anything unusual, let me know. Okay?"

-5-

THE RAT-TAT-TAT of speed bags, the slap of leather, and the heady smells of liniment and sweat. Sinclair stood just inside the gym door and took in the atmosphere. He had toyed with the idea of a boxing career during his teenage years, but too much had been going on in his life and he lacked the dedication required. He had remained a fan though, and was not above using his step-father's connections to acquire ringside seats for the big fights in Las Vegas. Sinclair winced sympathetically as Mikey Dandridge hooked a vicious left into his sparring partner's rib cage.

Leonard Stein rang the bell a little early. The sparring

partner was there to provide Mikey with a workout and to let him try some moves, not to be beat up. What was Mikey up to? He had been edgy and bad tempered all through training for this Bacca fight.

"That'll do for today." Stein held the middle rope up for the boxers to leave the ring then untied the laces on their gloves. "You okay?" he asked the sparring partner. "I'll live," the man replied, "but you're going to have to start paying danger money." They both laughed.

Dandridge had spotted Sinclair and walked over to him. "Are you the guy who phoned?" he asked.

"Yes, Art Sinclair. Is it okay to talk here or would somewhere more private be better?"

"Not here, that's for sure. If you don't mind waiting while I shower we can find somewhere more suitable."

"Take your time," said Sinclair. "I'm in no rush." And he settled to watch the boxers still working out while he waited.

Hook up, hook down. Jab and move. Double up and do it again.

Trainers barked orders. Boxers sweated. It was a tough game. Sinclair kept himself in reasonable shape, but maybe some of this hard discipline would not go amiss. Maybe when he was back in Rome he would undertake a proper training regime. At that moment his mobile buzzed.

"Sinclair…"

"It's Max. Max Kaufmann."

"Hi Max. Is this a message from Cully?"

"No, but it is about Mr Homeyard. You asked me to keep my eyes open."

"You got something for me, Max?"

"I might have. I'm not sure, but I don't want to talk over the phone. Can we meet?"

Sinclair wasn't sure how long he was going to be tied up with Mikey Dandridge. "I'm in a meeting at the moment and can't be specific on times. Give me another call in a couple of hours and if I'm free then we can arrange to meet. If not, I'm back to see Cully the day after tomorrow; though if you do have something I would rather have it sooner than later."

"Okay," agreed Kaufmann, "I'll call you again in a couple of hours."

Sinclair slipped the phone back into his coat pocket. Max was no bonehead and had been a diligent enough worker before being tempted to dip into Tibori's cash, so anything he had spotted would deserve full consideration. No good speculating though. Keep the balls in the air and everything in its right box, to mix a metaphor or two.

The Cardiff Kid was coming towards him. It was time to concentrate on Angstrom's business. They settled in a local café not far from the gym, with a steaming mug of coffee for Sinclair and tea for the boxer. "Let me make one thing clear, Mikey – I can call you Mikey, can't I? Good. Look, I am talking to you at the request of a friend. I am not actually a part of any … agreement that you have made. I have been asked to make sure that you are still conversant with the terms of that said agreement and that you still intend to comply in full. My friend has the impression that you are … concerned. But as I say, I am just the messenger."

Dandridge made a great play of stirring his drink, staring down at the mug. Finally he put the spoon to one side and looked up. "I take it you know what the agreement consists of?"

Sinclair nodded. "Just the basics," he confirmed.

"I've never thrown a fight before," said the boxer

bitterly, "and if they weren't holding all my markers over my head I wouldn't be doing it now. Lenny Stein reckons the Italian is made for me and beating him would get me some high-profile fights."

"Bacca is definitely beatable," agreed Sinclair, "but even if you did do a job on him you would still be the opponent in subsequent fights. You would just be a higher-class trial horse for a couple of bouts."

Dandridge visibly slumped. "You're probably right."

"You know I am." Sinclair sipped his coffee. "And it's not just having your debts cleared is it? There's a bonus for you too, money for old rope."

"You can tell your friends not to worry," said the boxer. "I might not like it but I won't back out. I will lose in round four, as instructed, and their boy can go on to bigger things."

"Only so far before his particular bubble bursts. Stick around, Mikey, and you might catch him on his way back down…"

Dandridge laughed but the sound lacked humour.

"I hear you did some consultancy work for the Cully Homeyard Organisation," said Sinclair, changing the subject, happy to accept that The Cardiff Kid would play it straight regarding the fix.

"Indeed I did. I put his security people through their paces and suggested improvements to their working practises. I've done it for a number of large outfits."

"I'm a former employee and it's Cully I am really in London to see."

"Great guy," said Dandridge, sounding enthusiastic for the first time. "He gave me a full set of signed CDs. I had some of them already, being a bit of a fan, but not signed of course. Give him my regards, tell him that if there's ever anything I can do for him, just give me a call."

After a final assurance from the boxer that the Milan fight would go to plan the two men shook hands and went their different ways, Sinclair heading back to his hotel. After a drink in the bar he made for his room intending to switch the television onto a news channel and catch up with what was happening in the big wide world.

The fact that Max had not rung back as arranged did not bother him unduly. If it really was important then he would call, but maybe he'd been overreacting and it was nothing worth bothering over.

He should have called again though. Sinclair rang his number but Max's phone was switched off. If the man didn't contact him before then he would see him when he paid his next visit to see Cully.

Sinclair settled in front of the television and was starting to nod a little when his phone woke him. Tossing a mental coin he decided it was either Tibori checking that he had spoken with Mikey Dandridge or Max finally making his promised call.

It was neither.

"Cully my man, what gives?"

"Come see me tomorrow, Art. Don't wait till the day after. It's got me all on edge."

He certainly sounded it. "What has?"

"You haven't heard? No, I don't suppose you have."

"Heard what, Cully?"

"Max Kaufmann: he's dead!"

-6-

SINCLAIR HAD ARRIVED at the Homeyard building early the next morning, only to be told that Cully was not in residence. Evidently a chauffeur-driven car had been summoned during the night and nobody knew where he'd gone or for how long.

The heavy he spoke with, who knew Sinclair by reputation and was more than willing to chat, seemed genuine in his lack of knowledge regarding his boss, but was more forthcoming with gossip regarding Max Kaufmann.

"Okay guy, was Maxie; friendly enough, good worker. He only got married a year ago. I expect Mr Homeyard will make sure the widow is taken care of financially."

Yes, Cully would certainly see to that. "What did Max die of?" asked Sinclair. "I heard he was dead but I don't know any details."

"Heart attack brought on by extreme misuse of anabolic steroids. The cremation will be later this week."

"That's quick! Aren't there formalities?"

"All employees are patients of the company doctor, A Doctor McGlade, who I assume has supplied the death certificate and smoothed the way. It's best to get these things over and done with as soon as possible."

And with undue haste, thought Sinclair, but kept it to himself. "I never tagged Max as a bodybuilder," he said aloud.

"Sort of goes with the territory. Don't do it myself, but a lot of the guys feel a need for bigger and better muscles."

"I guess so…"

Back at his hotel, later, Sinclair mulled over the pieces of irrelevant information he had gleaned from the bonehead back at Cully's place. Providing medical care was something a benevolent employer would offer; the existence of this Doctor McGlade wasn't a shock in itself. The same with steroid abuse, a common enough practise among people employed in the security sector. Max, recently married had been a surprise of sorts; but that was because you didn't think in terms of these people having private lives. Mrs Monica Kaufmann, widow – the idea seemed almost preposterous, but why?

Taken in isolation, there was nothing particularly suspicious about the man's death, but Sinclair had to factor in his own involvement. He had asked Max to keep his eyes open in relation to any problems Cully might be having. Then Max had phoned requesting a meeting, but had apparently died before making the second call.

It was enough to set his personal antenna twitching. If only he had not been tied up with the boxer when Max had first contacted him.

Sinclair knew that there was something not right in the mix, but what he had was too flimsy and insubstantial. Little more than intuition really; so, after a time spinning in unanswered circles he was not sorry to be interrupted by a call from an irate Tibori Angstrom.

"The fight is off!" he stormed.

"Off! How come?"

"That ingrate Faustino Bacca, after all I've done to further his career, has only gone and dislocated his left shoulder during training."

"How badly?"

"Severe. The doctor says it requires surgery."

"Tough. I take it Dandridge has been told?"

"That's the promotor's job but I would assume so," snarled Angstrom. "Look, Arthur, go and see the Britisher again. I don't want him getting beat by anyone else until we know the score on Bacca's career. The

Milan bill is cancelled but tell him he will be offered some easy six and eight round fights in European promotions in order for him to boast an unbeaten run in the event of the Bacca fight being rescheduled. In the meantime, I will continue to hold his gambling debts. The promoter will make a generous payment towards his wasted training expenses. Just make sure he realises he remains in our pocket."

"Will do."

"You're a good lad, Arthur. Your sainted mother would be so pleased at us working together."

My mother, the blessed Margaret, thought Sinclair ruefully, with her weakness for murderous gangster hoodlums. He thought it best to make no comment.

"I hear that one of Homeyard's men has died rather suddenly," continued Angstrom. "Someone who worked for us in the past."

"Max Kaufmann," confirmed Sinclair.

"Any connection to your business with the so-called singer?"

"Cully has shut himself away and I still don't know why he sent for me in the first place. Something is wrong though, that much is clear."

"Watch your step, Arthur."

"Always, Tibori."

-7-

SINCE DANDRIDGE WAS no longer in training for a specific fight Sinclair was able to meet him in a pub. "You can't beat a British pint," he said. "Italian beer is like gnat's piss. I have to stick with imported bottled stuff over there."

They both drank, replacing half-empty glasses on the table they sat at. "Bad luck for Bacca," said the boxer.

"Maybe but it won't do you any harm in the long

run, Mikey."

"Apart from now being owned by the Mafia, or whatever they call themselves these days."

"Boxing has always attracted criminal elements. They carried old Primo Carnera all the way to the heavyweight title, so it's claimed."

"Until he met Max Baer."

"Primo showed real guts though – knocked down eleven times while he was hammered in eleven rounds."

Both men were quiet for a moment, contemplating the savage beating given and taken in that old-time championship clash. Then: "Switching to a different Max," said Sinclair, "did you come across Max Kaufmann when working with the Homeyard group?"

"Yes." Dandridge nodded. "Okay sort of guy. He and a couple of others signed up for a keep-fit course run by Lenny Stein, my trainer-come-manager."

"You would have seen him at the gym, and in the showers?"

"I guess so…"

"Look, this might sound slightly oddball…" Sinclair hoped he could word the question sufficiently delicately not to offend "…but did you ever notice anything unusual about his balls?"

"What?" The boxer was halfway between being amused and insulted.

"Max Kaufmann died from a heart attack brought on by supposed steroid misuse, one of the symptoms of which is shrunken testicles. I'm not saying you take special note of men's bollocks but you probably wouldn't fail to notice someone lacking in that particular department."

"Since I can bring nothing to mind I can only assume

Max was pretty standard in that respect. He's dead though, you say? Heart attack and steroids? That is a shock. He didn't strike me as the type who would go in for that sort of nonsense."

"Nor me, to be honest." He continued, telling Dandridge about the second phone call Kaufmann had failed to make.

"You're going to be looking into this aren't you?" suggested the boxer.

"I'll probably dig around a little," Sinclair agreed.

"If you need a hand with anything, well I'm at something of a loose end at the moment."

"I'll keep that very much in mind, Mikey."

-8-

THE NEXT WEEK did little to resolve anything for Sinclair. He checked by phone daily, but Cully remained absent and his whereabouts continued to be unknown. Maybe the singer would turn up for his employee's funeral, he thought, but that didn't happen either.

Poor Max. He wasn't given much of a send-off. Along with the widow, whose grief did appear genuine, and a sprinkling of neighbours and non-work friends, there were only a few colleagues from the Homeyard Organisation plus Sinclair himself and Mikey Dandridge. The boxer, though he had not known Kaufmann that well, tagged along out of general interest.

In spite of the bad blood between them, brought about by the man's previous thieving, it did seem that Max had indeed straightened out his life, as he claimed when he had talked to Sinclair in the lift. Cully was a satisfied employer; Mikey Dandridge had found him okay to deal with; and Mrs Kaufmann was devastated.

A few days after seeing her at the crematorium, Sinclair called on the widow. He could not help but harbour doubts about the steroid claims and wanted her view on the official cause of death. Luckily, she too found it hard to believe so he was able to broach the subject openly. Monica Kaufmann had not noticed any mood swings and claimed that Max had suffered no erectile dysfunction, another symptom often associated with steroid misuse. She also pointed out that her husband disliked needles to such an extent that he would try and dodge any medical that might involve having to give a blood sample. She also confirmed that the Homeyard Group paid for the funeral and had been more than generous with a cheque in her name.

He had no actual proof, but the more Sinclair picked up on, the more uneasy he became. For instance, the steroid connection was beginning to look unlikely, in which case maybe the heart attack diagnosis was dodgy too. Was he thinking that Max's death might not have been due to natural causes? And did *unnatural* equal *murder*? Had Kaufmann discovered something worth being silenced for? Permanently!

The phone rang and he lifted it. "Sinclair!"

"Art, it's Cully."

"Where the hell are you, man? What's going on?"

"I know, I know, unforgiveable…" but he sounded more on edge than sorry "…I should never have involved you, Art. Go back to Rome. There's talk of a world tour next year. Maybe you would like a slice of the action…"

"Never mind next year," snapped Sinclair, "it's here and now I'm concerned with." He could hear a faint voice while he was speaking, someone besides Cully, who was talking to the singer at the same time. "Who is that?" he demanded. "Who's with you?"

"Nobody."

"I heard a voice!"

All Sinclair could hear now were noises of what seemed to be a scuffle, no words, followed by what sounded like Cully muttering something about a doctor. Then a new voice came on the line, not Cully's, a deeper more guttural sounding voice.

"Mr Sinclair," said the newcomer, "you really must take your friend's advice. Mr Homeyard is in no trouble; but he is mentally fatigued and is undertaking rest and meditation. He intends to remain incognito for now but promises to renew communication as soon as he feels able to."

"Put Cully back on, now!"

"Return to your life in Italy, Mr Sinclair," said the stranger, and the line went dead.

-9-

WHEN HE HAD first arrived in London, Sinclair made a curtesy call to Brian Hannigan, Tibori Angstrom's man in the UK. Now he called him again. Cully had used the word "doctor" when arguing with whoever had been with him during the phone call. Sinclair already had a Doctor McGlade figured as the Homeyard Organisation's Company doctor, so was hoping two plus two would not equal five. Hannigan said to sit tight and he would dig up whatever was known, which he did.

Donald Randolph McGlade, aged fifty and single, had never worked as a GP nor been employed anywhere within the NHS. He had gone straight into private practise upon qualification and there he had remained, adding a role with the Homeyard Group only a year before. As well as his London surgery, which he lived above, he owned a ten-bed rest home at a separate address, but which was currently mothballed.

Thank you, Brian Hannigan.

"That's the quick version, Art. Do you want me to dig deeper?"

"No thanks, Brian. That should do me."

Rather than let Hannigan supply backup, which the man also offered, Sinclair called in Mikey Dandridge to increase the muscle quota. The boxer was keen, might well be useful, and Art didn't want the Angstrom organisation too deeply involved with Cully's affairs.

"What I am suggesting, Mikey, is quite definitely illegal and might even turn nasty."

"So?" The boxer shrugged. "I've already agreed to throw a fight. Another misdemeanour or two won't matter either way."

"As long as you're sure—"

If this McGlade was holding Cully, either willingly or not, and Sinclair realised both were possibilities, then the mothballed rest home was a likely location. But would it be best to simply march up the drive and knock the front door, or jump the surrounding wall and engineer a more secretive method of entry? The latter seemed best. An element of surprise might be of use if any heavy-duty security was around.

Sinclair couldn't supress a tingle of anticipation, nor wanted to.

-10-

THE TWO GUARDS patrolling the grounds had been expertly dealt with. Both, when they woke, would find themselves bound, gagged, and out of the loop. Sinclair and Dandridge had jemmied a suitable window and gained entry into the building. Moving from the room, they edged into a darkened hall.

As a gang-lord's step-son who was being quietly

groomed to one day inherit the top job, Sinclair was well accustomed to the illegalities of criminal behaviour. Dandridge, though, was experiencing a high-octane buzz, this the boxer's first-ever slice of breaking and entering. Nervous tension crackled within him.

A faint murmur of voices could be heard from above and the two men quietly mounted a wide staircase. Stepping into a corridor they moved from door to door, letting the chatter of conversation guide them until they stood outside a room from within which they could hear what was being said.

"…too far. I didn't expect all this!" said a voice.

"That's Cully," hissed Sinclair to his companion.

"Nor me," said someone Sinclair did not recognise. "I want no more to do with any of it."

"Quiet, the pair of you!" This third person sounded like the man who had interrupted his phone conversation with Cully, who Sinclair assumed to be Doctor McGlade. "It's too late for cold feet now. Every-thing will proceed as planned."

"I won't do it!" exclaimed Cully, his voice raw with panic. "End of this; end of that! It's all gone too far."

The rest of the building was silent and there appeared no reason to wait any longer. "Ready?" asked Sinclair, taking a pistol from his pocket. The boxer nodded grimly, and followed as Sinclair swung open the door and rushed into the room.

Cully Homeyard stood at the centre of a painted hexagram and the only other person was a short bespectacled man who crouched in a corner.

Where was the third?

"Art!"

"It's okay, Cully. Where's the other one?"

"He's bad, Art, from the bottomless pit. We thought

we could control him…"

"What the hell is going on?" asked Dandridge.

The man in the corner started to laugh hysterically. "Hell indeed," he babbled, and his laughter turned to tears.

Sinclair could not take his eyes off Cully though, because as he looked his friend was changing. His eyes became steely, his chin jutted, dark lines etched his forehead, and the missing man's voice spoke through cruel lips. "I am Apollyon the Destroyer, Locust King, and I will not be denied…"

Cully's face seemed to blur for a moment, then realigned to that of the man Sinclair knew of old. "I'm trying to fight him, Art, but he's too strong…" His face changed again.

"Much too strong, and soon I will have taken over this body completely and be free of this symbol."

"Until he does he's bound by the hexagram," shouted the man in the corner.

Cully Homeyard had looked long and hard for a spirituality he could feel comfortable with, toying with various religions and beliefs over the years. It was no surprise to Sinclair that he had finally turned to the darker side: the occult, black magic, voodoo, whatever. What was a shock was the form it seemed to have taken: two-entities-sharing-the-same-body nonsense. How could he save Cully from himself?

Knowing full well he wouldn't use it on his friend, he nevertheless made a great show of pointing the revolver. Whenever Sinclair was faced with a choice his natural inclination was always to act. "Step out from there, Cully," he instructed.

The only weapon on view was the one Sinclair held. There was no other gun. Yet, with an explosive blast, half Sinclair's head, his face, disintegrated and disappeared in a crazy mix of jagged bone and flesh. His body dropped to the floor, his rib cage burst open scattering pieces of organs in a terrible confusion of blood and gore.

Mikey Dandridge watched mesmerised as what was left of Sinclair's dark skin and blond hair vanished under an oozing scarlet flow. Slowly, he dragged his gaze away from the corpse and towards the man in the hexagram.

"Art…!" cried Cully, fighting hard to control his own mind.

With a growl that started in the back of his throat and emerged as a roar of pain and horror, Dandridge stepped forward and hit Homeyard twice. The singer dropped, unconscious, offering no resistance as the boxer grabbed his head and twisted, breaking his neck.

The man in the corner screamed wordlessly as he watched a glistening insect crawl from Homeyard's dead mouth and fly purposefully at Mikey Dandridge's face. The boxer, in turn, felt his mind torn into raw and painful strips as the creature dissolved into him.

At that moment three men burst into the room, part of a team Brian Hannigan had organised to shadow Art Sinclair for as long as he remained in the UK. His boss's step-son warranted special treatment. They had decided to forget discretion and follow Sinclair into the rest home in case he needed assistance.

Dandridge, eyes bulging insanely as he fought for mastery of his own mind, took an aggressive step towards the newcomers, who themselves were shocked and trigger-happy at what they saw in the room. A volley rang out and Dandridge died in a hail of bullets. One of the men then fired at a large insect that appeared on the shot man's face.

"That looked like a big fucking locust!"

The two guards who had been gagged and tied earlier were dealt with execution-style and their bodies added to the room's carnage. The one survivor was removed from the corner where he still grovelled and was taken with them when they left. The building itself was torched. Let the authorities make of it what they will.

-11-

TIBORI ANGSTROM SAT in his hilltop citadel and brooded. Arthur Sinclair, child of his beloved Margaret, was dead. Torn from him by that fool Homeyard, who he wished had survived so that he could have killed him himself.

There had been other deaths, of course. Angstrom had insisted that Brian Hannigan execute the three men who had fired the building where Arthur had died. Their failure had been in not bringing out his body first and therefore depriving him of a proper burial.

The one person who had survived, a Doctor McGlade, had been of little use, jabbering about evocation rites going wrong and a Locust King from the pits of hell. Angstrom gave no credence to any of it, especially the part about two minds battling for one body. He preferred to put that down to insanity.

McGlade had been disposed of and his remains would never be found.

Locusts! Angstrom snorted angrily. His organisation, his private army, would sweep around the world devouring everything, just like locusts did in nature. The world had deprived him of the only two people he had ever cared for…

And the world was going to pay…

EVEN THE KLIN

SCATTERED THROUGHOUT WALES there are still a number of concealed churches surviving to this day. Places either hidden or so difficult to get to that they escaped the Puritan reformers of the seventeenth century, the well-meaning Victorian restorers, and the anti-religion pogroms of the Klin.

The same was true elsewhere of course. The Klin had not destroyed every single place of worship on the whole planet. Just most of them, and very few people had any interest in those that remained anyway. It was all so long ago.

Ben Davey huffed and puffed, glad his long walk was over, though he would have to make the return journey later. He had left Abergavenny that morning, initially in his electro run-around, which he'd parked after a thirteen-kilometre drive, then continued on foot.

A rough and overgrown lane climbed steeply before levelling, passing occasional derelict constructions, cottages and farm buildings at a guess. Soon after he was walking through woodlands, leading to a sharp drop into the valley below where the loudest sound was that of fast-flowing water. Alongside a river bridge were the oddly isolated remains of a building, the origins of which had him stumped.

Over the bridge and eventually right through another abandoned farm, then there it was. In a state of collapse but with enough still surviving for him to have worked out what it had been, and he had even found records confirming it. Partrishow Church, hugging the hillside, hidden, and well off the beaten track. No wonder it had survived, even through the troubled times before the pogroms; but it was redundant now. Anyone still in need of religious relief, and there were some, worshipped the Klin themselves.

BEN DAVEY HAD discovered the spot quite by accident during his teenage years. Always something of a loner, he liked the solitude it offered and enjoyed the feeling of peace he experienced there. It had been somewhere for an occasional visit back then. Now Ben was pushing forty and had been making the trip regularly, every eight weeks, for the past five years. Ever since he had been appointed Contact Manager for the South Wales Complex.

It was a position nobody wanted and few were qualified for. If Ben had been able to, he would have hidden his suitability but that had not been possible. Nothing could be kept out of sight, or out of mind.

It was amazing, in this day and age, to accept that mankind had seen fit to wage a military defence when the Klin had first arrived. Billions of humans died while the invaders lost no one. They hadn't wanted their demands to escalate into actual warfare but having claimed this particular star system for the Klin Empire they weren't going to turn tail and run.

Their superiority had been total.

Once every eight weeks Ben had to endure Contact. The following day he would suffer delirium and vomiting to such an extent he would wish himself dead. The day after that he would be physically easier but still in need of mental cleansing. That was why he came to

Partrishow Church. The hike itself helped sweat any lingering residue from his body and the peaceful solitude of the place calmed his mind.

It hadn't been how those old-time leaders had expected first contact to be. It had been hoped that wise beings from the stars would usher in an age of new enlightenment, not plant their flag and claim the planet as theirs. If Earth had spoken with a single voice then the bloodshed might have been avoided, however reluctant the surrender, but those were still the days of individual nations. A political structure which must have caused chaos.

Ben sat within the shadows of the dilapidated church, letting good vibes source the mental anguish lurking in hidden corners of his mind. Each Manager had his own way of dealing with Contact, and this was his.

Ninety-nine percent of humans could not survive close proximity with the Klin. They erupted into boils and their brains would fry; death was a welcome release. One percent had immunity though it was still a most unpleasant experience. All children were tested and those possessing the survival gene were trained in the ways of Contact.

There was no dodging it.

PARTLY VEILED BY the damaged structure, Ben looked out at a landscape within which he could imagine himself the only survivor of an apocalyptic event. Here, alone, he could dissociate himself from the controlled orthodoxy of the Klin's benevolence, something which was stressed throughout the worldwide education system.

Earth's doomed retaliation against becoming an

outpost in an ever-expanding galactic empire saw the planet itself, already suffering the ravages of ill-use, damaged seemingly beyond repair. In a final act of desperation-tinged madness, mankind had unleashed the accumulated nuclear arsenals of the previously competing nations. None had penetrated the Klin defence but the planet itself had been devastated – and defeated.

The new rulers had gathered the vastly depleted population into safe areas and proceeded to not only put right the immediate conflict-induced damage but also rectify the long-term ills that mankind had ignored for generations. With icecaps refrozen, sea levels dropped, deserts transformed into fertile land, it was little wonder that the Klin themselves were elevated from invaders into saviours.

Earth, in common, it could be assumed, with countless other worlds, was linked in to the Klin's industrial network. Thirty percent of output was geared to home planet consumption and seventy percent to Klin specifications, such produce being collected by automated star freighters at regular intervals.

Being attached to the South Wales Complex, Ben met his Klin supervisor every eight weeks to discuss targets, performance, and any matters arising. Though *met* was probably the wrong word. Nobody had seen any of the Klin in the flesh since the conflict, which was six hundred years in the past now. There were folk tales aplenty concerning their actual appearance, ranging from gigantic ogres to doll-like miniatures, but those assigned to Sol never left the palatial crafts that orbited the system.

Ben, when he entered the specialised chamber, met with a projection that appeared to him like a shining and glittering star. A voice emanating from it conversed with him in standard Earth language, but the physical being rested on a couch in a spaceship. Only Contact Managers could survive even this second-hand communication, and then at a cost.

The Klin had these factory planets dotted throughout space, all providing goods to their specifications. The worlds were well maintained and indigenous populations cared for. It was, well, a safe existence. Too safe, for some. Ben knew there were pockets of dissatisfaction, small groups who met in secret and talked about unworkable plans to free the Earth from what they saw as alien tyranny. He knew because he had once been approached, but had declined.

Ben had enough on his hands with spreadsheets and reports; with raw materials, finished products, achieving targets and quotas. And the eight-weekly meetings with his Klin Supervisor.

HAVING EATEN A packed lunch, he replaced the empty containers and refresher bottle in his rucksack. Ben never left any litter. The unspoilt nature of the site was one of its attractions. This latest meeting, the one he was just recovering from, had gone well. His Complex had matched the increased quota placed upon it and bonus credits had been granted to all employees. His personal two-day recovery period was now drawing to a close and he would be back at his desk tomorrow.

As much as was possible with a mechanically voiced glittering star shape, Ben thought he had a reasonable relationship with his Supervisor, who was currently in the fourth of its ten-year off-world contract. Another six and it would return to the Klin home planet. When Ben had first assumed Contact duties the then Supervisor had been nearing the end of its term of office. The new one had looked no different but there was a slight change in the voice and it had seemed keen that they should work in harmony.

By the time all work related topics had been dealt with, Ben would be starting to experience early bilious sensations, and stomach cramps would not be far away, but the Klin would always want a little non-work-related conversation to end up with. It took some sort of interest in Ben himself, and his life in general. Though none of the Klin ever used names in relation to themselves they used those allotted to their human workforce.

"How goes your life, Ben-jam-in?" The Supervisor always used Ben's name in full, though separating it into three distinct syllables. "Have you acquired a partner yet?" It was a subject of regular interest.

"No," Ben would reply, often with a wry chuckle, "much too busy with the new quotas you keep giving us." His stomach would be beginning to churn and bile would be burning at the back of his throat. Only once had the Supervisor kept him talking long enough for Ben to actually collapse in pain and anguish while still in the chamber. It had learnt from that and had since ended the meetings before that point was reached. Though sometimes only just.

Ben, lifelong loner that he was, had only once met someone he had wanted to sign a personal contract with and she had turned down his offer. As gently as she could, but a no was still a no. Ben often got the impression that his Supervisor would have liked him to have had a relationship to discuss. Klin lifestyles and habits were completely unknown. Ben didn't even know whether his Contact was a male or female, or even if the Klin had gender differences at all. Or if they did, how many!

"YOU HAVE A good world, Ben-jam-in," the Supervisor had told him, "better than many we have acquired."

Ben thought about that as he kept to a steady pace, hiking away from Partrishow Church on his return to where his electro runaround was parked, and he agreed. But history showed what a disjointed and terrible place it had been pre-Klin. Mankind fared better as a subservient race, when not in charge of their own destiny.

He wondered about the growth of anti-Klin cliques, when it was entirely due to the Klin that the planet had been cured of all its old ills. It was still only a tiny minority, of course, but rumour had it that membership of such groups had been growing of late.

Why?

Apart from anything else, it was absolutely pointless. Back when humanity had been both greater in numbers and more aggressive in nature, they had completely failed to inflict even a scratch upon the Klin. Such groups could never be more than a place to let off steam. No real uprising was possible, thank goodness.

Ben shook his head slowly, unable to understand why anyone would want to consider such a possibility. Making himself comfortable, he powered up the runaround and fed in his Cardiff address. It would be back to work for him in the morning.

AS THE CONTACT Manager, Ben Davey had to be aware of every facet of production in each Unit of the South Wales Complex. Departmental Heads might be hands-on, knowing their own segment of operation in detail, but Ben had to have the overall picture at his fingertips in readiness for his bimonthly Contact. So a copy of every report produced landed on his desk and each working day was filled with meetings.

He often had to take unread reports home in order to catch up. How anyone had time to join secret groups, Ben had no idea, but whispers against their Klin overlords seemed on the increase. There were even rumours of open criticism in some parts of the world though nothing like that had happened locally.

Colleagues sometimes asked if their Supervisor ever mentioned that the Klin knew of the growth of these subversive ideas, but Ben gave them short shrift. Even if they were aware, it would mean nothing to them. The Klin were indestructible.

Then, shortly before his next Contact, word came from Up Above, the euphemism for the Klin spaceships, that all production was to cease. Star freighters would be deployed to empty the Warehouse Bays of all stock. New productivity schedules would be forthcoming, but in the meantime to give the whole Complex a thorough overhaul and clean up.

A series of calls confirmed that the message had been worldwide.

Rumours were rife but there were no further instructions. Everybody looked to Ben, expecting him to discover what was going on, as he hoped to himself, at his next Contact.

As WAS NORMAL the Chamber was empty when Ben entered. He placed all the reports brought with him on the single desk and sat on the only chair. The rest of the room was empty.

It started as a slight movement in the air, a distortion which magnified quickly into a riot of twinkling and shimmering light. Like a star, Ben always thought.

"Greetings, Ben-jam-in," said the very formal metallic sounding voice.

"Greetings, Supervisor. All received instructions have been carried out. Where would you like to begin?" asked Ben, getting to his feet and taking hold of the report folder.

"Not on this occasion. I have news to impart. Be seated, Ben-jam-in."

Ben, all ears at this departure from their regular routine, sat as requested.

"We, the Klin," continued the Supervisor's voice from within the glittering mass of light, "do now revoke all claims to this planet. Earth is now yours again…"

"But why?" Ben had jumped to his feet. "What do you mean, ours again?"

"This is a shock, Ben-jam-in, but by what you call tomorrow we will have departed from this section…"

"But why?" Ben repeated, interrupting again. He could feel the colour draining from his face. The Klin had ruled for six hundred years. They couldn't just pack up and leave at a moment's notice!

"Be calm, Ben-jam-in. I have done as instructed and informed you of what is to happen. I will now tell you why, as will all other Supervisors with their Contacts."

"But…"

"No 'buts' Ben-jam-in. Please listen. It is important that you know these things."

Ben tried to calm himself sufficiently to take in what was said, though he could hardly credit what he was being told. "Okay," he muttered.

"We, the Klin, developed space travel sufficiently to enable us to explore and control our galaxy, creating what we thought to be the greatest empire ever known," continued the Supervisor. "We drew all other races into our control, either willingly or by force, but to the eventual benefit of all. Is the planet Earth not the better for our rule?"

"It is, of course," agreed Ben sincerely.

"This galaxy of ours is big enough. Not only were we not able to explore the vastness beyond, we had no interest in doing so either. But we have studied neighbouring galaxies and probed their workings."

This is all becoming too big, worried Ben, hoping he would be able to follow what was being said.

"We have discovered the existence of a new breed of conquering hordes. They call themselves, as near as we can interpret it, Quaaalism. Unlike the Klin they are not interested in incorporating other sentient beings into their realm. Each new planet they reach they cleanse completely of all life. They then adapt the planet as necessary and people it with their own species. Also, unlike us, they have developed inter-galactic travel. We cannot tell where they originated but are spreading from galaxy to galaxy like dust in a high wind."

The Supervisor's voice paused, giving Ben a moment to try and assimilate what he was being told. Then continued. "It is true to say, Ben-jam-in, that the Klin in comparison to this Quaaalism is in similar proportion to humanity as compared to the Klin. They will reach us, Ben-jam-in. The only question is when, and when they do they will destroy all. Unless they can be stopped. To this end we are retreating to a tight knot of planets surrounding our home world. There we will concentrate everything on new technologies of attack and defence in the hope that we can meet the invasion when it comes."

"But what about us?" exploded Ben. "Will you just leave us to be destroyed?"

The star-like visuals seemed to glitter with increased intensity.

"We cannot defend the whole galaxy. It would not be possible. It might be that we cannot even hold out in our home system, but that will give us our best chance of success. If we can defeat them then their plans for dominating the whole universe will be ended."

Which is fine, thought Ben, but if they reach us first then we are destroyed anyway. "How long before any of this happens?" he asked, trying to let his practical side take control.

"We cannot be specific, but not for many of your generations. You will not see it yourself, Ben-jam-in, but it might be that the children of your children's children will face the threat. We are giving both ourselves time to prepare and you also, and other species dotted through our galaxy. This is why we have genetically introduced rebellious and independent streaks into a small percentage of your species."

"You mean you were behind the anti-Klin groups?" Ben was starting to sweat and knew he would soon start to suffer from an overlong Contact; but he needed to learn what he could.

"Of course. They will provide the leadership needed after we depart tomorrow. And you Contact Managers will offer stability and practicality to the new rulers.

"You must go now, Ben-jam-in, before Contact sickness becomes too strong. I have become – what is your emotion for it? I have become fond of you humans. I wish you well. If we succeed, our descendants will one day meet. If we fail, then someone else will have to stop Quaaalism spreading. I think there will always be a more powerful race waiting."

The voice was becoming fainter and the shimmering

light becoming less.

"Wait!" cried Ben. There were still so many questions he wanted to ask, but the star shrunk to a dot and was then extinguished.

The chamber doors slid automatically open and he went through to where the various Section Heads and Departmental Managers were waiting, eager to find out what was going on with the Complex, all hoping he would be able to give them a brief update before Contact sickness laid him low.

Ben Davey stood before them. "It would seem," he said, tasting bile at the back of his throat and knowing the stomach spasms would soon start. "It would seem," he repeated, "that even the Klin are only human…"

HOUSE & LAKE

The house of high ceilings
Stands empty now
The green lake unused

Footprints give hints
But hastily placed
Cameras and tripwires
Reveal nothing

The house crumbles
A place of ghosts
The green lake
A bowl of poisoned water

Nothing moved
Nothing lived
Bar myself
And my pointless surveillance

Hoping to find something
Needing to find nothing

STATIC

At first I dreamt of static
Endless blocks
Rolling
Crackling
No rest and no sense
I woke tired

Gradually words
Faint at first
Breaking up
But getting clearer

The who and the what
The why and the where

We are the dead

There is no heaven
There is no hell
Just Planet X

We are the dead
And we're coming home

I begged for more
But their words were gone

[/continued]

Fading
Fading
Breaking up

Static

DARK LOVE

Gorgon like
You gorged a trail of men
Destroyed
Devoured

You had the power
Knew it
Used it
A puppeteer
Pulling strings

Like skeletons picked bare
Those chosen danced
A strange and weird
Ballet of your making

Spellbound
We blundered on until
Like Perseus
I rose to chop and hack
And hide you in
A secret place.

And still
Medusa's husband
Takes flowers to her grave

DUMMY

The dummy
A teaching aid
Was a private joke

He left it sprawled in an attitude of death
For me to find in that half-light
Where reality and pretence blur at the edges

I scribbled a note: *Goodbye cruel world*
Creating a tableau with my centrepiece
Collapsed with pen in plastic hand

It was when my joking adversary
Was placing a noose around its neck
That the dummy spoke

"No," it told him. "Not me … you!"
Plastic hands reached out
Fingers suddenly supple

MESSAGES FROM

WHAT DID I know about planets? Before I found out about my father's odd behaviour: nothing at all. Music is my bag, not space, and prior to this relatively recent strangeness, Dad had no special interest in the subject either.

Delving into pop history, I knew there had been two different songs titled "Venus". British singer Dickie Valentine and America's Frankie Avelon had battled with their versions of the first song in 1959. The second "Venus" charted three times: Dutch group Shocking Blue in 1970, Britain's Bananarama in 1986 and Don Pablo's Animals, from Italy, in 1990. Add in Mark Wynter's 1962 hit "Venus in Blue Jeans", and the famous Venus de Milo statue, and that was it. In other words, I knew nothing about the planet.

Then I found out my father claimed to be its representative on Earth.

Well, sort of…

WINTER HAD SUPPOSEDLY moved into spring when a message had me driving back to the town of my birth. A bleak and unfriendly place even when a busy industrial hub, which had worsened when the steelworks closed and unemployment had gripped the area in a bitter embrace. Not a good place for someone whose musical ambitions stretched far beyond the gobby punk limitations I'd grown up with.

Dad and I spoke on the phone at least once a week and he would visit me a couple of times a year. Once it had been the two of them but my mother had gone to her rest six long years before. It had been a phone call that had summoned me into this particular homecoming.

"Hello? Dan Jacob speaking."

"Dan? Danny? This is Arthur Hemmimgs. I live two doors from your father."

"Of course, Mr Hemmings," I responded, knowing full well that this was likely to be a bad news call. "How are you doing?"

"I'm fine, Danny. It's your father, he's in hospital…"

The long and the short of it was that Dad had suffered a stroke and if I wanted to see him before he died I had better hightail it there pretty damn quick. I called the hospital and had Mr Hemmings' account verified. Yes, someone confirmed, his lasting was being considered in hours rather than days. A few more calls put my life on temporary hold and then I set off.

It was cold and damp with a bitter wind blowing as I hurried from the car park to the entrance of the old King George Hospital. The seriousness of his condition ensured I would be admitted at whatever time I arrived and could stay as long as I wanted.

Though everything I'd been told should have prepared me for the worst, it was nevertheless something of a shock when I entered the small room leading off the main ward and saw him for the first time. Dad, ghostly white and unmoving, was attached to an array of medical paraphernalia. There were normal hospital noises drifting in from outside but within that small room there was only the beep and hiss of the mechanical aids.

"Dad?" I asked quietly even though I'd been told he was not conscious. My voice was out of place, almost like an intrusion.

There was no response.

"Dad?" I repeated a little louder. "It's Danny! I'm here now, Dad. For as long as it takes."

I had read of cases where supposedly unconscious people had known what was happening around them. So though Dad showed no sign of having heard me, or even being aware of my presence, I stroked his cold hand and spoke occasionally. Just on the off-chance that some sort of internal awareness might record that his son was with him.

Later, having been assured that there were no signs of any immediate change in his condition, though that could not be guaranteed of course, I made my way to the little terraced house where I had spent the formative years of my life. The hospital had both the house landline and my mobile numbers and would ring if need be. After switching on the living room's coal-effect electric fire, hoping it would at least reduce the chill, I went back out and rang the bell two doors away.

"Ah, Danny," said Mr Hemmimgs. "You made it then."

"Of course. I just wanted to thank you for letting me know."

"It's why I had your number. Your father asked me to let you know if anything ever happened to him. Have you been to the King George yet?"

"Yes," I replied, nodding. "I sat with him for a spell. I'm just checking the house now, maybe have a bite to eat, then go back in."

"I've just put the kettle on," said Mr Hemmings, opening the door wider and stepping to the side.

"Come on in and have a cuppa. There is something I think I should mention, about your dad."

IN THIS WAY I learned that my father had developed a strange fixation with Venus. I would not have guessed he even knew the planet's name let alone become interested in it.

"Ted got me to Google it and print off every scrap I could find," Mr Hemmings told me.

"Huh!" I snorted. "I wanted to buy him a computer but he wouldn't let me."

"You'll find a folder somewhere in the house, full of everything Venus related he could get his hands on."

We both sipped our hot teas. His, I'd noticed, well sugared. Mine, with an eye on my waistline, unsweetened. "He never told you what sparked this sudden interest?"

"No, afraid not."

I let the conversation drift into generalities and once my cup was empty I refused the offer of a refill and made my excuses. Back at Dad's house I heated a tin of soup in the microwave he had let me buy him, and after that made my way back to the hospital. I would look for the Venus folder some other time.

IT HAD BEEN a severe stroke, a doctor told me, and though they were doing all they could the prognosis was not good. To put it bluntly, my father was not expected to survive. It was possible he might drift on for a little while longer but the end could come at any moment. I guessed, though, that if he didn't die naturally it would eventually be suggested that his life support be turned off, a decision I would be expected to make. But could I?

It must have shown on my face.

"Don't worry, Danny."

He was still lying there, still joined to a variety of medical equipment, but his eyes were open and looking straight at me. "Dad!" I gasped. "Shall I get a nurse? Call a doctor?"

"Just listen to me, son. I have to try and tell you about where I go, and what I see…"

Bloody hell! I thought. Was this a miracle or what?

"I walk through a dry and desolate desert, passed large slab-like rock formations. I see evidence of volcanic activity…"

"Where?" I asked, surprised at his firm and clear voice, and wondering if I really should be reporting his sudden improvement to the nursing staff.

"Venus." He replied, bringing back Mr Hemmings words to me, and this from a man who would not even cross the channel and visit France.

"Nobody has been to Venus yet," I shot back at him. That much I did know.

"Not physically, lad. Of course not! The atmospheric pressure would crush me like a burst balloon. But, how shall I put it? Mentally, spiritually, in ways I would have previously considered mumbo jumbo and half-cocked nonsense. So the pressure, heat and carbon dioxide do me no harm."

Never mind the stroke, my father had obviously suffered some sort of breakdown. "I must get someone," I decided, backing towards the door.

"Hang on, Danny! Let me finish…"

But I was out of the small room and rushing to find a nurse. She, not unexpectedly, was surprised at what I told her and hurried with me to see for herself. Dad, eyes closed again, was as unresponsive as he had been since his initial collapse. She checked the machines and studied whatever information they processed. She checked Dad himself, finding no indication he had even been awake let alone speaking.

"You may have been mistaken," she suggested diplomatically. "There can be wheezing noises from the throat area. Even the machines make odd sounds at times."

"I can assure you..." I started to say but I could see the disbelief on the nurse's face, and when coupled with Dad's return to a coma-like situation I felt a sense of doubt myself. Maybe I had nodded off momentarily. Maybe it had been nothing but a dream. "It seemed so real," I finished lamely.

"Your father seems quite stable at the moment," she said, "and you are under a lot of stress, Mr Jacob. Why don't you go and get some rest? We'll call you if there is any change."

It seemed like a good idea.

POKING AROUND, BACK at the house, I soon found the Venus folder. Scientific papers, photographs, tabloid pieces on various crank connections; all indications of my father's interest but offering no explanation as to what had prompted it in the first place. At least it confirmed what Mr Hemmings had told me and I now knew where Dad got his odd bits of information. I personally could not have even made a guess at anything about the planet, so maybe I had not dreamt it. Maybe my father really had opened his eyes and spoke.

I rang Bernie after putting the folder aside. Bernie Lipton, head guy and owner at Triple D Records: Deep Down & Dirty, and you'd better believe it. I was a producer, songwriter, and general dogsbody with the company and had been due to oversee a session with a visiting American veteran bluesman. Bernie would either have to postpone the recording or get another producer in to take my place. His choice.

"Okay, kiddo, leave it with me," boomed Bernie.

"Sorry to drop you in it like this."

"Not your fault, Dan. I'll let you know what we decide and you keep me up to speed about your old man. Okay, amigo?"

"Okay, Bernie. Thanks for that."

THE NEXT DAY, back at the King George, I sat with my unconscious father. The doctor's round had already taken place and I stretched my legs when the bed linen was being changed. Back in his room I stood to one side when the regular BP and temperature checks were carried out, sitting back down when the nurse wheeled her apparatus trolley away.

"Right, lad," said my father. "With any luck we should be free from interruptions for a bit."

I knew I hadn't been dreaming before!

"What the fuck is going on?" I demanded.

"Language, Daniel!"

"Sorry, Dad." I felt twelve years old again. "But what is going on?"

"I was contacted by Venusian entities, son, a couple of months ago. Not in person of course. They didn't knock the door. It's all done by telepathy."

"Telepathy!" I managed to say, spluttering over the word.

"I know this must be difficult for you, Danny."

Difficult? Impossible would have been a more accurate word.

"I found it hard to accept myself, at first," he continued. "There have been others before me making similar claims. Some were charlatans, no better than criminals. Others were earlier contacts, individuals who collapsed under the volume of incoming knowledge. The Venusians had learnt a little each time so that when it came to me there was no mental breakdown. Instead, sadly, my physical frailty was such that I couldn't stand the shock of it all, leading to my stroke."

"Dad!" I shouted, interrupting him. None of this gobbledegook mattered. There was only one thing I needed to know. "Does this mean you are going to recover?"

It was as I spoke that I realised that only his eyes showed any signs of life. The rest of him remained unmoving, including his mouth, though his words continued to echo through my mind.

"I see it's striking home, Danny. That's good. I want you to understand. As to your question: no I'm not going to recover. If truth be told I should already be dead. The Venusians are keeping me alive for purposes of their own but their powers are not godlike and at some stage their control will fail."

"But Dad!" This was madness. "You want me to understand but I don't—"

"Everything alright?" asked a nurse entering the room.

My father's eyes had closed again and he had withdrawn from my mind, just another stroke victim barely hanging on. "Yes thanks," I replied bleakly. "As much as it can be."

It was a pattern we continued to repeat. Alone we could communicate but he reverted to his unconscious state as soon as we were interrupted.

OF THOSE WHO had publicly declared similar contact, my father told me, George Adamski had at least been genuine but his mind had cracked under the strain. Though correct in claiming that Venusians lived underground on their planet, he got little else correct. Orthon, the blond and tanned humanoid he met with, was a figment of his imagination, dreamt up when he couldn't accept the true physical nature of the beings he was in communication with.

Howard Menger, on the other hand, was merely a trickster looking for an angle. His "space brothers" were pure fabrication.

"But what is the purpose of it all?" I asked.

"I don't really know, lad. I think they are reaching out to Earth, through me currently. I assume I am some sort of channel but I don't know why."

Then there were the Venusians themselves. Existing under such extreme conditions, they had to be very different from us Earthlings, but my father was no help there.

"They enter my head the way I enter yours," he told me. "They've let me see the surface of Venus through their eyes but not underground where they live. I have never seen one of them."

HOW ALL THIS was achieved, or what it meant, was an absolute mystery. Yet, strange as it most definitely was, it had produced an extended timeline between my father and me, and for that I was grateful.

The hospital staff, however, were quite frankly bemused. Happily so since their patient was surviving beyond expectations, but bemused just the same. I had rushed down because Dad was only thought to have hours left and days later he was still alive. The doctors were scratching their heads but I could hardly tell them it was all down to interplanetary intervention. He wasn't improving but he wasn't deteriorating either.

A situation that was about to change.

I WAS SITTING in his small room, waiting for his eyes to open. I was convinced by then that all he told me was true. Where it was leading and what the Venusians intentions were, I had no idea. Neither did Dad but for now that didn't matter. This extra period of communication between us was sufficient in itself.

Then suddenly: "No! No!" His voice was screaming through my brain, full of fear and panic, repeating that one word over and over. I threw myself hard against the backrest of the chair, gripping my head as I tried to blot out the awful anguish.

I wish I could have looked away and not seen that his whole appearance was changing. His eyes bulged – seeing God knew what – while the rest of him started to shimmer, blurring at the edges, until it was no longer my father on that hospital bed.

My first horrifying impression was that Dad had been replaced by gnarled tree trunk, glistening and bark -like, oozing greasily from a multitude of cracks that covered its exterior. Fleshy-looking tendrils waved from top and bottom. A harsh sounding squeal filled the room.

I knocked over my chair as I scrambled to me feet, intent on trying to move as far away as possible from this monstrosity. As I did a nurse, probably summoned be the noise, rushed in, halting when she saw the thing.

"What the f—!" she managed to gasp before the tendrils snaked out, encircling and capturing her. I watched, paralyzed with fear, as she was lifted onto that trunk-like body, her screams fading as she was dissolved into those hundreds of cracks.

That was when I fainted.

BY THE TIME other members of the staff entered the room, I discovered later, Dad was back on the bed. Just his body because, yes, he was dead. It was assumed that the shock of his dying had caused me to faint. Nobody else had seen the Venusian, if that had been what it was. Nor had anyone seen the nurse enter the room and it was not until later that her absence was realised and investigated. I knew better than to volunteer any information. The police did speak to me as I had been on the ward when she had last been seen, but they didn't expect me to know anything and I did not disappoint them.

I placed Dad's Venus folder in the coffin with him, consigning both to the crematorium flames. I put his little terraced house in the hands of a local estate agent and said my goodbyes to Mr Hemmings. I returned to London and my work at Triple D Records, trying hard to convince myself that none of the Venus stuff really happened.

TROUBLE IS, I'VE started having these dreams. I walk alone through a dry desert-like, terrible landscape. I pass large slabs of rock while heavy clouds gather overhead and everything shimmers with a heat I cannot feel. I wake sweating and my mind in a panic. These dreams are becoming more vivid – and more often. I dread going to sleep and I know, with an awful certainty, that the messages will start soon.

TRUMPET INVOLUNTARY

THERE WERE LEGAL twists on offer, designed to heighten perception and sharpen the senses, but Gerry Armitage had decided against using any this evening. He would definitely not be blurring the edges of reality with illegal substances either. No, this was going to be historic, and he wanted to experience it without any artificial enhancement.

"Are they really dead?" asked Bette for what seemed like the thousandth time. "Are you sure they are not just impersonators?"

"Yes, they are dead. No, they are not impersonators."

When Bette got a bee in her bonnet, it took some shifting, as he knew from experience. She was convinced that tonight's concert would turn out to be a succession of tribute acts. Good, maybe, but copies just the same.

Gerry smiled inwardly while she tut-tutted her disbelief. Bette dabbled in interior design, which meant their apartment was an absolute picture; but she existed in something of a bubble, protected and pampered to a certain degree. He, though, was out in the daily cut-and-thrust of the city financial institutions, earning the big bucks that kept them in luxury. Being more worldly, Gerry was better able to accept the advances made in DNA techniques. That didn't mean he understood them, just that he didn't discount them as fairy tales.

This evening's concert was being billed as THE TRUMPET IN JAZZ. A star-studded band from all around the world would perform with guest appearances by Louis Armstrong, Roy Eldridge, Dizzy Gillespie, Miles Davis, Chet Baker and Maynard Ferguson. Initially it had been the promoter's intention to include a Special Surprise Guest, which would have been Buddy Bolden; sometimes known as the King of New Orleans, an unheard but legendary figure in the history of jazz development. Unfortunately, though he was said to be buried in an unmarked grave at the Holt Cemetery in New Orleans, the resting place could not be confirmed. So: no body, no DNA, no reconstruction.

"Dead is dead," muttered Bette.

IF YOU DEVELOP the means to do something, someone will surely do it. DNA, extracted from the dead, could be speed-developed in vats of life-enhancing nutrients with the timer set for the person, newly formed, to emerge at whatever age it had been decided best suited that particular subject. Just imagine: Winston Churchill, John F Kennedy, Nelson Mandela, all at the height of their powers, combining to offer solutions to world problems; William Shakespeare writing a Second Folio; Marilyn Monroe finally confirming which of the many theories concerning her death was correct. The possibilities were never ending.

Gerry Armitage, mixing as he did with the rich and powerful, heard all the rumours. The political giants provided no international insights. The Bard of Avon ignored the specially prepared quill. Even though all were medically considered to be fully operational, none of them would speak. Not a word. They ate, drank, performed the usual bodily functions, but wanted to do nothing more than sit in silence and stare at the horizon, or a wall.

"It's just science fiction hogwash," declared Bette, her mind made up.

The one exception turned out to be musicians. Though they too refused to speak, or write, or paint, they would play their instruments. THE TRUMPET IN JAZZ would mark the debut appearance of any of the reconstructed dead in public. Already a commercial bonanza, sell-out tickets were being sought at astronomical prices. The show was scheduled to tour the world, with follow-up concerts featuring a variety of other instruments already being planned: nineteen twenties/thirties star Frankie Trumbauer on his C-melody saxophone alongside altoists Johnny Hodges, Charlie Parker, Julian Adderley, Paul Desmond and Joe Harriot. What a line-up!

"Frankie who?" asked Bette, with studied in-difference.

"YOU'VE DECIDED what?" Gerry was beside himself – if not with anger, then definitely with annoyance. "You can't just make a last-minute decision like that!"

"I'm sorry Gerry, but my mind is made up."

They were so well suited, generally. Smart without being nerdy, intelligent without being academic, attractive without having to depend on over-glamorisation. At least that was how they saw them-selves. They knew the right people, were invited to the best parties, and were part of the *In Crowd*. Gerry loved Bette and had every intention of broaching the twin subjects of marriage and children as they moved further into their thirties, but she could be both stubborn and annoying at times.

"Do you know how difficult those tickets were to get hold of? And what they cost?"

Bette shrugged, waving an elegantly dismissive hand. "You know I've not been keen," she said. "I'm not going, and that's that."

It wasn't the money. Hell, even at this late hour Gerry could turn on his computer and make a tidy profit. Tickets for this show were like gold dust. He would still go himself, but Bette knew how much he disliked going to something like this unaccompanied. Comparing notes afterwards was often as much fun as the event itself.

"You're just being childish," he snapped.

"For goodness sake, Gerry, I simply don't want to go. If I'm right then it is all make-believe and mimicry, and I'm not enough of a jazz fan to want to spend an evening listening to copycats."

"But it has been scientifically and medically confirmed as genuine. They are the real thing!"

"Which would actually make it even worse."

"Worse? How?"

"Dead things! Zombies! Playing trumpets!"

When Bette started speaking in exclamation marks Gerry knew he was beaten. He put the ticket up for sale and quickly got twice what he'd paid, which itself had been well over the face value. Everyone wanted to be there for this first public appearance. Everyone, that is, except Bette.

THOUGH IT STILL rankled that he was there alone, Gerry was too enthralled by the sheer audacity of it all to let it spoil the thrill of anticipation he was feeling. He even chatted to the elderly gent sat in what would have been Bette's seat, finding out that the ticket had changed hands another twice after he had sold it, and for ever increasing sums.

"The money is immaterial," said the old chap. "This is history in the making."

Gerry had just enough time to murmur an agreement before the auditorium lights dimmed and the stage curtains opened.

"Did you know," continued the chatty pensioner, "that they refused to rehearse?"

"The dead guys?"

"That's who. I've heard whispers. The house band is having to leave spaces for their solos. Sort of hoping for the best, I guess."

Some *house band* though, thought Gerry, a gathering of top living musicians from all around the globe. Everybody wanted a slice of tonight's action. It was a fifty-strong ensemble that included a string section. Even larger than Stan Kenton's early nineteen fifties Innovations Orchestra, which should at least make Maynard Ferguson feel at home.

A band this size, he realised, while capable of massive volume and highly structured arrangements, could also fragment into whatever backing requirements were needed for the star turns. And there they were, the centre of attention, summoned on stage by the eminent jazz critic who was acting as commentator for the evening.

They shuffled into view slowly, each seemingly a parody of the others. They looked to neither left nor right, only straight ahead, focussed on something out and beyond. Gerry suppressed a shudder, bringing to mind Bette's use of the word *zombies* in her dismissal of the whole event.

The six of them sat on chairs at the side of the stage.

The orchestra would play, it was explained, with open-ended invitations worked into the scores which would hopefully entice the trumpeters into the spotlight. And if this did not happen, an orchestra member would fill in with a solo. The whole performance would be seamless and the audience was in for an absolute treat. So it was hoped.

The six men sat, apparently unresponsive, showing no awareness of either the audience or the occasion. They could have been in a barbershop waiting their turn for a trim.

Was the whole thing going to be a complete dud?

Gerry was convinced that everyone present was holding their breath, as he seemed to be doing himself. Waiting on tenterhooks, on edge; eager to hear that first blast of brass back from the grave.

Two numbers in, Louis Armstrong stood and lifted his horn.

THOUGH IT WAS claimed that those regrown retained the memory of their whole lives, their chosen physicality was aimed at a snapshot in time that encapsulated their burgeoning artistry. The Louis Armstrong who stood up was as he had been at twenty-five, when his Hot Fives and Sevens were recording music that changed the concept of what jazz was about.

But, to quote the title from one of the many albums he had issued during his long career, this was no *Laughin' Louis*. Not even a smile, yet the blank bodily disinterest he projected paled into insignificance when he started to play. The audience, like a fully choreographed assembly, had been sitting forward, brimming with eager anticipation. Those first few notes, however, speared expectation, squeezed air from lungs, knocked everybody into the backrest of their seats.

All the Armstrong technique was there: his range, structure, fierce attack, astonishing volume; all characteristics of the audacity with which he had transformed jazz into a soloist's platform. It was spot on, great ... too great!

Gerry gasped for air as he realised he had been holding his breath.

The trumpet ran the full gamut of ideas, full of intriguing sub-plots and soaring statements; but it was cold and clinical, lacking in humour and passion.

"What the hell...!" muttered the old bloke in the next seat.

And so it continued. One or other of the six would stand, not in any particular order and not for any prescribed time, and play. All note perfect but without feeling. It was as if they were playing to a mathematical formula.

Roy Eldridge looked like the thirty-three-year-old who played with the Gene Krupa and Artie Shaw Big Bands, one of the first black musicians to feature with what had previously been all white concert orchestras. Bridging the gap between Armstrong and the modernists, he still played it high with a rasping attack, but with his once admired emotion removed.

Dizzy Gillespie flew in imperious patterns. Miles Davis was still the Epitome of Cool. Chet Baker could make his horn almost whisper. Maynard Ferguson blasted through the stratosphere. All as expected, but hard and cold. No soul, and their faces as sterile as their technically accomplished playing.

"They might have brought them to life," said the old man, "but the jazz elements are missing. The music is dead."

Gerry could only nod his agreement. An icy chill was starting to spread from the main reception points in both his brain and his stomach.

"HOW DID it go then?" asked Bette.

"It was … strange."

"In what way?"

She hadn't wanted to go so why was she showing an interest now? "I don't know," he snapped crossly. "Strange, odd, unusual, unnerving; take your pick."

"Hey! Untwist your knickers, lover."

"Well you weren't interested enough to go yourself so stop asking questions about it."

Bette spun on her heel and stalked from the room. Alone, Gerry switched off the television but flinched at the slamming of cupboard doors and the rattling of crockery emanating from the kitchen. He knew Bette was angry but did she have to make such a hullaballoo about it?

All he wanted was to be given some space, alone and in silence, so he could begin to evaluate what he had witnessed that evening. The music: cold and clinical, had been so … planned. Every trill and growl, each cleanly hit high C: all lacking the spark of spontaneity that marked true jazz. It had been a hybrid, almost, and maybe new classifications would be needed to encompass it.

The elderly gent who had occupied the seat originally intended for Bette had appeared upset, or at least uncomfortable, at the end of the performance. Less open minded, maybe, at his age. Gerry, though initially shocked, had been more willing to assimilate and now to consider.

The door swung open with a creak that annoyed his

eardrums and a whoosh of displaced air that assaulted him as sound waves. "I'm off to bed. If you want any supper get it yourself," snapped Bette in loud and strident tones that caused him almost physical hurt.

When Gerry didn't answer she turned and left the room, banging the door shut with an echoing crack that shuddered its way through every part of his body. And this was the woman he had wanted to bear his children?

By the time he turned and walked to stand at the window, Bette had been banished from his thoughts. Their apartment was on the fifteenth floor of a luxury tower block, so afforded him an outstanding view of the surrounding city skyline. Unbeknown to Gerry there were others doing exactly the same thing, either that or staring at a wall. Some were alone, as he was, or with another, or others, physically together but in individual isolation. All had been present at THE TRUMPET IN JAZZ. All had heard the dead men play their music.

BETTE HAD EXPECTED Gerry to follow her to their bedroom. He was always keen to make up after one of their rare and usually pointless arguments. He would apologise even when she had been the one in the wrong. Bette, in her turn, would pout and play at being badly treated, gradually allowing herself to be won over by his ardent entreaties. The love making that followed would be both athletic and satisfyingly entertaining. But on this occasion he did not follow her to bed, and when she got up the next morning and found him still in the living room, staring out of the window, she felt a strange conviction that he had been standing there all night.

If that's the way he wants it! Bette decided when

Gerry failed to even acknowledge her presence. She could dish out the silent treatment for as long as he could. What she didn't know was that Gerry wanted it to last for ever.

It was with an overriding sense of relief that he realised that, for now at least, Bette was keeping to an angry silence. If only she would wear slippers and learn how to open and shut doors quietly, then life would be bearable. He flinched as she slammed her way into the kitchen, her heels clip-clopping on the Paris Café style cement tiled floor.

Why wouldn't she go out and leave him alone? Preferably permanently!

"Stupid…" what was her name? "…woman!" But his tongue felt thick and awkward in his mouth when he spoke, and though he had only muttered the words they echoed like thunder through his head.

Where was he up to in reliving the concert? Ah yes, Dizzy Gillespie, and the way he slid a semitone away from the chords of the tune under examination, at such breath-taking speed, too. Like shards of ice.

Cold was good … cold was good…

What on earth was wrong with Gerry?

Bette had considered ringing one of her friends, have a good moan, maybe meet up for a coffee and a chat. But this was her home too. Why should Gerry's bad mood drive her out? Inconsiderate sod!

She had thought he was *The One* but this was a side of him she hadn't seen before. Bette wasn't the sort to let bad feelings simmer, preferring confrontation and getting things out in the open. Determined to do just that she strode purposefully back to the living room.

"It's all to do with that bloody concert, isn't it?" she demanded.

Concert? What concert?

"Just because I wouldn't go and see those dead trumpeters!"

Trumpeters? What trumpeters?

"I don't think it's reason enough for such bad behaviour!"

Why did this woman speak so loudly? Why did she have to speak at all?

The fact that Gerry didn't answer was unsettling in itself, being so unlike him; but when he looked at her there was no flicker of recognition. His face was strangely blank. Indeed, he appeared almost unaware of his surroundings or what was happening. Bette hesitated a moment, experiencing a definite sense of unease.

"Are you having some sort of breakdown?" she asked.

Goddam this woman, bombarding him with words that echoed like artillery fire.

"It's all down to them," she continued loudly. "That Louis *Bloody* Armstrong, Miles *Sodding* Davis, and…" Bette couldn't remember any more; "…the others," she finished lamely.

All Gerry wanted was total silence and this woman was preventing it. Her and her non-stop gibberish! It wasn't anger, however, that prompted him to shuffle in her direction; emotion, of any sort, having drained from his understanding. All he wanted was for her to contribute to an absence of noise.

If he had come towards her with an angry expression on his face, or with any other emotion for that matter, Bette felt she could have dealt with him.

But – she had to admit it – the total blankness of his features scared her, that and his slow but deliberate movement.

"Keep away, Gerry."

Please be quiet, woman.

"Gerry!"

He reached out his hands and took hold of her by the neck; anything to shut her up and stop the flow of words. And as he held he automatically squeezed.

As the full realisation of what was happening struck home, Bette fought like a tigress. She tried to prise his fingers loose but failed. She scratched at his hands and face, her nails gouging red lines of broken skin. She kicked out wildly and tried to scream – but couldn't. Gerry's hands continued to apply pressure, causing damage to her larynx and both thyroid and cricoid cartilages. Gradually her violent struggling grew less as air hunger overtook her bodily responses.

Whether she finally died from asphyxia or reflex cardiac arrest was not apparent and was of no concern to the man who had killed her. The black and white opposites of life and death had little relevance to the non-person he had become. Only the difference between noise and silence had any real meaning.

Since she was now being quiet, Gerry let Bette's limp and throttled body drop to the floor, immediately relegating her to the forgotten. Stepping slowly over her sprawled shape he moved sluggishly back to the window where he stood staring at but not really seeing the panoramic city view spread out before him.

His fellow concert attendees from the previous evening: audience, staff and performers, were all trapped in a similar fashion. All who had heard the dead trumpeters play their music; all seemingly mimicking the dead who now walked among them. Gerry Armitage, like the others, no longer had any concept of self, of who he was or ever had been.

Some hours later he closed the curtains on the window and turned to face one of the walls. The concert was forgotten, the dead trumpeters and their music banished, Bette and her murder obliterated from his mind. All that mattered was the chill that filled him and the quiet that surrounded his very existence.

The cold of the churchyard earth…

The silence of death itself…

LATER THAT EVENING, BBC1 was showing a filmed recording of THE TRUMPET IN JAZZ. From a couple of thousand at the actual concert there would be millions watching it on their television screens. Not Gerry though, nor the others already infected. They stood in cold and silent isolation, mimicking the grave.

DARK-HAIRED ITALIAN GIRL

She's a dark-haired Italian girl
A dark-haired Italian girl
When sighing sighs or flashing eyes
She's a woman … yes she's my woman
She's a dark-haired Italian girl

She set out from S'Angelo and brought her Latin
charms
She set out from S'Angelo and ended in my arms
She's the girl in my life … and she's my wife

She's a dark-haired Italian girl
A dark-haired Italian girl
One-minute thrills, next minute chills
From this woman … oh what a woman
She's a dark-haired Italian girl

She set out from S'Angelo to travel overseas
She set out from S'Angelo and brought me to my knees
She's the girl in my life … and she's my wife

She's a dark-haired Italian girl
A dark-haired Italian girl
Sweet loving slips from her sweet lips
She's a woman … yes she's my woman
She's a dark-haired Italian girl
A dark-haired Italian girl
And she's my wife.

BOY WITH A GUN

No time for loving ladies … boy on the run
No time for might's or maybe's … no mother's son
This time the tension's growing … boy on the street
This time the cracks are showing … here comes the heat

Boy with a gun now, baby … boy with a gun

No image no reflection … boy with no face
No saviour no redemption … no saving grace
Time soon to face his showdown … boy can't take more
We'll read the tabloid lowdown … blood death and
gore

Boy with a gun now, baby … boy with a gun

Mad dog, they don't want you 'round
Mad dog, they're gonna shoot you down

They'll say:
Shoot him
Kill him
He's just a boy with a gun

THE WINE WAITER

The wine waiter smiles as he fills your glass
But the smile is a mask
Things are not as they seem
The wine waiter thinks his act is first class
The smile is a traitor
On the face of the waiter

The wine waiter thinks he's been betrayed
Nothing turns out just as displayed
He will hear no voice, there is no sign
The wine waiter is waiting for the wine

The wine waiter laughs when you tell a joke
But the laugh has a crack
He is not full of fun
The wine waiter's mainspring seems to be broke
And sooner or later
Time will tell for the waiter

The wine waiter thinks the world is to blame
That other people should feel the shame
He'll trip the wire, he'll walk the line
The wine waiter is waiting for the wine

EL HOMESTEAD NOTORIOUS

TROY ALARADO WAS pissed off and not in the mood to take the kind of bull that Henry Parker was trying to lay on him. It wasn't as if he actually liked Lil' Rosie, or her him. There were times when he actively disliked her, a feeling she seemed to reciprocate, but some strange magnetism sparked a connection that neither could quite shrug off. So okay, Rosie worked out at El Homestead Notorious, five miles outside the town limits; maybe not the best cat-house in all of New Mexico but it had little competition locally.

"Why don't you find a proper girlfriend, Troy?"

"You mean like yours?"

Betsy Bloomfield was overweight and, well, *homely* was as kind a description as one could come up with. "Take that back!" snarled Henry, clenching his fists and standing away from the counter.

"Calm down, the pair of you," interrupted Big Irish. It was his bar they were drinking in. Some said it was the roughest dive in Roswell, and only one step up from places like the cat-house, but it was probably the most trouble free. Big Irish was not a man to be messed with. "Out in the street if you insist on fisticuffs, you hear me?" he continued. "Within these walls the only punches thrown are mine."

"I didn't mean nothing about Betsy," muttered Troy. He had known Henry since their schooldays and had no real wish to fight him. "You got no cause to keep on about me and Lil' Rosie though. There's no courtship going on there."

"Just joking with you, Troy, though maybe I did go on a bit."

"Okay."

Troy still felt edgy, maybe because some of Henry's teasing had struck home.

"Did you hear about that rancher who had something crash on his land?" asked Big Irish, offering a new subject up for discussion. "Only a couple of days ago; surely one of you lame-brains have heard something about it!"

"Guy named Brazel, from over near Corona," called someone sitting in a booth.

"I should have guessed you would know about it, Johnny," said the bar owner. "I suppose you'll be doing a broadcast about it – local interest stuff."

The radio reporter snorted and shook his head. "I wanted to, believe me, but the story has been killed, stone dead."

"What do you mean, killed?" asked someone else.

"This Brazel character came into town and reported the crash to Sheriff Wilcox, and he contacted the Army Air Force Base in case it was something of theirs. Then Brazel came and told me about it, and you can bet I was working it into broadcasts. It was a bit more lively than most of the news items I get to work with."

"I heard one mention from you but nothing else," called a voice, "and the KOAT station at Albuquerque didn't seem to carry it at all."

"And I'll tell you why, shall I?" offered Johnny McBoyle. "Not that I'm supposed to say a word but what can they do? Shoot me!"

"Okay Johnny, you've got us hanging on your every

word," said Big Irish. "What's this all about?"

"Officialdom stepped in and stomped all over me," claimed the radio man. "Bigwigs from the AAF threatened to get the authorities to remove my broadcasting licence if the subject wasn't removed from all further transmissions, and the same at KOAT. They took Brazel himself over to the camp for questioning and his ranch is now off limits to anyone bar military personnel. It all smells of some sort of cover-up to me."

"Covering up what?" asked Troy.

"Well, Brazel said the wreckage material was thin and light but wouldn't bend or crease, no matter how hard him and his son tried," said McBoyle, frustrated that he wasn't able to cover all this in a broadcast. "He'd never seen nothing like it and thought it maybe came from someplace else."

"You mean like Russia?" suggested Henry. He had always been a bit bookish, even at school.

"Or Europe?" called someone else.

"No, Brazel meant like the moon, or Mars!"

"Come on now, Johnny," said Big Irish, "you don't believe that sort of shit, do you?"

"I've probably said too much as it is," continued McBoyle, pushing himself up from where he sat. "Keep your eyes on the *Roswell Daily Record*. Those bastards might have silenced the radio stations but the press is not so easily controlled." And so saying, he left the bar.

"Well that was interesting," said Big Irish, but while customers were talking they were doing less drinking. Coming round from the bar he stuck a nickel in the juke box and selected The Harmonicats hit record "Peg O' My Heart", a favourite of his since it seemed to have a flavour of the old country about it, though that was only supposition on his part since he had left the

Emerald Isle while still only a babe in his mother's arms.

As expected, empty glasses were soon being placed on the counter for refilling. It was back to being just another mid-day session in the dusty town of Roswell.

THE VERY NEXT day, just as Johnny McBoyle had hinted, the local paper splashed it big. *RAAF Captures Flying Saucer on Ranch in Roswell Region* screamed the headline. Hey, maybe that radio man had known what he was talking about, thought Troy Alarado. Suddenly there was only one topic of conversation, and it upped to an even more hysterical level when a Public Information Officer at the base issued a press release confirming that a crashed Flying Disc had been taken into military possession. People were looking up rather than down, seeking signs of a *War of the Worlds* type invasion.

The wreckage was moved, photographed, moved and replaced, then photographed again, but by then it had been officially downgraded to being only a weather balloon. There were no Little Green Men coming from space, and the claims of an engineer named Barney Barnett that he had seen a damaged disc that contained alien bodies was considered a step too far, especially in the light of strong official denials and explanations. Thus amid hearsay, contradiction, claim and counterclaim, the original paranoia died away. The subject was maybe good for a laugh; there were still some who took it a bit more seriously but in the main it was a source of embarrassment that the locality had been hoodwinked into believing something so far-fetched.

"It shows what boring lives we lead, to have been taken in by such nonsense," decided Troy, a true sceptic now.

Henry was not quite so sure. "That Barnett bloke wasn't the only one to claim to see those bodies. What about the archaeology students from the University of Pennsylvania?"

"Students?" mocked Troy. "Smoking pot and drinking moonshine, if they were there at all."

"Well what about the Air Base ordering those child-size coffins. I know that's true because I heard Mr Dennis, the undertaker, talking about it myself."

"Midgets? Dwarfs? Even children die sometimes. It wasn't proof of nothing."

"Your trouble, Troy Alarado, is that you've got a closed mind."

"And yours is that your brain is leaking out faster than you can replace it. Are you coming out to the old Notorious with me later? You could do with lightening up a little."

"No, can't risk it." Henry shook his head firmly. "Betsy gave me hell the last time she found out I'd been there. She reckons you're a bad influence on me."

"You're no fun these days, Henry, do you know that? Tell you what though, I'll tell that Dinah-Jane you said hello. Don't think it hasn't been noticed the way you make moon-eyes in her direction, when you do manage to sneak out from under the thumb."

"Shut up, Troy! Betsy would kill me if she heard that sort of trash talk."

Troy didn't really like going to El Homestead Notorious on his own. When he had company he could avoid seeing every single time Lil' Rosie disappeared upstairs with a customer. He occasionally went with one of the other girls, hoping against hope that if she noticed it would burn hurt and pain into her heart, the way it did with him. And on his own he would usually drink too much, sometimes being thrown out, or even beaten up. The heavy mob there were not as smart as Big Irish when it came to defusing trouble before it even started.

Troy often wondered why he went there at all. Sometimes Lil' Rosie would speak to him and smile, sweet as cherry pie, and let him buy her drinks. But at other times she would be cold as ice, ignoring him as if a stranger. Whatever her mood though, if he paid his dollars and took her upstairs she would mostly be neither hot nor cold, but merely business-like, and that hurt more than anything.

He was twenty now, out of his teens. He couldn't keep on, drifting like this, forever.

PERSONNEL AT THE 509th Bomb Camp of the Eighth Air Force, Roswell Army Air Field, were on high alert. Top brass kept coming and going, and had done from the time they'd brought in the wreckage found on that local ranch. It had been hoped that transferring it all to Fort Worth in Texas would allow the Roswell Base to return to relative obscurity but that had not happened. There were still parts of the camp off limits to ordinary servicemen, security was tight as a drum, and visiting generals still kept popping in.

Major Jesse Marcel of the Group Intelligence Office had taken the original call from Sheriff Wilcox. He had examined the downed craft himself and had okayed its transfer to Texas. He had accepted his posting to the arid state of New Mexico because he was a career serviceman and went wherever the powers-that-be saw fit to send him, but he had not expected anything out of the ordinary to occur here. The crashed vehicle had been a proper humdinger, but the alien occupants had taken it all to a level never before experienced. Marcel was not sorry that a general had been flown in to take overall command. He was more than content to be kept near at hand as the person who knew the area.

There had been six of the strange creatures: humanoid in general appearance, no more than four feet tall, bald, piggy-eyed, with large heads, and virtually colourless in pigmentation. They all wore grey one-piece suits. Marcel had seen them where they were found, and had contained the site with maximum security until the general had flown in with a special medical team.

There were three males and three females, it was discovered. The three females and one male were dead. Of the survivors, one died shortly after his secret arrival at the Roswell Camp and the other was making good progress towards recovery. Initial examinations and one full autopsy were carried out at Roswell but then the five dead ones were packed in ice and transported to specific medical and scientific facilities across the country where highly secret investigations were already in motion. 1947 was going to be a very important year even if the population at large knew next to nothing of what was going on. It was deemed too risky to move the one living alien, which meant that Roswell remained at the centre of what was growing into a national conspiracy.

DRINKING AT EL Homestead Notorious was a lot more expensive than any of the regular bars back in town, but nobody went there just for the booze.

Lil' Rosie, all four foot two inches of her, felt in an expansive mood. "Why do you come here so much,

Troy Alarado?" she asked, sipping the drink he had bought her, "when you don't really seem to enjoy yourself."

Was she asking him a straight question, he wondered, or was there an underlying twist to it? "That's a hard one to answer," he responded, dodging the issue.

"Sometimes I think you come just to see me, even though I don't give you any encouragement."

"You certainly don't do that!" Troy laughed a little, but without humour. "I don't especially like you and I don't like what you do here, but you're like a magnet to me and I can't fight the attraction." If it's love I feel, he thought but did not say aloud, then I definitely do not like it. Love or hate: they were so mixed up in his mind he could not tell one from the other.

Lil' Rosie half smiled, half grimaced, making wrinkles around her pert and tiny upturned nose. "I'm being nice to you tonight," she said, "though I don't know why, so don't spoil it. If you want sex choose one of the other girls. Pay for me and the spell will be broken and my bitch-half will float up like oil on water."

"But it's only you I want, damn it!" exclaimed Troy. "You've got me so I don't know day from night, left from right, black from white."

"That almost sounded like poetry," said the cat-house girl, but with a piss-take sarcastic edge to her voice. She reached out and stroked Troy's cheek. "I must be your muse, or something."

He jerked his face away from her hand. "Something, for sure," he agreed bitterly. "More likely a devil-girl than anything else."

Lil' Rosie finished her drink and stood up. "Time to

get back to work," she remarked.

Troy felt his insides twist and turn as he watched her walk away. If I had a gun, he thought angrily, I'd shoot her. I'd shoot her dead!

GENERAL TOM LEWINGTON brought his fist down heavily, sending papers flying in all directions. His face had turned red, he felt near to exploding; and his voice, when he finally spoke, was full of anger. "What do you mean by *He/it needs to have sex*? And choose your answer very carefully. Are you saying that part of my function is to take on the role of a pimp, that I should have to procure female company for the thing?"

The team of experts, all top men in their respective fields, each waited for one of the others to speak first. The general's temper was well known but this promised to be his biggest outburst yet. There was, however, no way to avoid this particular issue.

Though the linguists had not yet managed to establish a full and comprehensive dialogue with the alien they were able to pick 'n' mix with sufficient expertise to have achieved a basic form of communication. Rudimentary and slow it might be, but with patience and hard work a proper exchange of ideas and information was achievable. In this way they were able to learn a lot about the alien's home world and the nature of its civilisation.

He was part, it seemed, of a male-dominated society where their females were owned, on a par with slave status. Sex was not an everyday occurrence, not even potentially, males being physically unable to couple, a situation which resolved itself only during an individual rut period, which apparently happened twice during each planetary orbit made by their world.

This was why the three alien spacemen had brought a female each with them, now all dead of course, and the one surviving male could sense his next rut was nearly upon him.

"That might be the way of things up there," thundered General Lewington, "but it's not our way. Our world, our rules!" AAF Group Intelligence training had not prepared him for anything like this.

"There are physical and psychological differences, General. He is a different species, after all."

"If the fellow becomes that frustrated can't he hide in a corner and jerk himself off?" Which was what they'd done back at military academy, he remembered.

"Masturbation is not part of their culture, sir."

"Goddamn it, man! Never mind your objections, start seeking solutions!"

It was at this point that Major Marcel joined the discussion. "I am correct in understanding that the alien is biologically able, when the rut is upon him, to perform sexually with a human woman, aren't I?" he asked.

"Most certainly," confirmed one of the boffins.

"There is an establishment I know of, El Homestead Notorious, a cat-house. It even has a girl working there, just about the same height as the alien. I'm sure if I were able to wave handfuls of dollar bills under various noses, arrangement could be made to satisfy all our needs. Not very savoury maybe, but when needs must…"

"No, Major!" shouted the general. "We can't have prostitutes coming here to the camp. This is the nineteen-forties and we are AAF officers, not ranch-hands hitting town in the Old West."

"General, let me arrange it." Major Marcel could

already see how his own needs could be seen to, as well as those of the alien. "I'll fix it for him to be taken to the girl. Disguised of course so no-one will know what he really is."

"It needs to be done, and in ten days' time," interrupted one of the experts. "If he doesn't rut when due he'll run amok, with no telling what results."

"I'll leave it all to you then, Marcel," said the general, making the first panic-stricken decision of his career. "I'm not sure that I want to know any of the details."

"HAD A COUPLE of Mud Puppies in here yesterday," said Big Irish.

"Uh?"

"Military Police. Didn't they teach you guys nothing?"

"Sorry," said Troy, "I've got things on my mind."

"Where's your pal, Henry? I thought you two were joined at the hip."

Troy pulled a face. "He's only gone and bought that fat Betsy Bloomfield a ring. He's got himself engaged. Idiot!"

"Don't knock it, lad," said Big Irish with a laugh. "Someone to cuddle up to on a cold winter night? I'm partial to a big-boned woman myself."

But Troy didn't want to talk about Henry Parker's love life, not when his own was such a disaster. "What were the Military Police doing here then?"

"Oh them, yes! In town to pick up a bad lad from the Camp who the Sheriff had locked up overnight; called in here for a drink first."

"They are not still talking about that weather balloon, are they?"

"No, not mentioned once but there are still oddball

things going on out there."

"Such as?"

"Part of the base is still sectioned off, and no ordinary servicemen are allowed to go near it."

"They've probably got atom bombs stockpiled there. Or the officer's special rations."

Big Irish smiled at that. "There is something funny going on though, Troy. After a couple of drinks one whispered to his partner, quiet-like, but I could hear. He said 'What's this secret El Homestead Notorious detail all about?' and the other snapped back 'Beat your gum, bigmouth'. They both glanced at me, but I just carried on cleaning glasses and making out I hadn't heard a thing."

Troy didn't think too much about it. He'd seen a few dust-ups when the military had turned up heavy handed. As long as they didn't make no beeline for Lil' Rosie they could do what they liked. "Just soldier boys looking to let off steam," he said.

"I've got a nose for these things," said Big Irish, sniffing deeply, "and I think there might be more to it than that. There are strange things afoot and they might be linked to them being closed down for a day next week."

"Who? The camp?"

"No!" Big Irish winked knowingly. "El Homestead Notorious, on Wednesday next week. For a private function, so it's said, and most of the girls are being given the day off. See what you can find out, Troy. I assume you'll be out there once or twice before then."

The big bar owner liked to know what was going on in that place, and Troy was keen to find out for himself anyway. "I'll do my best," he offered, and of course he did.

THE RUMOUR, AS it happened, turned out to be right. Two girls, Lil' Rosie and Dinah-Jane, plus one of the owners, would be in attendance. Everyone else was on unpaid leave for a twenty-four-hour period. "I'm not supposed to talk about it," said Lil' Rosie but she was intrigued by it herself. "You've got to promise to keep quiet." Troy nodded, crossing his heart and swearing silence.

The girl leant close, her voice no more than a murmur. "Dinah-Jane is only coming in to pass time with an employee. I will be seeing to the actual customer ... and I was asked for specifically." She was proud of that.

It didn't ring true with Troy, though. "Anyone who wants to spend time with you, all they got to do is come in as normal and pay the going rate for as long as they want. I don't understand this need for secrecy."

Lil' Rosie moved even closer and whispered in his ear. "The guy is a cripple, or deformed, or something. He keeps himself covered and won't appear in public places. That's why!"

It sounded like a ten-cent pulp novel to Troy. "Pull out, Lil' Rosie," he suggested, "let one of the other girls do it. Somehow it doesn't come across as right to me. You don't know what this guy might want."

"For what they are paying me all he'll have to do is ask. This is a top-dollar gig, Troy. No way am I handing it over to someone else." And when he continued to argue against it, Lil' Rosie got angry and stormed off.

ALF ALARADO - CHRISTENED Alfredo but shortened at an early age – was part of the 30th Infantry Division when the Allies had been caught unprepared by the Ardennes

Counteroffensive, the last major German attack of WW2. America suffered their highest casualties of the war but the battle was won after two months of bloody fighting.

Private Alarado returned home, luckily unscathed but, as with many ex-servicemen, unable to settle back into civilian life. When he died, in a major traffic pileup while driving for an organisation of ill-repute, the only thing he left for his brother Paul to remember him by was a souvenir of his time in war-torn Europe. The Walther P38 was a German Army semi-automatic pistol. It, and a number of ammunition clips, were locked in a box, Paul Alarado's prize possession. His son, Troy, however, knew where the key was kept, and the weapon was in his pocket as he made his way to El Homestead Notorious. Just why he'd felt the need to take it, he really didn't know; apart from an overriding conviction that something was wrong with what was going on at the cat-house, and since Lil' Rosie was involved it left him in his usual state of unsubstantiated contradictions. Damn her to hell and back; stupid little whore. Stupid lovely little whore.

Settling himself down within wooded cover, far enough away for safety but close enough for observation, he had no plan other than to wait and watch. Any action on his part would depend on what he saw, if anything.

With no sound or movement the place gave an impression of being an empty building.

Troy was patient though and eventually the main door opened and Max Adams came out. The part-owner of the establishment just stood, chewing on an ever-present fat cigar, as if waiting, and soon enough two vehicles arrived, both carrying military insignia.

The first was an ambulance and the second an open-backed truck carrying a number of uniformed soldiers.

Someone, who at a distance looked and dressed like an officer, left the ambulance and spoke with Max Adams. Then a stretcher carrying someone well covered under blankets, was brought out and carried into the building. The soldiers clambered down from the truck and spread themselves out, apparently on some sort of guard duty. Max and the officer had followed the stretcher in through the door. A little later Dinah-Jane came out with the part-owner, both handing out bottled beer to the soldiers. Then they went back in. The guard duty lounged around, drinking and smoking, but nothing else could be heard or seen, and Troy was becoming more and more agitated.

Cripple, she'd said.

Deformed, she'd said.

Lil' Rosie might well be in there with some sort of grotesque monster, or maybe not, and the not knowing was driving him crazy. Finally he could stand it no longer and moved out in a carefully controlled circular route. There was a broken latch on a window in the downstairs toilet at the rear. It had been busted for a year or more and never mended. That could be the means to getting in, should he need to.

MAX ADAMS WAS siting at the bar, puffing a cigar and twiddling his thumbs, waiting to dispense drinks as and when required. He had no intention of giving the outside soldiers anymore, and the two couples upstairs would be too busy fooling around to think about drink for a spell yet. He hoped Lil' Rosie would be able to help the sad guy on the stretcher get his jollies. It was costing him enough, whoever he was, and that was all that mattered to Max.

The scream, when it came, chilled him to the bone. Whether male or female, human or animal, wasn't clear, but it was terrible to hear. As Max trotted up the stairs a bedroom door swung open and Major Marcel hurried out, struggling into a dressing gown, with Dinah-Jane behind him.

"What's going on?" Running up the stairs behind Max Adams was Troy Alarado, who had clambered through the broken toilet window as soon as the scream had started.

"Who the fuck is that?" demanded Marcel.

"Alarado!" exclaimed Max Adams. "What the hell are you doing here?"

Downstairs, the front door burst open and the guard detail came bursting in, adding to the general confusion. Max, meanwhile, ignoring everything else, reached the room where the awful noise seemed to be coming from.

"No!" shouted Major Marcel. "Let me!" But Max Adams took no notice and opened the bedroom door, and out stepped a ... creature: four foot tall, bald, large head, naked, deathly white except for the scarlet liquid oozing around its mouth and dripping down its squat body.

It looked at the people milling around the corridor ... and ended the scream. "The rut, it was good," it said, in a close approximation of English. "Not as expected, and the ending was different, but it was good. Thank you."

"What is it talking about?" shouted Troy, pushing his way to look into the bedroom. And then there was screaming again but this time it was him as he looked at Lil' Rosie, or what was left of her dead on the bed.

Troy was pulling his Uncle Alf's pistol from his

pocket as the alien creature spoke again. "It was good," the thing repeated. "Thank you."

Troy shot and shot and shot, pumping bullet after bullet into what stood before him and didn't stop until a bullet from a different gun took part of his head off and he died too. Both Marcel and Adams were holding weapons now. "There can be no witnesses," said the Major, and they both opened fire on the soldiers who had been on sentry duty earlier, not stopping until they were all accounted for. Dinah-Jane had also been hit in the gunfire.

"How are you going to do it?" asked Max Adams. "Will you handle the clean-up through the army, or do you want me to see to it?"

"When I said no witnesses, I meant none at all," said the Major, firing three further shots. Then, as the only survivor, with all the death and mayhem around him, he made his way down to the building's office and telephone.

"I'm sorry, General," he said into the mouthpiece after dialling and being connected. "El Homestead Notorious calling. Things did not go to plan."

DIAGNOSIS

JANE KAVOTNY SHIVERED. The gallery was cold, too cold, though it probably suited the series of anticipated death scenes the artist had produced for this particular show: ten for the pop singer Lucinda, ten concerning movie actor Jeff Halliday. Neither had actually posed for the paintings, but both had endorsed them after private viewings. Kavotny shrugged mentally; that had been their public posturing but she wondered what had been their inner feelings. She, personally, would not want to see her potential death splashed in larger-than-life and vibrantly coloured canvases. The artist Leonard Sargasso had talent, there was no denying that, but with a morbidity she did not appreciate.

"Jane, my dear, I'm late. Do forgive me."

She turned to face Doctor Parry.

"Have you had a first look?" he asked. Kavotny nodded.

He had been seeking her company, and opinions, a lot lately. Either he valued her input, or she herself had become the focal point of one of his investigations. "What did you think of the painting of Halliday, the one with the twisted metal of the crashed helicopter?"

That caught her off guard a little. "You've seen them already?" she asked, surprised.

"Oh yes! Leonard Sargasso is … er … a friend of long

standing. I was in the background when both the subjects had their personal introductions to the paintings. They both knew what Leonard was doing, of course, but their first look at such realistic representations was most interesting."

The hesitation intrigued her. Either it was genuine and his relationship with the artist depended upon interpretation, or it was a deliberate attempt to guide her in a direction that Parry felt unable to suggest himself.

A number of smartly attired mannequins had been placed throughout the gallery; some sitting, some standing, all posed in slightly different ways. The dead-studying-the-dead symbolism was too obvious, she thought. There had to be more subtle meanings, but at this moment in time Jane Kavotny felt that she was being manipulated like a shop window dummy herself.

"I thought the idea was that we would compare our initial reactions," she complained, wondering how long she should stay before good manners dictated she could leave.

WHALE SONGS FOR THE BROKEN-HEARTED

ALAN BUXTON NEVER tired of listening to his recordings of male humpback whales. The plaintive sounds spoke of watery depths, and moved him in ways very little else could. Sweet Gloria, the love of his life, had drowned at sea, with others, and he hoped with all his heart that sad whale songs had accompanied their transition from life to death.

Doctor Parry had handed Buxton a small printed business card at the end of that week's group session. "Go to this gallery," he had suggested. "You have yet to challenge death face-to-face. The paintings currently on show might help you."

Jane Kavotny, who took notes during the sessions, stopped Buxton as he was leaving. "Are you familiar with the work of Leonard Sargasso?" she asked.

"Leonard who?"

"Sargasso, the artist. It's an exhibition of his work the doctor wants you to visit."

Buxton shook his head. "Never heard of him," he replied. "I know nothing at all about art."

"Well, be warned, Mr Buxton, his paintings do not make for easy viewing."

He remembered the brief conversation now, as he glanced at the programme purchased as he had entered the gallery. Ten paintings each, he read, featuring the images of Jeff Halliday and Lucinda in various death scenes. He had heard of her of course: Lucinda, the current pop sensation, more famous for her costumes than anything else. To the best of his knowledge, he had never actually heard her sing. The Halliday character was said to be an actor, but Buxton had not been to the cinema since losing Gloria, and even before that had only tagged along to see films of her choice.

The dummies were an initial shock: still, not breathing, but horribly lifelike at first glance. Only a closer examination revealed them to be manufactured. Buxton grimaced, trying to ignore the figures as he looked in turns at the paintings.

Most of the Halliday series portrayed him dying in action-man settings: unopened parachute, crashed helicopter, mountaineering accident, and others, though there was also one showing him dead in a hospital bed. Those featuring the pop singer incorporated more fantasy elements, ranging from her being devoured by zombies to her corpse being attended by fairies. Whereas they were obviously very well painted, there was no hiding that Buxton could not see that anyone would want to hang one on their living room wall.

The very last painting was of Lucinda being turned to stone by the Gorgon, but he didn't see that one. The canvas before it was a seascape of sorts, with the drowned pop singer sinking to oceanic depths. It hit Buxton like a hammer blow to the head and as he looked, staggered by the upswing of horror and grief brought bubbling to the surface of his mind, so the dead face morphed from the singer it was meant to be to that of the woman he had loved and lost.

His throat felt constricted, gasping for air, and his voice was dry and cracked. "Gloria!" he called out, and when he finally dragged himself away from the painting he found that the nearby mannequins had taken on her features too.

"Gloria," he repeated, this time in a whisper. Turning sharply, barely keeping his feet, almost falling, he rushed from the gallery and out into the horn and engine noises of a busy thoroughfare.

SEX DREAMS FOR SALE

DOCTOR PARRY HAD initially been a father figure for Jane Kavotny and she had experienced severe self-disgust when her feelings for him had taken on sexual overtones. Since he was such an expert in the theoretical needs of both the male and female, she granted him Casanova status, and the more she fantasised about him the less guilty she felt. In the end, the paternal viewpoint faded completely, but so did his sex-bomb standing.

Everything the doctor did had multiple reasons and seemed so planned. Jane wanted spontaneity. To be swept off her feet, to be surprised, even in her imagination. No, more than that: *especially* in her imagination. The darker and deeper layers of Jane's personal extravaganzas were for inward consumption only. Nothing intruded into the real world.

She had never seen the point in fantasising about singers or movie stars. Jane wanted the added thrill of genuine possibility, even while acknowledging she would never act on these secret desires. So when the good doctor fell out of favour, she cast around for a replacement, looking first at the male members of Parry's self-help groups.

The forlorn and wasted figure of Alan Buxton was an early possibility. Gaunt, troubled, pining for a lost love and unable to move on from her death. Jane pictured herself as the one woman capable of breaking him free from the crippling chains of loss that weighed him down. It was quite a satisfying dreamscape in that she cast herself in a Good Samaritan role, almost on a par with nurses and missionaries. But however illuminating it might be to be good, it didn't quite match the shivering excitement of a badass partner, and that made her look at Eric Landreth, a relative newcomer to Doctor Parry's circle of troubled souls.

Landreth, bristling with dark moods and a sense of resentment, was troubled by acute anger issues. Jane felt a delicious thrill as she considered the violence that bubbled beneath his brooding exterior. She could see something of Emily Bronte's Heathcliff about him. Cue Lucinda singing her cover version of Kate Bush's "Wuthering Heights", which in turn brought Sara-gossa's exhibition to mind. Eric Landreth could well be the only person she knew, apart from Doctor Parry, who might actually like the twenty paintings on show. She wondered if Alan Buxton had gone to the gallery and, if so, what his reaction had been?

BLUES IN THE NIGHT

THE COOL SPOT was two evenings a week – Mondays and Tuesdays, traditionally quiet in the pub trade – in the upstairs bar of The King's Head Tavern. Trad Jazz and Blues Bands pulled in the most punters and Swing Nights did okay, but Harry "Bugs" Bonney was committed to featuring jazz in all its shades and genres. He usually lost money on the Modernists, who had their followers but did not pick up as much passing trade as the others. That was fine though; it all evened out in the end, and Harry stayed true to his ideals.

Breathless were playing tonight, alto and tenor leads backed by double bass and drums. Not that a piano-less group was anything new; Gerry Mulligan was doing it back in the nineteen-fifties. These lads weren't bad though, making a good fist at reproducing the delicate traceries of counterpoint that Mulligan and Chet Baker had pioneered back in the day. The audience was small but enthusiastic, and Bonney could live with that.

"The boys are playing well tonight, Bugs," called someone as the group finished their deconstruction of a standard blues motif.

His surname being so close to that of the well-known cartoon rabbit, he had been nicknamed Bugs from schooldays on.

"Where's the action, Bugs?" asked Eric Landreth.

Bonney knew it went on, but did his best to discourage it. "Nothing going on here," he replied, knowing it to be a lie but wishing it were true.

"Uppers, downers, all over towners; where's the Dealer, the man to see," recited Landreth, paraphrasing lines from an old poem he had read years before in a small press magazine.

"You're always throwing that quote around!" Bonney was hoping to move the conversation on. "Who was the writer?"

"Just a Welsh idiot with poetic delusions. I don't remember his name."

"Dylan Thomas?"

"No, man, it wasn't anyone you would have heard of."

That one suggestion had exhausted Bonney's knowledge of Welsh poets. "Sounds more like Lou Reed lyrics than a poem to me," he said irritably, but Landreth had already moved on, circulating the small crowd as he tried to find someone he could score from.

THE HOUSE ON THE HILL

OAKWELL HAD BEEN in the Parry family for generations. It boasted fantastic views of the surrounding town, and a banqueting hall large enough to hold dances. It must have been an imposing building in its day, set in spacious grounds and lording it over the immediate area. Doctor Parry's father had often reminisced about the big parties and dances held there when he was still only a boy. "Ah, Trevor, they were really grand affairs," he would say. "I would creep from my bed and sneak a look at everything that was going on; such laughter and colour. Your grandmother was an absolute beauty, my boy, and everybody said what a lucky chap your grandfather was."

But that was then, and this was now.

Bad investments and a conviction that nothing would ever change both contributed to what started as a gradual decline in the family fortunes, and ended with an almighty rush. By the time Trevor Parry returned to Oakwell to bury his father and accept his inheritance, the grounds were overgrown and the house in a dilapidated state of disrepair. As a single man whose every thinking moment was devoted to his profession, he tried to keep tidy the few rooms he used and let the rest continue to deteriorate. Such mundane things were of no interest to him at all. Only his investigations mattered.

Leonard Sargasso, he decided, could be put down as a partial success. A depressive drunk who no longer lifted a paintbrush when they had first met more a decade previously, the artist would always look on the dark side, but was drink-free now and had re-established himself as a painter of note. Doctor Parry had not seen Leonard for the last couple of years and had been quite touched by the level of involvement his former patient had given him for his latest exhibition.

As he had known it would, the painting of Lucinda drowning had sent Alan Buxton spiralling downwards. He needed to turn off the whale songs and face the reality of death, and maybe this shock tactic might do the trick. Either way, Parry would pick up interesting data, and that was always his prime objective. The prim and proper Miss Kavotny, for instance, had provided him with so much information when being hypnotised, sessions she personally had no memory of.

Doctor Parry smiled, maybe a little ruefully. Jane Kavotny had got it so completely wrong when granting him super stud status. It had been a relief, almost, when she had lost interest in him and started to consider other options. It was just as well she only wanted fantasy lovers. Eric Landreth would almost certainly show cruel and nasty tendencies in a real life situation.

A, to B, to C, to D. One thing often led to another. Doctor Parry visited The Cool Spot early, hoping to pick up information regarding Landreth's drug use. The man himself denied he was still a user, but addicts were notorious liars. As it happened, the promoter fellow, Harry Bonney, was more than willing to chat. He obviously didn't like Eric so didn't hold back, providing the doctor with a wealth of additional data, and also enabling a file to be opened on him too. Bonney was an interesting jumble of psychiatric jigsaw pieces and Parry could see many challenges in trying to make them all fit.

Jane Kavotny, Alan Buxton, Eric Landreth, and now Harry Bonney; there were others on his books, but these were the really interesting ones. Parry wondered if a more informal setting might pay dividends. Maybe a dinner party at Oakwell? The more he thought about it, the more the idea appealed.

A SET MENU

THE LARGE BANQUETING hall, with its long central table: dusty, unkempt, unused, reminded Harry Bonney of Miss Havisham's wedding reception room in Dickens' *Great Expectations*. What potential though! Tidied, modernised, repaired, a lick of paint alone would work wonders, and he could see himself putting on some great jazz gigs here.

Doctor Parry had invited Harry Bonney earlier than the others, hoping some time alone would help fill in the background information so important for both diagnosis and treatment. Bonney smiled slyly, secretly amused that the doctor thought he could keep his motives hidden. Maybe it worked with the others, but not with smart-arsed Bugs. "Quite some place," he said.

"It was once!" Parry had enjoyed giving his guest a guided tour. "The decline started in my grandparent's time, according to my father." They had returned to his living quarters and he poured a glass of beer for them both.

Bonney toyed with his drink, knowing that soon he would have to come to a decision. This doctor fellow was no fool, smarter than most, but not quite as clever as he thought himself to be. He had spotted Bonney's unusualness, for which he deserved full credit, but was confident of keeping his own strange tastes secret.

Ha! Bugs Bonney was as well versed at reading the signs as Doctor Parry. The difference being that the doctor did not realise it. He glanced at a clock ticking away on the room's mantelpiece. If he was going to act, it had better be now.

"What's up Doc?" asked Bonney, putting on his best Bugs Bunny voice.

"Pardon?"

As Parry turned towards him, Bonney struck his forehead as hard as he could with a metal hammer he had taken from a bag he had brought with him. Stunned, probably fully unconscious, his feet were expertly tied and he was hung, head down, against a door, with the rope going over and being knotted around the opposite side's handle. Placing a bowl from the kitchen under the doctor's head, he cut his throat, severing the arteries to facilitate blood removal from the incapacitated body. While that was happening he cut away Parry's clothing.

"Were you going to eat me or cure me, doctor?" murmured Bonney, taking down the slaughtered cadaver. It was time to dress the flesh.

"It takes one to know one," he said, continuing the one-sided conversation while first of all making the primal cuts, with minimum wastage of course. "You were so pleased with yourself, spotting my cannibal tendencies, that you missed realizing that I could see the same in you."

Next he trimmed the primal cuts, in preparation for cooking. The other three: Eric Landreth, Alan Buxton and Jane Kavotny, were in for a special treat tonight. Bugs just about had time to tidy up the place while the meal was cooking, and then the other guests would be arriving.

AFTERWORD

DURING A RECENT Facebook discussion I described my-self as a "Short Story Hobbyist", and I think that sums me up fairly well. For as far back as I can remember I always had an interest in putting words on paper, which meant I could ignore the grammar side of English at school because my compositions usually scored well enough to bring up my average mark. Peter Coleborn, who has edited both my collections for The Alchemy Press, probably wishes I had paid more attention during those distant lessons.

Many of those bitten by the writing bug treat their short story years as a form of apprenticeship, during which they fine-tune their art before moving on to try and crack the novel market. These are usually the ones hoping for a writing career; I never looked in that direction. For one thing, I have never been a prolific writer and dread to think how long it would take me to write a hundred-thousand-word novel. I would de-finitely be starving in a garret long before the book was finished. Also, I do enjoy the short story format, both as a writer and reader. Do I read novels? Well yes, of course I do, but an author who can say it all in four or five or six thousand words holds me enthralled and gains my respect.

Long-time favourites such as Raymond Carver, Cordwainer Smith and William Gibson inspired me. Current practitioners such as Nathan Ballingrud and

Laura Mauro show that the dark art of short story writing is still there to be discovered, and small publishers of the independent press provide opportunities for writers such as myself to see their work in print, for which I am eternally grateful.

Those who know me will be aware that my writing hobby has been, to use a footballing term, a game of two halves. I come from the old school of manual typewriters, sheets of paper, carbon copies, and submitting by snail-mail. The independent press was largely non-existent, with very little between roughly produced fanzines and the paperbacks that filled the shelves in WH Smiths. But you knew where you stood because everything was more-or-less genre related. If you wrote a horror story, you tried it with Pan or Fontana. Science Fiction went to *New Writings in SF* or *New Worlds*, depending whether your story was traditional or new wave. Other short-term series and magazines tried to muscle in occasionally but usually flared briefly before fading away.

When I started to write again, after several years away, it was as if I had landed on an unknown planet. For one thing I had to buy a computer and banish my typewriter back to the attic. The independent press had blossomed during my absence and strict genre guidelines had become blurred, with themed anthologies becoming a publishing staple. I massaged the aching joints of my fingers and tried the alien concept of producing pages on a screen.

"Where do you get your ideas from?" is probably the question a writer gets asked more than any other. In many cases it is sufficient that a particular theme, specified by an editor or publisher, stirs the juices and prompts a reaction. At other times an idea niggles away until I write it. Not having a particular market in mind, such stories are filed away in the hope of one day finding a home. Then there are tribute stories, when something I've read makes me want to jump in and splash around myself, even if only at the shallow end. "The Place of Small Misdemeanours", for example. George Saunders prize-winning *Lincoln in the Bardo* was my favourite novel of 2017 and was the inspiration behind my subsequent story.

With poetry, some of my jazz-themed lines were written specifically for *The Song Is...*, run by Marianne Szlyk, who kindly nominated my poem "No Valentines for the James Dean of Jazz" for a Pushcart Prize; but it is very rare for me to write a poem with a definite market in mind. "Dark-Haired Italian Girl" was originally the lyrics to a song which was played at Maddalena's funeral.

According to my family, I am easier to get along with when I have a story on the go, and can be a crotchety old sod when I haven't, but I personally think that to be a privilege of old age. I must admit that I do enjoy all that goes into writing: the research when needed, and even the constant self-editing.

Yes, a "Short Story Hobbyist" sums me up and I'm happy to be one.

Before closing these few words, I would like to thank Adrian Cole for his brilliant introduction. I was my daughter's favourite writer until she discovered his Nick Nightmare stories, which she can't get enough of. Plymouth Argyle made a late run for the playoffs in League One but just missed out in the end. Newport County, after two seasons of barely escaping the drop into non-league football, settled for mid-table security and a good cup run. We both think that next season will bring success.

It has been a great pleasure to be published again by Peter Coleborn's award-winning Alchemy Press. The whole process was as smooth and enjoyable as I expected it to be. I really do enjoy my hobby and my thanks to everyone concerned, readers included, and that means *you*.

Bryn Fortey
Newport, 2018

16475697R00199

Printed in Great Britain
by Amazon